TRICK YOU

REBEL INK #2

TRACY LORRAINE

Copyright © 2020 by Tracy Lorraine

All rights reserved.

No part of this book may be reproduced in any form or by any electronic or mechanical means, including information storage and retrieval systems, without written permission from the author, except for the use of brief quotations in a book review.

Editing by Pinpoint Editing

Proofreading by Gem's Precise Proofreads

Photographer Wander Aguair

Model Isaac Dawson

A NOTE

Trick You is written in British English and contains British spelling and grammar. This may appear incorrect to some readers when compared to US English books.

Tracy xo

Andy and Amelia x

PROLOGUE

Danni

I didn't want to get back into online dating. I'd closed my profile down months ago for a very good reason: all the guys I'd been matched with were wankers. They said all the right things via message, made me think that they were actually interested in more than what was between my legs, but when it came down to it, none of them wanted anything more than a quick fuck before ghosting me. I get it. The need for a bit of mindless fun, some easy sex with no ties. I'd done it a time or five myself. But that wasn't what I wanted these days. I want something a little more fulfilling. I'm not talking a ring on my finger and a bun in the oven by the time the year's out, just someone I can spend time with—outside of the bedroom—and for a sustained length of time. Actually get to know them, not just how big their cock is.

But it turns out that guys outside of internet dating

didn't really exist. Or at least not in my world. The guys at uni didn't really make me look twice, and I refuse to even consider the possibility of dating someone from work. That's a huge no-no in my book.

I blow out a breath and stare at myself as I lower my straighteners. My hands tremble slightly at what tonight might hold for me.

Carter has been nothing but incredible over chat, but I'm not naïve enough to think it's going to be that simple. It can't be, nothing ever is.

I take a sip of my wine before letting another layer of my hair down and continuing to straighten it within an inch of its life.

I finished work early to ensure I'd be ready, but in my excitement I'm now well ahead of time, and I'm worried that if I stop, I'll overthink everything and cancel. My previous experiences will scare me off when I really want to meet this guy.

I don't want to say that he seems perfect, because I just know that'll jinx something, but… he really does.

He makes an effort to ask about my job like he really cares. He checks on my family, despite him not having a clue who any of them are, and he seems to share my hopes and dreams for the future. *Of course, all of that could be total bullshit,* a little voice in my head says.

Pushing the thought away, I continue with the task at hand and try my hardest not to drink too much as my nerves begin to get the better of me.

By the time I leave the flat, I'm two glasses down and things are just a tad fuzzy.

It'll be fine. Open the window in the Uber and you'll be right as rain when you pull up to the restaurant, I tell myself.

I fidget with the clasp on my bag as the car stops and

starts in the evening traffic. It only increases my nerves as I look at the time and realise that, after almost being ready too early, I'm now probably going to be late.

We're only two minutes out when my phone vibrates in my bag. I'm tempted to ignore it, not wanting a distraction before this date, but needing something to do aside from breaking my bag, I pull it out.

His name illuminates my screen, and my stomach drops. *Please, for the love of god, don't cancel now.*

With trepidation, I swipe the screen. I hold my breath as the app opens, trying to tell myself that I'm prepared for the rejection I'm about to read. I'd like to say it won't sting, but I'd be lying. While the realistic side of me has been trying to prevail, my inner romantic can't help swooning every time this guy says something so perfect.

Carter: I need to tell you something.

My heart pounds as I read the words for a second time. Okay, so he's not ditching me at the final hurdle. I guess that's a good sign. Right?

I stare down at his words. *Fuck.* I knew this was too good to be true. No guy can be that good looking, have his body fill out a suit quite like he does, and have the perfect words every single time. It's just not possible. That guy who mostly lives in my dreams... he does not exist.

I'm still considering my options when the car pulls to a stop. I look out of the window and find the restaurant I chose for tonight staring back at me.

The temperature in the car seems to have risen all of a sudden, and my need for fresh air gets the better of me.

Before I think better of it, I shoot back a reply.

Danni: I'm outside. I guess I'm about to find out first-hand...

My stomach turns over as possibilities of what he needs to tell me run through my mind. I've had so many bad dates over the years that I'm sure it'll be nothing new. *What if he's a woman? Or one half of a couple hoping for a good night?*

I shake the thoughts from my head, thank my driver, and step from the car. Dropping my phone back into my bag, I slide it over my shoulder and wrap one slightly clammy hand around the strap as I hesitantly head for the entrance.

He told me that he'd wait for me at the bar, so the second I step inside, my eyes scan all the people standing along the length of it.

I don't find him. I tell myself that it's busy, and I'm panicking as I step forward.

I don't hear any noise from the restaurant as my blood races past my ears and my stomach churns. I'm about halfway across the space when a guy steps from the bar in my direction. I dismiss him the second my eyes land on him, because he's wearing ripped jeans, a shirt that's open at the neck and has the arms rolled up, exposing tattoos on every bit of visible skin.

I continue walking, my eyes scanning all the bodies, but no one seems to be looking for anyone. None are recognisable in any way.

I take one more step but am forced to stop when the guy with the tattoos gets in my way.

"I'm sorry, I—" I look up to his face, and my words falter. His eyes. They're the same hypnotising green ones I've been looking into online for weeks. But the rest of him? I shake my head. No, it can't be him.

"Hey," he says nervously as he stares down into my

eyes. It's almost like he's willing me not to freak out, but as reality hits me, that's exactly what I want to do.

"You've got to be fucking shitting me." My voice is an octave too high to be in the middle of a restaurant. I feel everyone's attention turning my way, but I don't pay them any attention. My angry, betrayed eyes stay firmly on his.

Carter James. Or at least that's what he told me his name was. But looking at him right now, I see that the man he was claiming to be doesn't exist. He's not the prim and proper banker with the perfectly styled dark hair, five o'clock shadow and designer suit. He's just... he's just a tattooed bad boy who will promise to break your bed and, inadvertently, your heart too. There's a reason I stay away from those types. I've been burned one too many times for a return visit, thank you very much.

"Danni, please just let me explain." His voice is quiet, almost pleading, but I don't care. He tricked me. He promised me time and time again that the person I was talking to was real. Yet here he stands, looking nothing like his profile picture. Well, aside from his eyes, and his cheekbones, and his full lips.

Who is this guy?

"I'm leaving." I turn, but his warm fingers wrap around my wrist before I can take a step. My heart aches, but it's stupidity that reigns. How could I have been so naïve to believe all his bullshit? "Get the hell away from me. I should have listened to your warning message and never stepped inside this place. Everything I thought I knew about you, you've just ruined. Goodbye, *Carter.*"

1

Carter (aka Titch)

"Zach, open the motherfucking door," I shout for the millionth time. The wanker's locked himself inside ever since his brother's wedding last weekend. He only emerged for a mysterious client the other night, then quickly retreated back here again. "Who was she, huh? If you're fucking about on Biff, I'll rip your fucking balls off."

Silence.

My lips purse as my frustration gets the better of me. I've been in a perpetual state of pissed off since *she* walked out on me that night. I know I looked different, but I didn't trick her. Not really. Everything she knows about me, aside from my job, is true. The person she's got to know? That's me. I thought we had a connection. I know it was only through the dating app, but I still felt it was there—even more so when I looked up and saw her. Fuck, her profile picture didn't do her any justice, because she was fucking gorgeous. Thick, dark hair that surrounded her shoulders like a curtain, and she had huge, chocolate eyes that I swear looked right into my soul in those few seconds she was standing before me.

Jesus, as my mind conjures up my memory of her standing there with her tiny fists clenched at her sides, my cock jumps. I still want her just as badly now as I did that night when her sweet, alluring scent was surrounding me.

"Fine, asshole. You refuse to come out, I'll find someone who can push their way in," I bark in warning before waiting another couple of minutes to see if it'll get him moving.

My best mate is a moody fucker, and I'm not ending another day without him at least attempting to sort his shit out, whatever the fuck it might be.

With a sigh, I run down the stairs that lead up from the tattoo studio below to the flat he's locked himself inside of. I can't even make use of the spare key, because the wanker's locked it from the inside, probably knowing that I'd try to force my way in.

I've already cancelled my couple of clients tonight. I was fed up, knowing he was dealing with some shit while Biff had apparently decided not to turn back up to do her job. The other guys can cope if any walk-ins turn up.

I don't bother going back to my room to grab anything or tell the others, I just storm through the front door and head in the direction of Biff's flat. If anyone knows what the fuck is going on, then it'll be her, seeing as she's avoiding the studio just as much as Zach is.

I hit the buzzer the second I'm outside her building, expecting to have to convince her to let me in. This shit is seriously getting boring. I've been calling and messaging her since she disappeared, but everything has gone unanswered.

To my surprise, I'm instantly buzzed in. She doesn't even ask who it is. Not wanting to argue with this easy entrance, I push the door open and start heading up the stairs when I discover hers is at the top.

The second I'm in front of her door, my patience snaps.

"Biff, open up," I call at the same time my fist rains down on her sleek black and chrome door.

The second she pulls it open, I'm inside and demanding she get her arse to the studio to sort Zach out. I can tell she's concerned, but the moment another person comes into view behind her I almost forget the reason I'm here and why I need her.

"*You.* What the fuck are you doing here?" The words are out of my mouth before I have time to compute anything.

I've not seen or heard anything from her since she walked out of that restaurant almost two weeks ago. By the time I'd ordered myself a drink and pulled up the dating app on my phone, her profile had already vanished. The only communication we'd had up to that point had been through the app, and now it was gone I had no way of contacting her. All I knew was that her name was Danni Lou, she was twenty-six and an operations manager for a business I knew nothing about because she didn't disclose the details.

She stares at me, her eyes hard and filled with hate at having to even look at me once again. I know I look different to the photo I used online, but I also know that I'm not exactly hard on the eyes.

"Dan—"

"Don't," she barks with such venom that it makes Biff's eyes widen in shock.

Our eye contact holds, mine begging for her to give me a chance and to hear me out. I know I shouldn't care so much, but there's just something about this woman. I knew it from the moment we started chatting. Something was... different to all the others who had come before, and I really thought my risk might pay off, despite Spike's warning that it was a dumb arse idea.

"Err... what the fuck is going on right now?" Biff asks, looking between the two of us as if that will help her work it out.

"Nothing," Danni snaps, dragging her hate-filled stare from me to look at Biff. I don't miss that her features immediately soften as she silently begs her not to ask any more questions.

Without her stare, I'm able to regain my own thoughts and remember why the hell I'm standing here in the first place.

It takes some convincing, but eventually I manage to get Biff out the door and heading towards where Zach is. She's not happy about it, but I can see the concern in her eyes knowing that something's not right. Neither of them may want to admit that there's something between them, but I see through both of them.

Convincing him to let her in is easier than I thought it was going to be, but with Biff now inside with my grumpy arse boss and my clients cancelled, I have nothing left to do. Unless...

Without thinking, I'm back out of the studio and heading in the direction I just came from. I've no idea if she lives there, if she's Biff's roommate or even sister for that matter, but right now I don't really care.

My one short memory of her has been driving me crazy since that night, and my need to explain myself to her is uncontrollable now I know where she is.

I jog the short distance back, afraid that she might be one step ahead of me and have already left—or, if I'm lucky, on her way out so I can intercept her when she's not expecting it.

As I turn the corner for the building, I come up behind a delivery guy. I wait a few steps back and watch as he lifts his hand to ring the buzzer for whichever flat he's delivering to. I can't believe my luck when he presses for Biff's.

I stand with my heart damn near in my throat as I wait to see if she'll answer, if she's still there. And two seconds later she does.

"Delivery for Biff?" the guy says into the speaker.

"Yeah, come on up." I wait for the crackle to say she's released the button, and he's pushed the front door open before rushing over.

"Hey, is that for Biff?" I ask, coming to stand next to him. "I'm her boyfriend. Cosy night in," I say with a wink. "I can take it from here. Thanks, man."

I don't give him the opportunity to refuse me. I take the bag from his hand and walk away.

"Thank fuck for that. I'm running so behind tonight."

"Glad I could be of help. Enjoy the rest of your evening." I give him a friendly wave as he turns and rushes back to his moped.

With a smile curling one side of my mouth, I take the stairs two at a time.

I knock again, but unlike last time I'm not quite so forceful. I need her to believe that I'm just a delivery guy with dinner.

"At last, that took—oh, fuck. No, no, no," she chants as I jamb my foot in the door at exactly the moment she realises it's me.

"It seems I owe you dinner, and look what I have here," I say, lifting the bag of what smells suspiciously like Chinese.

"No. You're not welcome in here." She stands tall in front of me, which in itself is amusing because she can't be more than five foot four to my six foot two. She squares her shoulders and sets her jaw ready for a fight.

"We can either do this here for all the neighbours to hear, or we can do it in there. The choice is yours, doll." It's the term I used in our messages, and I like to think that her cheeks flushed just like they are now every time she read it.

She holds her ground for a few seconds before eventually conceding and stepping back, allowing me to enter.

The flat itself is incredible. It's obvious the building's been converted from its previous use, and whoever's completed the work has done a great job of keeping some of the original features.

The moment she takes a step in front of me, though, all thoughts of the building we're currently inside leave my mind as my eyes lock onto her arse, swaying as she walks. It seems I lucked out with this one. If she's even half the person she came across as on the internet, I may have found exactly what I was looking for without too much effort—especially with that little banging body.

"You're not staying," she states, turning on me. Her eyes are still hard, her shoulders pulled tight.

She looks fucking hot.

My heart rate increases just looking at her, all pent up and ready to fight.

"Aw, come on, doll. There's too much in here for you to eat alone." She glances down at the bag of food that's still in my hand before looking back to the door.

When she opens her mouth, I'm convinced she'll be sending me on my way, but much to my surprise, it's the opposite.

"Fine. But only because if you leave that here then there's a good chance I'll eat the lot."

"And we wouldn't want to ruin these curves now, would we?" I take a step towards her, allowing my eyes to drop down her body. She's wearing a pair of fitted joggers and a loose cut off sweatshirt, showing off her smooth stomach and the incredible curve of her waist.

She sucks in a breath as I get closer, and it tells me everything I need to know. She feels this crazy thing between us just like I do.

"Am I interrupting a yoga class or something?" I say, looking back to her outfit.

"Um... no. Just a long day, and I need to be comfortable." At no point does she meet my eyes, and it pisses me off.

Reaching out, I touch my finger gently to her chin and tilt her face towards mine.

"I'm sorry. I'm really fucking sorry. I—"

"Don't want to hear it. Let's eat, and then you can leave, knowing that you helped me out by not allowing me to be a fat pig. That's all this is. I don't care why you did what you did, or why you turned up here. But nothing is going to happen." Her eyes hold mine before narrowing as if she's trying to make me believe her.

"Okay, fine. Fine," I say putting my hands up in

surrender. My voice is totally insincere, and if she believes it then she might not be as intelligent as I think she is.

She takes the bag from my hand before rounding the kitchen island and lifting her glass of wine to her lips. She swallows an insanely large amount before turning and getting out some plates. I smile to myself. I'm totally getting to her right now.

"Drink?" she asks politely.

"Sure. Whatever you've got will be great."

I help carry everything to the table and laugh when she sets herself down a fresh glass of wine and me a pint of water.

"Wow, thanks."

"Trust me, it's more than you deserve."

I can't really argue, so I don't. Instead I watch her as she pulls the tops off the takeout containers and fills her plate, leaving me to have what's left. I'm not going to complain, it's better than the crap I would have probably got for myself tonight. Plus, it's free.

"So..." I say, desperate to break the heavy silence surrounding us. "This place is nice."

"It's not mine." Her voice is cold, and even though I don't really know her, I know it's not her usual tone.

"So Biff lives here alone?"

"Yeah."

I blow out a breath. "I work with Biff," I say, hoping to fill in some blanks she might have.

"Great."

"Danni." I sigh. "Just give me a chance."

"You had one. You fucked it."

"I know, but—"

"No. You don't get any buts. You eat up and then leave.

If I was interested in hearing you out, then I'd have stayed that night."

"I had no idea you'd be here. That you knew Biff," I admit.

"I know. If I thought you were stalking me then you most definitely wouldn't be sitting there right now."

"So you'd get fat to keep a stalker away," I quip.

"Stop it."

"Stop what?"

"Stop trying to be funny. Stop trying to be the person you pretended to be online."

"That's just the thing though, I am—"

"Nope. La la la. Not listening." Danni pushes her empty plate away, grabs her wine, and stands from the table.

Rushing to join her, I stand and cut off her journey towards the sofas behind me.

"I have every intention of making you."

"Carter, get out of my way. If that's even really your name," she mutters as I allow her to step around me. It feels so strange that this is only the second time we're met in person, yet I feel like I know her better than many others in my life already. It's unnerving.

"It is. I am Carter James Wright. Everything you know about me aside from my picture and my job is true. Everything. The person you got to know is me."

"Not good enough. You still lied. You still tricked me."

"I know, but..." I trail off, expecting her to cut me off again. "Fuck, Danni. What do you want from me? I'm sorry. It was a stupid thing to do but—"

"But what?" she shouts, slamming her empty glass down on the coffee table and taking an angry step forward.

"But I can't regret it." Her brows draw together with confusion. "I can't regret it, because I met you." She opens her mouth to argue again, her eyes burning with fire so I know she's not suddenly going to soften—and to be honest, a part of me doesn't want her to. I like the fire. It's almost like a challenge for me to try to put it out. "This is me, Danni." I reach behind my head and pull my shirt off, dropping it to the floor beside my feet so she can see me in all my tattooed glory. Her eyes immediately drop from mine to take in my exposed torso. I've no idea if she's aware of the move or not, but the second she sees me, she sucks her bottom lip into her mouth.

2

Danni

"What you see is what you get." He holds his arms out from his body to allow me to take my fill. "I'm not a banker, I'm an artist. And this," he says, pointing at himself, my eyes powerless to resist, "is my face. Messy hair, scruffy jaw and all."

"But everything else?" I ask hesitantly, thinking of all the things we talked about. Our hopes and dreams for the future. Where we want to be in ten years' time. What we want from life.

"All me, doll."

My heart thunders against my chest, my head swimming with the amount of wine that's currently flowing around my body and lowering my inhibitions and rational thinking.

"Everything I said, aside from some very vague details

about the bank, was all from here." He lifts his hand and places it over his heart. "What about you, doll? Everything you said true?" He takes a step forward, and I swear he sucks all the air out of the apartment with it.

He reaches out and gently tucks a lock of loose hair behind my ear. Had I known I would have been spending one-on-one time with a guy quite as hot as him tonight I might have turned up to my best friend's dressed slightly more appropriately than I am. My grey joggers and cropped sweatshirt don't exactly scream sexy. I'd pulled my hair up into a messy bun before leaving the office, and that's exactly how it's stayed. Why he's looking down at my body right now like he could devour me is beyond me. But as I stare up into his eyes, I can't help but get lost in their green depths.

I want to tell the truth, to tell him that everything I told him was who I am. But seeing how things have turned out when I speak something very different comes out.

I shrug. "I guess that's for me to know and for you to never find out."

Excitement tingles through my veins. Why is standing up to this guy so much fun?

We were already so close that the heat from his very naked chest was seeping into my body, but with my words he gets even closer.

"Is that right?"

My head spins. His manly scent, his deep rough voice. His full lips and playful emerald eyes. They push away everything I was feeling when he first stepped inside this place. That and the wine I've almost downed since in my need to cope push me to do something I really shouldn't.

I lift my arm and wrap my hand around the back of his

neck, pulling him down so that our lips meet. He stills at first, probably expecting me to knee him in the bollocks or something, but I'm lost to him and my need for what he can give me.

I know I wasn't looking for a one-night thing, but right now, it's exactly what I need. So I'm going to use this guy for what he's more than likely capable of and then kick him back to the curb where he belongs for lying to me.

Our lips part simultaneously, and our tongues meet. Fire ignites in my belly, and I press my entire body against him. My breasts squash against his solid chest, and when his arm wraps around my waist it only goes to prove just how into this he is, because his hard length presses into my stomach.

I forget all about what he's done, how much it hurt after I truly believed he was honest with me, and I put everything I have into at least getting something I deserve from this man.

The second his hands slide down my body and grip onto my arse, I jump into his arms. My legs wrap around his waist, his length now pressing in a much more satisfying, yet frustrating, place.

His fingers squeeze into my flesh as he lowers us to the sofa and settles so I'm sitting astride his lap.

"Danni, I—"

"Shut up. Just shut up. Can you do that?" I grind down on his cock, and his eyes flicker with pleasure.

I don't wait for his verbal answer—it should be obvious anyway while he's half-naked beneath me.

Taking his strong jaw in my hand, I stare into his eyes, our noses only a breath apart.

"You want to attempt to apologise for lying to me?

Maybe start by showing me what skills you've got besides tricking women into meeting you."

He flips us, and before I know I've even moved, I'm on my back with him staring down at me.

"One: I don't trick women into my bed. Ever. Two: I've got more skills than you know what to do with, doll."

"Less talk more action, Trick."

A laugh rumbles up his throat before he dives for my lips.

His kiss is all-consuming. He licks into my mouth, teasing my tongue, biting and sucking with just the right pressure, making me impatient to find out how good he might be with it on other places of my body.

"Carter," I moan when he kisses across my jaw and down my neck.

"Oh fuck," he barks, the roughness to it causing my thighs to rub together to quell the persistent ache that's formed. His large, calloused hand lands on my waist before skimming up, causing goose bumps to erupt in its wake until he finds my breast. My back arches with my need for more.

Pushing up the fabric of my top, he lifts me and drags it up over my head so I'm lying in just my lace bra.

"Jesus, you're so beautiful." He peppers kisses across my collarbone before dropping to the swell of my breasts. My breath catches as he licks along the edge of the lace before tucking his finger inside and pulling the fabric away.

With his eyes locked on mine, he leans forward and runs his tongue around my nipple.

All the air rushes from my lungs, and at my reaction he ups the ante and sucks it into his hot mouth.

"Oh fuck." My fingers dive into his mop of hair, and I

grip hard to keep him in place as he goes to town. My hips grind on nothing and my back arches to try to get more, to get anything. He reaches for my other breast and pinches that nipple between his thumb and forefinger. "Oh god, oh god."

"So fucking sweet."

Sadly, he releases me and stops, forcing me to pull my head from the pillow to see what he's doing.

He's still hovering right over my breasts. His eyes are dark and glittering with naughty thoughts that I'd love to hear him say out loud.

"What are you—" My words falter when he drops a kiss between my breasts and then descends down my stomach. The second his lips hit the waistband of my joggers, his fingers wrap around and he starts tugging them and my knickers over my hips. The moment he uncovers my pussy, he sucks his bottom lip into his mouth and stares at my recently waxed mound.

"I knew you'd be fucking perfect. Bet you fucking taste like heaven, too."

"Guess there's only one way to find out." Heat hits my cheeks as my words register. I've never been shy when it comes to sex, and I've had my fair share of utterly forgettable one-night stands, but I've never been quite so brazen about what I want.

"I guess I will." He throws my discarded clothing to the floor before dropping to his knees and twisting me until I'm at the perfect angle for him.

My chest heaves as my breaths race past my lips in anticipation for what's to come.

His palms press against my thighs and he pushes my legs as wide as they'll go before licking his lips.

He manages to drag his eyes from my core and up to

mine. His pupils are shot, totally lost to his own desire, and fuck if I don't want to drag him back up here to kiss the shit out of me. That is, until his finger presses against my clit. He ever so fucking slowly drags it down until he circles my entrance.

I'm embarrassingly wet for this guy despite the fact that he's a fucking liar, but I can't help myself. I need what he can give me more than I need my next breath. This week at work has been hell, and it's been entirely too long since I've had a man between my legs.

"Carter, please. Come on."

"You sound so fucking sexy, begging for me."

"And to think, you're the one on your kneesssssss," I squeal as he dives forward and sucks my clit into his mouth. "Fuuuuuck." My hands thrash at my sides, needing something to hold on to. I find a cushion with one, but the other goes for his hair again.

As he starts licking at me, my grip gets tighter and tighter, but at no point does he complain. He just keeps giving me the pleasure I need.

"Yes. Fuck. Yes. Keep going." When I lift my hips from the sofa, his giant hand grabs my hip to keep me in place while the other plunges into my wet heat. My muscles ripple around him, the sensation almost too much to bear after so long of nothing. I've not even had the time recently to take care of myself.

Words fall from my lips, but I've no fucking clue what they are as he drives me higher and higher.

"I've been thinking about doing this since that night," he admits against me, the vibrations from his deep voice sending shudders through me.

"Carter, don't," I warn, not wanting him to ruin this

with reality. I just want to be two people going after what we need. No drama, no lies, and no betrayal.

His fingers thrust once more, but this time he bends them and fuck, if I don't see stars.

A squeal of pleasure passes my lips before I shatter beneath him. My chest heaves, and my body convulses as pleasure stronger than I've ever known rocks me down to my toes.

"How's that for skills?"

"It was okay." I shrug, attempting to look bored, but it's pointless after all the noises I just made as I fell apart.

"Good job I've got a few more *tricks* up my sleeve." I roll my eyes at his corniness, but when he stands and pops the button of his jeans, I forget all about inappropriate jokes and focus on what he's hiding beneath his clothing.

And to give him credit, when he drops everything to the floor, I discover that it's really quite a trick he's rocking between his legs.

He pulls a condom from his pocket and quickly rolls it down his wide length.

"I'm glad you're pleased, but there is more of me than just my cock," he quips when he realises that I've not taken my eyes from his length since he exposed it.

"I'm just surprised. The cocky ones are usually hiding something."

"Hmmm... hiding it sounds like such a good idea."

If I weren't already so far under his spell I might tell him to get out at his lame joke, but as it is the only thing I want him to do is what he just suggested.

Thankfully, he has the exact same thought, because not a second later is he shifting me on the sofa to accommodate his large frame. I could suggest moving to the guest room, but that would mean stopping, and like fuck am I allowing any reality to seep into this situation until I've had at least one more orgasm.

No sooner is he settled between my legs than he's teasing my entrance with the head of his cock.

"Now." The demand comes out of nowhere, but he obliges. One second he's driving me crazy with desire, and the next I'm so full of him I don't know what to do with myself. "Fucking hell. Fuck." I squirm beneath him, trying to adjust to his invasion and size. Thankfully he allows me a few seconds before he starts to move. And when he does, sweet Jesus, it's fucking mind-blowing. He strokes each and every one of my nerves with every move he makes, and before I'm expecting it, I'm right on the edge of what promises to be another earth-shattering release.

He leans over me and captures my lips just in time to swallow down the cries of his name that fall from my lips.

"Fuck," he grunts as my pussy pulsates around him. "Fucking Christ. A man could become addicted to that," he moans in my ear as I come down from my high. He slows his pace to drag every last ounce of pleasure from me before sitting. "Ready for another?"

"What do you think you are? God of orgasms?"

"Something like that, doll. All I know is that I'm not pulling out of you until I've felt that again."

He slides his palms under my arse and tilts me until everything around me blurs and the only thing I can think about is another release.

He picks up the pace until he's slamming into me, his hair flopping all over his face and his skin covered in a delicious sheen of sweat from the work he's putting in. I might prefer my men suited and booted, but fuck if there's not something about a man who puts in some serious hard work. And my view right now is to die for. The muscles in his neck strain as he throws his head back in pleasure. His abs pull tight, the definition only getting clearer, and my mouth waters to trace them with my tongue.

Reaching around, he presses his thumb against my clit and circles, building me up as his cock swells inside me.

The second before I crash, I have the fleeting realisation that this already hasn't been enough. I'm not sure a lifetime would be enough, if I'm being honest, but that's not what this is.

His cock twitches once, a growl rumbling up his throat, and I lose control. I don't even get to watch him because my eyes slam shut as pleasure renders my body useless. When I do drag my heavy lids open and get a look at him above me with his chest heaving and his hungry eyes, I realise that I might forever regret not seeing him consumed with pleasure.

3

Carter

The moment she opens her eyes, I know my time is up and my stomach drops. I'm not ready for this to be over. Not by a long shot.

"Well…" she says, pulling away from me and sitting on the edge of the sofa. "That was nice. At least I've got a better memory of you now than you just being a liar. You're a talented one at least."

"Danni, please. I—"

"No. We're done. It's time for you to leave. Find your clothes—or don't, whatever—and get the hell out." She stands, righting her bra before looking for something else to cover up with. Spotting her joggers beside me, I kick them away, not wanting her to put up her walls and cover up.

"Mature. Thank you."

"The photograph is of my twin. He's the banker. I just thought that—"

"I don't care," she screeches, making me wince. "How many times. I. Do. Not. Care. You fucked up, and we're done here. Thanks for the shag, it was... forgettable."

I scoff at her words. There was nothing about that that could described as forgettable.

"You're lying."

"Am I? You don't know me, so stop pretending that you do. Oh, and put some fucking clothes on. I've had my fill of your cock." Rolling her eyes, she makes a show of looking to the other side of the room. Only, when I do reach down to grab my clothes, I notice her flick her eyes back and drop to my arse. Smiling, I shake my head at her.

"You're a terrible liar, you know that?"

"You don't know me, Carter, so stop pretending you do."

"Oh, doll. I know you better than you think I do. You challenged me to find out who you really were, but I didn't need to. You've already given me everything I need to know."

"You know nothing. You've no idea where I live, where I work."

"None of that matters. A job is a job. A house is a house. It's what's inside you that I know, and that is exactly what I want."

"Jeez, you're such a guy. One dip in my pussy and you're fucking addicted."

"I'm not talking about your pussy. I'm talking about what's in there." I point at her chest, my hand trembling slightly with frustration and the restraint it's taking for me not to have her again. I know the second I touch her she'll be like putty in my hands, but I won't do it. Not while she's lying to herself like she is right now.

"You're delusional, you know that? A few messages online and what? You think we're a match made in heaven? Well, let me tell you something." She takes a step towards me, her eyes narrowed in frustration, her fists curled in anger. "I don't do bad boys, Carter. Why do you think I went for your twin?"

"Oh, you don't? What was that then?" I lift my chin to the sofa behind her.

"A one-night stand I'm going to regret." Her eyes flash with something, but it's gone too quickly to be able to read it.

"Bullshit," I spit. "If you're really the kind of girl who doesn't 'go for the bad boys'," I say, mocking her, "then you never would have allowed me to fuck you on your mate's sofa." Her face flushes red. "Too late to regret it now. Your juices are all over that." She snarls, and I can't help but keep going, wanting to push her into admitting what she really wants. "You think any suit-wearing motherfucker could do what I just did to you? You think my pansy ass twin could? He might look like he has everything, but there's no fucking way he can make a woman scream like that."

"Get out," she shouts, stepping up to me and raining her tiny fists down on my still-naked chest.

"Careful, doll. You don't want to hurt yourself." She growls, and I can't help but laugh. "Okay, fine. I'm leaving. But this isn't fucking over."

"Yes it fucking is."

I back away from her, running my eyes down her bra-clad body. Fuck, she's fine. She's got all the curves in all the right places. I lick my lips, still able to taste her, and my cock swells. How I would like to bend her over that sofa and fuck her defiance right out of her.

Reaching down, I make a show of rearranging myself. She doesn't miss it, and her dark eyes are engulfed with heat.

"Just so you know, I fucking love fiery women."

"Fuck you," she barks.

"Aren't you glad you did?"

Her teeth grind as I pull my shirt on. "I'll tell Biff that I kept you company while she sorted her man out."

Her lips part in shock as if she's forgotten how I ended up here in the first place. I can practically see the cogs turning in her head as she tries to make sense of all this.

"This might not be your place, but I now know you're close enough to Biff that I'll be able to find you again."

"Don't," she says in a panic. "Don't you dare say anything to Biff about this. Not if you intend on keeping your job."

"You threatening me, doll?"

"You bet your fucking arse I am. Keep it quiet, you hear me?"

"I don't know. I'm sure all the guys at the studio would get a kick out of this. I might give them every single detail... down to just how tight your pussy is." She pales, and all her fight seems to instantly drain away.

"Please. Please don't do that."

I have no intention of telling anyone about this, but her reaction to me suggesting it sure is interesting. "Meh, I'll see how I feel."

She takes a step forward, her lips parting to say more, but no words form.

"Well, unless you want another round, I guess this is it for now. But rest assured, doll. There will be another time.

Maybe not tomorrow, or next week, but I will claim what's rightfully mine."

Her fire returns. She's just about to retaliate when I turn and march from the flat. The only thing I hear is her frustrated growl and then something smashing behind me. A chuckle falls from me as I let myself out of Biff's flat. I'm certainly much more satisfied than when I arrived, but fuck if I'm not a hell of a lot more confused. Who the hell is that woman? I fully intend on finding out, because this isn't over between us. Not by a long shot.

4

Danni

After pulling my clothes back on, I fall down on the edge of the sofa and drop my head into my hands.

What the fuck did I just do?

I drag in a deep breath but instantly regret it, because all I smell is him. He's everywhere: on my skin, under my skin, and in my head.

"Fuck." I bark, thinking that Biff could return at any moment. I jump up, make quick work of tidying the place up, then grab my bag and the rubbish to dump in the bin on the way out so her place doesn't stink of the Chinese we'd eaten while she was gone.

I shut my mind off as I make the short journey back to my flat. I refuse to allow myself to think of what I did or what the consequences might be until I'm safely inside, behind my locked door.

The lights from the house above mine shine bright, and, as I pass the window to head down the stairs, movement catches my eye and I find Harrison, my older brother, and his wife dancing in their kitchen.

Curling my lip up in disgust that it can be quite so easy, I make my way down.

Dumping my bag on the unit in the hall, I make my way to my bedroom, run the bath, and strip from my clothes. I shove the lot in the laundry, fully prepared to have to burn it all to successfully remove his scent from them.

I walk naked to the kitchen to locate a fresh glass of wine, knowing that it's very unlikely anyone will see me down here baring everything before I return to the bathroom and sink down into the too-hot water.

My skin prickles, but I refuse to blast any extra cold in. I need the pain. I need it to wash him away and as some kind of fucked-up punishment for what I did tonight. I guess it's karma. My best friend allowed my brother to fuck her while I was in the next room, so I allowed her friend—his employee—to bang me on her sofa.

I groan, placing my wine on the side and sinking down so it's only my face above the water line.

How could I be so fucking stupid?

I run the events of the evening through my mind and mix them with the little hints of things I've gathered over the years but never bothered to look into.

Him turning up at Biff's door demanding that she follows him because there's something wrong with Zach. That's not news. He's been MIA since the wedding. All of us have tried to get in touch with him, but none of us had any success. Then I combine that with his admission at the wedding that he was Biff's boss, and Carter telling me he worked with Biff. Zach's secret makes sense. He spent all his childhood with a pen or pencil in hand, and it takes me back to a few years ago when a friend told me that he'd inked her boyfriend. I didn't think any of it at the time, too focused on my own life and not what my idiot brother was doing, but I guess it goes to prove that the signs were there the whole time.

So what happens now? I know the studio—Biff told me which one it is. I could turn up and confront him, demand he tells me the truth like I did on Saturday at the wedding, or I could just let him be. He clearly wants to keep his two lives separate, and who am I to force his hand? He's happy. Or is he? The only reason Carter appeared tonight is because something's going on.

I ask myself again. Do I turn up? Try to see him and find out what's going on? Then the image of Carter standing before me tonight with his top off appears, telling me that 'what you see is what you get', and I change my mind.

He has no way of finding me. Well, he has Biff, if he goes against my demand not to say anything.

Fuck. Fuck. Fuck. My head spins with everything, and I fear that only a very large amount of wine is going to slow it down.

What I do know is that I never should have slept with him tonight. I shouldn't have turned up to that date after his warning that he had something he needed to tell me, and I shouldn't have answered Biff's door tonight, let alone let him in and allow him to get his hands on me.

My skin prickles as I remember just how good it felt. I bite down on my bottom lip as I vividly recall how his lips felt against mine, brushing over my breasts, kissing my pussy.

Heat heads south as I think about his tongue, and I squeeze my thighs together. Shit, I shouldn't have been turned on with him in front of me, let alone now when all I have is memories. He shouldn't hold that kind of power over me.

I talk myself in circles about what I should do from here, but by the time my wine is empty and the water is cold, I'm still no closer to having any answers.

All I do know is that Carter James Wright is not my type. Should our paths cross again, I need to stay as far away from him as possible.

———

It might have been a month now since the night I try to forget, but he's still just as under my skin as he was the moment he stepped inside Biff's flat.

Tonight is Zach's birthday meal that's been organised by our mum and Biff, who's now officially Zach's girlfriend. Is it weird that my best friend is banging my brother? Yes, very. Biff and I have shared everything since we bonded at uni a few years ago, but that's had to come to an abrupt end because I really, really don't need all the sordid details of how things are with my brother. Watching them kiss openly in front of me is weird enough. I do not need to know about anything else they do behind closed doors.

Thankfully, Biff's been totally preoccupied with him since the truth came out about what sent him into hiding: being dad's illegitimate son. While everyone else was shocked by Zach's announcement about him owning a very successful chain of tattoo studios, the other one that came out that same day rocked me to my very core. It seems the perfect relationship Mum and Dad have had all these years hasn't always been quite so. I guess we all have skeletons hiding in our closets, and it's best to remember that the people we look up to aren't always perfect. Things aren't always as they seem.

That final thought takes me back to Carter. Was he right when he claimed that he didn't lie to deceive me but to find something different? And if that is the case, could I ever overlook it to give him a chance?

No. No, you can't. He's not your type, remember?

My hands tremble as I lift the zip on the back of my dress for tonight. I've not asked for details of who's going to be there, but I overheard Mum telling Summer that she and Biff were arranging to bring both of Zach's families together: his real one as well as his work one. So there is a very good chance that he's going to be there. I tell myself that he's not the reason I spend an inordinate amount of time ensuring my hair is perfectly straight or that my make-up is flawless, or the reason why, when I chose my underwear for the night, I pulled out the tiniest, sexiest set I own. *It's for confidence*, I try convincing myself, but I've always been a shit liar.

Happy with how I look, I sneak a shot of vodka to steady my nerves before heading up to Harrison and Summer's house for a lift to the restaurant Mum has chosen.

My stomach is in knots as I trail behind the rest of my family to find our table. I've no idea if we're first or last, and to be honest, I'd rather not know. Mostly, I just want to run home and hide. I can only imagine it's going to be hard enough to ignore him if he's here, let alone try to appear unfazed by him, when in reality I'm not sure if I want to hate him or fuck him.

I'm a strong, independent woman. I always have been. So this tattooed bad boy being able to unnerve me so much is unsettling to say the least.

I don't want him. He's not my type. He tricked me. That should be the end of it. I don't do liars or cheats. That's my one hard limit when it comes to men, and that's exactly how this started, so there's no way there can be anything else between us. No way, no chance— The moment my parents part, our table comes into view, along with one very amused pair of green eyes. I don't need to look down to his lips to know he's smiling as our eyes lock, although I don't miss the confusion that fills them.

Something sits heavy in my stomach. I want to say it's dread that I've got to spend the evening in his company, but I fear the reality of it is very different.

Movement finally makes my eyes drop, and when they do, I find him suggestively running his tongue along his bottom lip. My thighs clench as the memory of what that tongue can do hits me full force.

I've no idea how much time passes, but the next thing I know, Biff is beside me as everyone stands to greet the birthday boy. He does a round of introductions, but apparently that's not enough for Biff, who insists I get to know everyone better.

"Danni, come and meet the guys," Biff says, winking at me, telling me that she didn't miss what just happened between me and Carter. She wraps her hand around my upper arm and squeezes just to nail home the point. "This is D, he's the sensible one who keeps everyone in line."

"Hey," Zach shouts from behind us. "The boss keeps everyone in line, I'll have you know."

"Whatever you say," Biff mutters with a roll of her eyes. "This is Spike," she says, gesturing to the guy sitting beside Carter. He smiles and nods politely. "And this is Titch, but I think you two already know each other, right?"

"Something like that." I risk a glance in his direction, seeing as it's the polite thing to do when being introduced.

"Guys, this is Danni. Zach's little sister." Carter's—or Titch's, as he seems to be known—chin drops in shock. That one move tells me a lot about him. His shock means that he's not had a conversation with Biff, much like I haven't, about what was obviously off between us that night in her flat. I've only managed to achieve that by mostly avoiding her since the event. It's not been all that hard seeing as she's been preoccupied by Zach.

I can see the curiosity in her eyes every time she so much as looks at me—how he's managed not to get a grilling from her god only knows.

"Zach's little sister? Whoa," Carter says, openly checking me out.

"And that's code for keep your eyes to your fucking self, dickhead," Zach snaps, coming to stand beside me and staring daggers at Carter.

"That's rich, seeing as you're fucking *my* best friend," I mutter under my breath, but Zach doesn't miss it.

"Not the same, sis. Not the same."

"Really?" I turn to him, staring into his light blue eyes. I don't know why I'm fighting with him over this. I can only hope it's the principle of the thing, that it's okay for him to have my best friend without me batting an eyelid —kind of—but I couldn't possibly go near his friend. I mean, that has to be the only reason, right?

He rolls his eyes at me and turns back to his mates.

"I'm fucking watching you two." He points his fingers to his eyes and then theirs, making everyone laugh, although I don't find it half as amusing as the others.

If Carter is at all bothered by the warning, then he doesn't show it.

5

Carter

I find it hard to take Zach's warning seriously. Plus, it's too little too late, because I've already had a taste of his sweet sister and I have every intention of having another. Tonight, if this incredible turn of events is anything to go by.

I had no fucking clue she was connected to my life in any way aside from being Biff's friend. Maybe if I'd have gone against what she asked of me before I left Biff's flat that night, I might have discovered the truth. Christ knows Biff's tried to dig for information. It seems she forgot to mention the one piece of information I could have done with.

I watch as Biff and Zach happily chat with his parents —who happen to look exactly as I'd imagined all these years: perfect—and I wonder if Biff kept her lips shut on purpose. She knows too well how private Zach is about his life. Hell, she managed to insert herself right into the middle of that clusterfuck, so maybe she's still protecting him—or her.

She excuses herself from Zach's mum and turns to Danni. The two have what looks like a few tense words before Danni looks around the table to find a seat.

There are only two left that are vacant. There's one next to Spike and opposite myself, or there's one at the other end of the table. I laugh to myself when she locks eyes on the one the farthest away from me and marches towards it.

"What's amused you so much?"

I turn back to Spike, trying to decide how much to divulge. Seeing as he was the one who helped me set up the damn dating profile in the first place, despite his warning that it would probably end in disaster, and the fact that he knows all about the clusterfuck date that followed, I decide to be honest.

"So, funny story..." He quirks an eyebrow, and I lean towards him to ensure no one overhears. "You know the girl I met online?"

"The one who curbed your arse the first time she saw you?" he asks with amusement and an 'I told you so' dancing in his eyes.

"Yeah. That one. Turns out she's Big Man's sister."

His eyes fly to the other end of the table. "Fuck off. It's not."

"It is."

"She's the one who only wants a swanky banker?"

"Apparently so."

"I mean, she kinda looks a bit stuck-up, so I can understand her preferences for a slick Rick."

"Trust me," I mutter, "she's not stuck up when you strip away the designer clothes."

Spike gives me a double take. "T, you been holding out on me?"

I spot Zach heading this way out of the corner of my eye and panic. "Shut the fuck up, yeah? The less he knows the better."

Spike opens his mouth to say something but must change his mind, because no noise comes out.

"So..." Zach says looking totally out of his comfort zone. "I guess meeting my family was a little overdue."

"They're awesome, man. I don't know what you were so worried about," Spike says, slugging him in the arm.

Zach nods, glancing over to where Biff's chatting to his parents. "This is all her fucking fault," he mutters to himself, but a wide smile twitches at his lips.

"Mate, we always knew a good woman would sort you right out."

"Now that's where you're very wrong. There's nothing good about Biff. She's all bad." He winks. I groan and roll my eyes just to wind him up, but since he got the girl he seems resistant to my piss taking, unlike when she first appeared at the studio and I could make that vein in his neck pulsate with just a look in Biff's direction.

Everyone takes their seats, and most of us go silent as we check out the food options. She might be at the other end of the table, but that doesn't mean I'm not aware every time she looks at me. My skin heats and desire tingles just below the surface. I refuse to look up, resulting in her glances getting longer and longer. It's as if she wants me to look over.

My need to see the look on her face when she's caught

eventually gets too much, and I drag my eyes from the menu I was pretending to stare at.

Our eyes lock immediately, proving that I was right about her staring at me, and her chin drops in shock. Yet she seems powerless to pull her eyes from mine.

A smirk curls at my lips. She can keep her distance all she likes, but her body tells me the truth. She wants me. She might think I'm all wrong for her and a liar, or whatever, but her desire is clear.

Pursing my lips, I mimic kissing her. That move finally pulls her from her trance as she looks around the table, making sure everyone's distracted. Zach, at least.

"Right, how are we all doing? Ready to order?" the waiter says, pulling his notepad from his back pocket.

Zach's mum opens her mouth to reply when a little rocket comes rushing towards our table.

"I'm so sorry. The tube just stopped in the middle of a tunnel and gah!" she says, lifting her arms out to the sides, looking totally flustered. My eyes drop from her face down her petite body, but they soon lock on her tatted arms. She's cute, that's for sure.

"Whoa, who is that?" Spike whispers, leaning over the table to me. I shake my head and turn back when Zach stands up to introduce her. "Everyone," he says, turning his back on the waiter who has his notepad poised to take down orders. "This is my little sister, Kas."

"Fuck me, how many sisters has he got exactly?"

"Two. Just two." I know about Kas. Biff gave me the run down one night when my client didn't turn up. I'm yet to have a conversation with Zach about it, though. Since he pulled his head out of his arse and admitted how he feels about Biff, it's kinda like he's forgotten I exist. It's fine. I get it. He's got regular access to pussy. I'd probably ignore everyone around me if I ever found a woman to put up with me.

"She is..."

"Off limits, I'd imagine. Just like the other sister."

Spike turns to me, his face expressionless aside from the heat in his eyes. "That's a damn shame."

"Mate, you see the size of her. You'd break her."

"Hey, I'll have you know that these hands can be soft and gentle when they need to be," he says, wiggling them in front of me.

"Fuck off. Don't forget that my bedroom backs onto yours. I don't hear a lot of 'soft' and fucking 'gentle' coming from it when you've got company."

He shrugs and looks back over when Zach points Kas in our direction. His eyes run the length of her before he looks at Zach, I can only assume in the hope he wasn't caught.

"Be nice," Zach warns, pulling her seat out for her.

"When are we anything but nice?"

Zach shakes his head and returns to his seat as the waiter finally begins taking orders.

"Hey, tiny. Nice ink," Spike says, his voice a little deeper than I'm used to, and I just about manage to stifle a laugh.

Sitting back to watch his attempt to pick her up, I can't help but smile. I've no idea what he's thinking—she's clearly too young for him, and Zach would kill him for even looking at her the way he is right now. At least if he continues then it should take the attention away from me and the woman who's still insisting on looking over at me.

Ignoring them, I glance back over at Danni as she places her order and take her in. Her make up is flawless and, much like the first time we met, her long dark hair is hanging straight down her back. The little black dress she's wearing is fitted and doing a fucking fantastic job of showcasing her tits. I bite down on my bottom lip as I remember just how soft her skin was when I kissed it. Just how she tasted when I sucked her nipples into my mouth.

I shift in my seat, giving my thickening cock some space in my jeans before the waiter comes over and wants to know my order.

It's a nice enough evening as family meals go. It's a hell of a lot better than any I've been forced to endure with my own family, that's for sure. More than anything, I'm just happy for Zach to finally pull both parts of his life together. I know I'm not really in a position to criticise how he dealt with his family, seeing as I hardly see my own, but after the number of times he'd told me they were good people, I couldn't help but try to convince him to open up to them. Seeing the pride on both his mum and dad's faces every time they look at him just proves my point. He should have done this years ago.

After a short argument from everyone around the table, we all eventually concede and allow Zach's dad to pay for our meals before his parents, brother and sister-in-law bid us all goodnight and leave the restaurant.

"What's next then, boss? Fancy hitting up The Avenue?"

Zach glances at everyone left around the table before his eyes land on Biff.

"Let's do it," she announces, pushing her chair out behind her and standing.

We all fall into step behind the happy couple, and I manage to ensure that I'm right behind Danni as we make the short journey down the street to the club we quite often end up in.

Her sweet scent blows down to me, making my mouth water as I watch her arse sway in that sinful little dress she's wearing.

She laughs with Kas, who's walking beside her, but every time she turns to look at her, she twists her head just a little too far and I know it's so she can keep an eye on me. I'm making her nervous right now, and I fucking love it.

6

Danni

Safe to say that was the most awkward meal of my life. I knew it was going to be bad, but I never could have predicted just quite what his presence and constant attention would do to me.

I was surrounded by family who all wanted to chat, but the only thing I could think about was him. My body might have been in that restaurant, but my head was firmly back on Biff's sofa all those weeks ago with his hands on me.

I shouldn't be like this. He shouldn't affect me.

Every time I glanced over at him, I was reminded just how much he doesn't fit my ideal type. I want a good guy who's going to treat me right, not a fuck 'em and chuck 'em bad boy. Yes, he was a good lay, but I need more than that right now. I want someone who's up for a few dates, maybe even a little romance. I doubt he would know that if it bit him in the arse.

The food I'm sure was great—at least everyone else cleared their plates and made all the right noises. I just poked my salmon around the plate, too consumed with the arsehole a few seats down and his burning stare that seemed to become an almost constant thing.

Thankfully—I think—Zach didn't notice. But as the night went on, I was starting to wonder if him noticing and taking Carter out of the equation for just looking at me that way might be exactly what I needed.

My intention was to go home as soon as the meal was done, but the second he mentioned The Avenue I found myself nodding and following Zach and Biff from the restaurant.

The Avenue is like my second home. I've spent almost every weekend there for as long as I can remember. Lauren, my old school friend, and I were trying to get in with fake ID before we turned eighteen, and nothing's really changed since then, aside from the fact that we can now legally walk inside with no issues.

My intention was to be first out of the restaurant to get well ahead of him, but sadly, Biff called me back as I attempted to make my escape, and I'm now stuck behind her and Zach while Carter quite obviously stares at my arse as we make our way down the street.

After a slightly awkward conversation with Kas, mostly because my head's in the clouds, an uncomfortable silence descends around us.

"I'm so sorry," I say, turning to her, feeling awful that she's probably just had her mind blown meeting everyone like that and needs some reassurance. "My head's a bit of a mess right now. Work's been crazy."

"It's fine," she says with a soft smile. "I totally get it. I'm not much of a talker really."

I want to tell her that usually that's exactly what I am, but I can't even find those words. All I can hope is that once we're inside, I can get a drink—or ten—and that Lauren will be here so I can make my excuses to hang out with her and Ben, her boyfriend.

Carter and... the other one who's name I've already forgotten, order us two rounds of shots once we get to the front of the crowd at the bar, and after a round of happy birthdays to Zach, we all down them.

With the Jägermeister warming my stomach, things seem a little better. That only increases when Biff wraps her hand around my upper arm and begins dragging both me and Kas out to the dance floor, leaving the boys behind.

"You having a good night?" she shouts in my ear. I've never been more grateful for the pounding music, because it means she can't question me like I'm sure she's desperate to.

"Yeah. I think Lauren's here tonight." Thankfully that's enough to distract her. I've no idea if she's seen anything between Carter and me tonight. I had every intention of totally ignoring him, but I know I've failed. What I don't know is just how obvious I might have been looking over at him. I know he knows. He's caught me more than once and nearly gave me a bloody heart attack when his green, hungry eyes met mine.

"Well, tell her to come and meet us."

Dragging my phone from the bottom of my bag, I shoot her a message to tell her that we're in the basement on the dancefloor.

Only minutes later, arms wrap around me from

behind. I still. My first thought is that it's Carter, but when I hear a female squeal in my ear I turn around and throw my arms around her.

The two of us used to spend all our time together. We met when Lauren started sixth form at my school. We clicked immediately. But her man and their business monopolise most of her time now, so we don't get to see each other as much as we'd like.

"It's so good to see you," I shout, holding her tightly.

"It's been too long."

Pulling away from her, I allow Biff to say hi before attempting to introduce her to Kas. Lauren smiles and nods, but I've no idea if she hears a word that comes out of my mouth.

When I look over her shoulder, I find the man responsible for taking up her time. I smile at him and he nods in response, but not before Zach descends on him. I knew they were in the same year at school, but I had no clue they were still friends until I called Lauren for a catch up after everything blew up and she confessed to knowing all along. I wanted to be angry at her, but to be quite honest, I couldn't find it in myself to care.

Lauren winces as she glances at the two of them. I smile back at her to tell her that everything is good. I think she thought I was going to fly off the handle when I found out, but really, I'm just glad Zach was able to open up. I can't imagine how hard it's been for him over the years to keep everything he does a secret.

A few of Lauren and Ben's friends join us, and after a bear hug from Joe and a few more shouted introductions, we all start dancing. That is, until everyone around me seems to pair off into their couples.

Even Kas' attention has been captured by Spike, who's showing her some slightly questionable moves.

Each couple smiles at each other as they move in time with the music, and a pang of jealously hits me. I want someone to dance wi— When I look up again, my eyes lock with Carter's, and all thoughts leave my head.

A smile curls at one side of his mouth, and my stomach twists with desire at knowing exactly what that mouth can do.

He looks around at the couples much like I did only a few moments ago before he mouths, "Shall we?" and holds both his arms out for me to step into.

I'm torn. A huge part of me wants to throw caution to the wind and walk straight into his body and start moving against him. That's the irrational side of my brain that needs to be locked down. I need to be listening to the sensible side that's telling me to run away from him as far as I can.

We stand, locked in our stare for what feels like the longest time as I fight my internal battle.

When I eventually manage to drag my eyes away from him, I find Zach's concerned ones where he's dancing with Biff's back to his front. The way his hips are moving against her makes me want to throw up a little in my mouth, but the happiness that oozes from him stops me.

"You okay?" he mouths, forcing me to plaster a fake smile on my face.

"Toilet," I mouth back before stepping away from our group and walking to the other side of the huge space. The temptation to take a left and leave the entire club is strong, but I don't want to do that to Biff or Zach.

Instead, I find myself in an annoyingly long queue for

the ladies. At least while I'm standing there, I can't feel his heated stare.

By the time I get to do my thing and am staring into the mirror above the basin, I almost feel like I've got my shit together and am able to walk back out onto the dancefloor and put him and everything he makes me feel to one side. I'm here for Zach. That's it. *You are also going home alone,* I instruct myself. Temptation might be in touching distance, but I'm stronger than it is. I will not cave to Carter James Wright again. He is off limits.

I walk out of the bathroom, intending on getting myself a drink and finding the others once again. Only, as I turn the corner, I walk straight into a wall of flesh. I don't need to look up to know who it is. I'd remember his scent anywhere. My mouth waters and every muscle south of my waist clenches. So much for that little pep talk.

"What do you want?" I shout into his chest, refusing to look up into his eyes.

That's not good enough, because I soon find his warm fingers tilting my chin until I've got no choice but to look up. I keep my eyes over his shoulder at the women walking back to the bar.

"Doll, come on. You've spent all night staring at me. I'm right in front of you now. You can take your fill."

"Fuck you," I spit.

"Yeah. That's the exact thought in my mind too."

A frustrated growl rumbles up my throat. Who does he think I am? Some cheap hooker who'd do anything to spend the night with him? He was good, but he wasn't *that* good.

Liar.

"How about we get out of here?" He takes a step closer until the heat of his body seeps into mine. My nipples pebble, knowing that another inch and he'd be brushing up against them.

"Thanks, but no thanks."

"I'm pretty sure I could convince you." His hand lifts until he's cupping my cheek, and he drops his head so his lips are to my ear. "I know you've not forgotten how good it was. That's why you can't keep your eyes off me." I flinch when his palm lands on my waist. His touch burns but in such a good way.

I open my mouth to respond, my compliance right on the tip of my tongue. It would be so easy to agree and to take him back to my place for an hour or so to finish off the night, but I can't. Thankfully, my rational side perks her head up and reminds me of the list of reasons why that would be a bad idea. The only positive outcome from allowing it to happen would be the orgasms, but I've got a perfectly suitable rubber vibrating friend in my drawer specifically for this kind of situation.

"I really doubt that, Trick. There's not enough alcohol in this place to make that mistake again."

He pulls back and looks at me. His brows are drawn together, but he's way too cocky and arrogant to be hurt by that comment. His ego probably just took a bit of a hit, that's all.

"You know my name is Titch, right?"

Dropping my eyes from his, I run them down his body. "Riiight. See, I think Trick suits you much better. Although, I'm sure I could come up with a few more options."

I tilt my head to the side as he chuckles at my comment.

"Oh, doll. Do you know how irresistible you are when you get all fired up?"

"Good to know. Now enjoy the last of it, because I'm about to walk away and never look back."

I take a step around him, but his hot fingers wrap around my wrist.

"This isn't over, doll. And you damn well know it."

I straighten my back and square my shoulders in an attempt to appear unphased by his words. I hate to admit it, but I'm already getting a little excited about the next time we meet. It's wrong, but it is what it is.

Pulling my wrist from his grip, I walk away exactly as I told him I would: without looking back. It damn near kills me.

7

Carter

Zach: I need you in Vegas. Flight at 12.30. Biff's cancelled your clients. Check your email for check in info.

I stare down at his message, my brows pulled together in confusion. I thought he was in LA with Corey. Why the hell are they in Vegas? And more importantly, why do they need me?

Rolling my eyes at him, I swing my legs from the bed and head towards the shower. It's already long past lunchtime seeing as Spike and I sat drinking long into the early hours after our shifts last night.

Stripping out of my boxers, I stand under the water while it's still cold in the hope it'll help rid me of the lingering effects of the whiskey.

My mind wanders as I stand there, and as always it's to *her*. Biff and Zach disappeared first thing the next morning on an impromptu trip to LA, so I haven't even had a chance to convince Biff to tell me where I can find her. I've searched all social media sites now I know her full name, but she's got them locked up tight with her security settings and, surprise, surprise, she's not accepted my friend request.

I really thought she was playing with me that night. I expected to find her back on the dancefloor with everyone else when I re-joined them not long later, only she was nowhere to be found. Spike had no idea where she'd gone, not that he was paying much attention while he danced with Kas, and I daren't ask Zach.

It turned out that she'd made an excuse about not feeling well and disappeared the second she returned from the bathroom. Biff could see I was concerned, but still, she refused to give up the information I needed.

Every minute since our interaction in that hallway, I've regretted allowing her to walk away. I thought it was just the beginning of an inevitable end to our night. Turns out it was the end.

After checking what the weather is like in Vegas right now, I pack a small carry-on with a few necessities, leave a note on the fridge for Spike, and head out to grab some food on the way to the airport.

Why he couldn't have given me some damn warning fuck only knows.

It's not until I'm standing at the security gate that I have time to really focus the email Zach forwarded with all my booking information on.

"Fucking hell," I mutter when I see that he's booked me first class, much to the annoyance of the family behind me. This trip might be last-minute, but at least he had the forethought to send me in style.

I get through security without much hassle and I'm soon heading through departures, following the signs for the first-class lounge. Like fuck am I buying myself a drink when I can get it for free.

I've never flown first class before. Hell, it's been years since I've flown full stop. Zach's always told me that he'd organise for me to head to one of the US studios for a bit, but it's never happened. We're always too busy, which leads me to wonder what the deal is right now. It's not like we're quiet in London and he needs my talented hands elsewhere; we're pretty much booked solid. Or at least, we will be now we're two artists down.

The large electric doors open as I walk up to them, revealing a very sharp woman sitting behind the desk. She looks like she's got a stick shoved so far up her arse I'm surprised it's not coming out of the top of her head. She takes one look at me with my creased t-shirt, inked arms and piercings and turns her nose up. Apparently, I don't fit her ideal customer.

"Hi," I say, plastering my fakest smile into place.

"Good afternoon, sir. Please could I see your boarding pass."

"Certainly." I hand it over, smug as fuck as she flicks her eyes over it.

"Well… okay then, sir. The lounge is just through there on the left. You're welcome to any of the refreshments on offer. I hope you have a wonderful journey to…" She looks back down at my phone and rolls her eyes. "Las Vegas."

"I can't wait. I hear there are strippers and hookers everywhere," I announce loudly, knowing that the doors have opened at least twice behind me in the time I've been standing here.

She blanches and quickly returns my phone before

looking over my shoulder to her next victim. He's probably some square in a suit, a type I'm sure she's much more used to. Someone just like my brother, no doubt.

I take in the over-the-top arrangement of flowers on a side table as I make my way through the doors she pointed me through. It's a bit like I've walked into Narnia. The loud noise and excitable screaming kids are long gone, and in their place is soft music, businessmen sitting at their laptops, comfortable-looking seating, and a vast array of food and drink. Walking over, I get myself a bottle of beer and grab a couple of cakes to pass the time.

Just about managing to juggle both along with my small pull-along case, I turn and look for a seat, but I don't get very far because everything stops.

What the actual fuck?

I stand there, staring. I'm probably right in the way, but I'm too shocked to care about the square behind me.

I'm dreaming. I've fucking got to be.

I blink a few times, thinking that my vision is going to clear and the woman sitting before me staring down at her tablet isn't anyone I recognise, let alone *her*.

Twelve days I've been desperate to find her without much luck, yet I walk into the first class lounge in Heathrow and there she fucking is.

My mouth opens as my heart starts to race. This is a coincidence, right? I think back to Zach's vague message and ideas about being set up start firing off in my head.

She either gets bored of what she's reading or she senses my stare, because after a few more seconds of me trying to figure out what the fuck is going on, she looks up and right at me.

She doesn't register anything for a few seconds, but I

see the moment reality hits her. Her eyes go wide, her lips part, and every muscle in her body tenses.

She drops her tablet to the table a little too harshly as she stands. "Carter, what the hell?"

"I was going to ask you the same thing, doll."

"Why are you even here?" She glances around, probably noting, exactly like I did when I first entered, that I don't really fit in.

"Why? Am I bringing the tone of the place down a notch?"

"What? No, that's not what I—" She shakes her head, trying to gather her thoughts. "Why are you here?"

"I got a message asking me to be. You?"

Her eyes narrow at me before she mutters, "Same."

I open my mouth to say something, but the reason why we're both being summoned to Vegas suddenly hits me. "They're fucking not, are they?"

"Trust me, I have no fucking clue what they're playing at."

"Is anyone else here?" I ask, thinking of the rest of her family who I'm sure would be desperate to be there if what I'm thinking is correct.

"Nope, just me. Biff said she needed me and emailed me these flight details. I was in the middle of work, for fuck's sake. I love that they think I can drop everything and come running."

"Well, you have."

"Yeah, silly me. I'm questioning that even more now."

"Ouch."

She blows out a frustrated breath. "Go and find somewhere else to sit. I've got work to do." After righting her jacket, she drops back down into her seat and puts her tablet back on her lap, making a show of staring down at it like she's actually reading something on it.

Sadly for her, she's not woken it back up, so all she's staring at is her reflection in a black screen.

"You know how to use that thing, doll?"

"Fuck you. This is a fucking disaster."

"Oh, I don't know. I think it could be a lot of fun."

When she looks back up at me, her teeth are bared in frustration. "How's that exactly?"

"We're heading to the City of Sin. What's not fun about that?"

"You're clearly going to be there."

"Jeez, it's no wonder you're single. Not only have you got a stick up your arse, but you're a bit of a bitch." I tilt my head, allowing my hair to flop into my eyes, hoping that I look innocent.

"Don't give me that look. Nothing I can say touches your massive ego."

"I think you could do with some loosening up, doll."

Dropping my stuff on the sofa beside where she's sitting, I turn on my heels and set about softening her rough edges. If I'm going to have to spend the next fuck knows how many hours with her, then it's in my interest to make her at least a little more compliant.

I pull a small bottle of sauvignon blanc from the chiller, and a wine glass.

"Here, have this. If you're nice, I might even let you share my cake."

"I don't want your damn cake."

"I'm sure I can tempt you. It's triple chocolate." I wave it under her nose, and despite the fact that she wants to look indifferent, I see the way her pupils dilate. Almost like they did when they locked on my cock that night.

I drop down right beside her, stretch my long legs out, and make a show of eating my first piece, moan of satisfaction and all.

"You're a real fucking pain the arse, you know that?"

"It's not news to me, doll," I say, I keep my tone light, not showing the emotions that statement threatens to erupt inside me.

"Carter, why can't you be more like your brother? You're a pain in my arse, boy."

Shaking the memories away, I focus on the explosion of chocolate in my mouth and the tempting woman beside me.

"Of course it's not. You drive everyone else crazy too?"

"Probably, but I have a feeling the crazy you're experiencing right now is for you only."

Her head snaps over to me, irritation filling her eyes. "I'm not feeling anything right now aside from crazy mad that you're here ruining my peace, and apparently my impromptu trip to Vegas."

"Vegas isn't Vegas without a little temptation, doll. You need to embrace your inner wild child or you're going to miss all the fun."

"Let's get something straight. I'm going for my brother and my best friend. I'm not going to lose everything I have on the tables or to get so wasted I forget the whole trip. Now, I've got work to do, so if you don't mind shutting the hell up, I might go a little easier on you."

This time, when she turns back to her tablet, she does at least turn it on, although I have a suspicion that she doesn't read a word of the document that's open in front of her.

Silence stretches between us while the chemistry that's

been sparking since our first disastrous meeting is still crackling away nicely. And that's how I know she'll give in to what she wants eventually. It might be easy to avoid when I'm not around, but sitting inches from her... I'm all she can think about right now, I'd put fucking money on it.

I eat half of the cake, enjoying every mouthful. But as sweet as it is, I can't help craving a taste of something even better.

"You really should try this. It's incredible."

"Carter," she warns, her voice low and husky. It does things to my body that probably shouldn't happen in the first class lounge.

"Come on." I elbow her in the arm. "Open up."

I hold the fork full of chocolatey goodness out between us. After huffing a breath, she turns to look at it. Her eyes bounce between it and my eyes as she tries to weigh up her options.

"If I eat this, will you shut up and let me do some work?"

"Sure."

She rolls her eyes before leaning forward. Her mouth opens, and fuck if my own doesn't mimic the movement. She wraps her red-stained lips around my fork, and a groan rumbles up my throat at the sight alone. Her eyes shoot to mine, the brown impossibly dark as she stares up at me before she pulls the chunk of cake free and sits back.

"Hmm..." she says once she's swallowed, quirking her lip. "I've had better." She sits back in place, but I don't miss her quickly checking me out before looking back at the boring shit on her tablet.

"I very much doubt that. I'm an expert when it comes

to... *cake*, so I know for a fact that you've experienced some good shit."

"Why are you still talking?"

I wince, making a show of zipping my lips shut before returning to finishing off both the chocolate cake and the Victoria sponge I also grabbed a slice of. I moan in delight with every mouthful. It's good cake, but it's not really *that* good. What amuses me so much is the way her shoulders lock up each time she hears the growl come from the back of my throat.

Once I'm done, I lean forward to place the plate on the coffee table, but just before it connects, the fork falls off the side, clattering right beside her foot.

I glance up at her when I feel her hate-filled stare burning into the back of my head.

"Whoops." It was a total accident, but now I'm reaching forward to pick it back up, I can't help but notice the opportune situation it's put me in.

My knuckles brush the bare skin of Danni's ankle a beat before she gasps and swiftly moves it away.

"I know what you're doing," she warns, "but I should tell you now that it won't work."

Placing the fork back onto the plate, I look back at her. Her pupils are shot from me just sitting beside her, her chest heaves, and her breasts press against the light fabric of her blouse.

"You might want to give your nipples the memo."

Truth is, I can't see them. I can only imagine how pert and ready they are. That's only confirmed when Danni looks down at her chest in a panic.

Sitting back, I ensure my knuckles trail up as much of the bare skin of her calf as possible.

Leaning over, I brush a lock of her curly hair from her

ear. "Your mouth can tell me whatever you want. Your body, however, tells a very different story, doll."

"That's enough." She goes to move, but my hand landing on her thigh stops her as she's about to lift her arse from the seat.

"This is only the beginning." She shudders as my breath tickles over her sensitive skin and her muscles clench under my touch.

"I can't believe this is happening."

"Well, you'd better start believing, because it's real, doll." I sit back and once again stretch my legs out, my thigh pressing against hers as I rearrange my jeans, ensuring she knows exactly what I'm doing.

"Excuse me. I need to— No. I'm not explaining myself to you." With her chin tipped up in defiance, she marches across the room to the bathroom. Her hips sway deliciously in her fitted skirt, and her legs look killer in her heels.

"Fuck," I moan to myself. This trip could be fucking epic.

8

Danni

The second I read the message I knew there was a very good chance of this happening. There's only one reason why Zach and Biff could want me in Las Vegas at the last minute, and I'm pretty sure it's not to help out in his studio—which, coincidentally, it seems he set up whilst Harrison and Summer were there pulling a very similar stunt to what I'm assuming they're about to do.

Our parents are going to fucking kill him. They were devastated when they discovered that Harrison married Summer without them there to witness it. It's the reason Summer was ambushed into the huge wedding they had a few weeks ago.

I lift my eyes from the water pouring from the tap and to the mirror in front of me. They're dark, and my cheeks are still heated. If I can see that, then there's no doubt that he could.

Fuck. Fuck. Fuck it all to hell.

I had one thing to do when it came to Carter James fucking Wright, and that was to avoid him. Easier said than bloody done when he just keeps appearing in my life despite the fact that he has no way to contact me. His friend request on Facebook taunts me every time I open the bloody app. I knew it was him immediately, despite the dark profile picture. He's in the shadows, but even still I could almost feel his green eyes staring at me, demanding me to give him more than I'm willing to.

He's had a night from me—well, an hour at most. What more does he want? He's not exactly the forever, or at least for a decent amount of time, kind of guy I was looking for.

Rolling my eyes at myself in the mirror, I pull my gloss from my jacket pocket and top up my lips just as an excuse to waste some more time. Glancing at my watch, I see that we've not got much longer until hopefully we can start boarding. I just pray to God that Zach and Biff got these tickets so last minute that we're sitting as far apart as possible.

"You've got to be fucking kidding me," I say, coming to a stop beside the two empty first class seats with the corresponding numbers to our boarding passes.

The seats themselves look incredible, and I might actually be able to get some sleep seeing as they're the ones that turn into a bed, but they're right beside each other. It seems there's no getting away from him.

"Wow, look at that. We're going to be flying buddies," he announces, stopping so close behind me that his groin presses against my arse. I jump forward, but his hand lands on my hip, stopping me from escaping. "Looks like you're stuck with me for a few hours yet."

"There's a screen. I can shut you out."

He chuckles behind me. "I thought you'd already been trying to do that. It doesn't seem to be working out all that well for you, does it?"

"I've got work to do, and I need to sleep. The time difference is going to fuck me up, so I need to get on US time as soon as possible. What I don't need is you chatting bullshit in my ear for the entire flight."

"Okay, okay," he says, lifting his hands in surrender and thankfully backing away from me. "I've gotta say, I'm looking forward to spending our first night together."

"Glad one of us is," I mutter. I sort my belongings out, drop my tablet and diary to my table, and, after kicking my shoes off and carefully folding my jacket, I drop into my chair in the hope of catching up on some of the work I should have done this afternoon before that text came through from Biff.

He remains silent, watching the other passengers get comfortable and then the flight attendants as they do their safety demonstration and final checks.

The second I'm able to, I lift the divider between us to block him out. The last thing I need is his smug as fuck face looking over at me every few seconds. He thinks he's got me all figured out, he thinks he knows what I want, but he couldn't be more wrong, because this right now is what nightmares are made of. All I can hope is that I'm going to wake up soon and find out it was all some fucked-up dream.

I manage to work and sleep through almost the whole flight, and to my amazement, he allows me to keep the screen up until the flight attendant insists I lower it before we start our final descent.

"Miss me?" he asks with a wide smile playing on his lips.

"Like you wouldn't believe," I deadpan, rolling my eyes.

"I'm glad you had a nice sleep and are now in a better mood."

I shoot him a glare, but instead of taking it as the warning I intended, he just laughs at me.

"I love it when you're angry. It makes you even hotter."

"Whatever you say," I mutter.

The second we're allowed out of our seats, I'm gathering all my things and making my way towards the doors. I don't bother looking to see if he's following, because I already know that I'm not lucky enough to lose him that easily.

"Anyone would think you're trying to run away from me," he says, stepping up beside me as we walk down the tunnel towards the terminal.

"That's because I am."

"Aw, I'm so glad we're enjoying this trip together." He wraps his arm around my shoulders and pulls my body into his. The move has my muscles locking up. I remember all too well how his body feels against mine, and it's not what I need to be imagining when I should be getting as far away from him as possible.

"And if you want to end this trip with your balls still attached to your body, then I suggest you get your hands off me," I say, shrugging him off and picking up my pace a little. I'm unlikely to outrun him, seeing as his legs are just a little longer than mine and I'm currently wearing heels, but any amount of space between us right now is a bonus.

He stays back and allows me to breathe some air that's not tainted with his scent and follows me all the way to luggage collection.

"Why are you even here? You've got your case," I spit, looking down to his tiny carry-on. I've no idea how anyone fits what they need into one of those things, even for one night. It's insane.

"Correct me if I'm wrong, but I think we're going to the same place. Plus, I thought I'd do the gentlemanly thing and carry your cases for you."

"While I appreciate the gesture, this is twenty-twenty. I'm more than capable of manoeuvring my own case."

"I don't doubt it for a second, doll."

"Do you have to keep calling me that?"

"Sure do, doll."

"You're exasperating, Trick."

"I'll prove that you want me eventually."

Rolling my eyes is turning into a regular exercise around this man. I come to a stop at the luggage belt and drop my laptop bag to the floor at my feet. He steps right up beside me, his arms lightly brushing mine.

"I do hope they've booked us one room. That will be so much fun."

"There's something wrong with you," I say, turning to look at him, and I'm glad I do because just for a spilt second, I see a crack in his armour and a hint at the guy hiding beneath the humour and sarcasm. I open my mouth to ask something, but he beats me to it.

"Oh, there's plenty, but right now my biggest issue is that it's been six weeks since I was inside you, and that's entirely too long."

My cheeks flame as my mind immediately returns to Biff's flat. Thankfully, movement in front of me is the perfect distraction. "Oh look, here come the cases. Let's hope mine comes quick."

"I'm sure I could make you come quick."

A growl rumbles up my throat, but a response fails me because all I can focus on is the clench of my muscles and my body demanding that I take him up on the offer, despite what my brain tells me.

Thankfully, my case only takes a few minutes, so before we know it, we're heading out towards the awaiting taxis so we can head to the hotel to find the two people who instigated this whole palaver.

"Go and grab a cab, I just need to shoot to the little boys' room," Carter says once the exit is in sight.

"Fine," I mutter as he veers off to the right.

When I get out in the fresh air, there's a line of taxis all waiting for passengers. I walk straight up to the first one and, without thinking twice, I give him the hotel name Biff included in her message and jump inside.

"I'm sorry, do you mind being as quick as possible? I'm in a bit of a rush."

"Of course, ma'am. We'll have you there in a flash."

"Thank you." I sit back and look out of the window. Just as the car pulls away from the curb, I spot Carter walking out of the terminal and looking around for me. His brows draw together in confusion before he finds me. Our eyes lock. Mine probably sparkle in amusement while his harden in frustration. His head shakes slowly from side to side, but I don't miss the smile that twitches at his lips.

Game on, baby. Game on.

I'm first to the hotel, no surprise there. After thanking the driver and giving him a generous tip for doing as I requested, I hop out and head inside. The second I push the door open, I spot her.

I just about have time to drop my bags before Biff collides with me.

"You're here. You're here." She squeezes me tightly, her excitement palpable despite my exhaustion.

"Not sure I had a lot of choice," I say with a laugh into her hair.

She pulls back and looks at me with a wince. "Yeah, sorry about that. It's all a bit crazy."

"You're telling me."

"Talking about crazy, where's your travel buddy?"

"Ha, funny story. So... I killed him."

"Joke away, but I should warn you, I've got our whole afternoon planned and it won't end until you tell me everything. And I mean *everything*."

Groaning, I allow her to pick up some of my bags and lead me across the reception towards a lift.

"Don't I need to check in?"

"Zach's got you covered. You're mine this afternoon."

"Why do I get the impression that it's not going to be as fun as it sounds?"

"I guess that all depends on how easy you give up the information I need."

"You've got some making up to do to me, first."

"Why? We just got you here first class, what could possibly have gone wrong?"

"You've no idea." With yet another roll of my eyes, I step into the lift beside her and we descend towards what seems to be the spa a few floors down. I can't really complain about that after the day I've had.

9

Carter

I shouldn't have been surprised to see Danni disappear off in a cab without me. She's made it clear since the moment I found her in the lounge that she didn't want me here. I probably should have been angry that she'd abandon me quite so easily. Part of me was, but a bigger part of me was excited. She was playing a game, but she didn't know me well enough yet to know that I never lose. All she just did was up the challenge. If I wasn't already sure that this trip wouldn't end until I was inside her, then I was fully confident now. She wants to run, to avoid this thing between us... well, I intend on reminding her every chance I get.

By the time I turn to grab my own cab, all the ones that seemed to be empty and waiting when I first walked out to find her have vanished and I have to wait in line for another.

I must be a good thirty minutes behind Danni by the time I arrive at the hotel.

"Took your time, didn't you? Dan was here ages ago."

"Don't remind me," I murmur as he pulls me in for a hug.

"How you doing, man? Feels like it's been forever."

"It's not even been two weeks. I'm surprised you noticed while having full time access to Biff."

"She lets me out of bed every now and then." The smug as shit smile that graces his face makes my fingers twitch into fists to wipe it off. It seems he's getting more than necessary while I'm being cock blocked by the woman who should be enjoying it.

"Speaking of, where is the little lady?"

"Taken Danni to the spa for the afternoon to get ready."

"So I guessed correctly then. You putting a ring on it, man?"

"Too fucking right. I'm not letting that one go. Here," he says, handing me a key card. "For your suite."

"Suite? Fucking hell, you're really pushing the boat out."

"Stop complaining or I'll keep the bottle of Patron that's sitting up there for myself."

"Most definitely not complaining. The others are going to be pissed, though."

"They'll get over it. If we're doing this, then it's going to be our way."

"Wouldn't expect anything else."

I follow him to the lift before he hits the button for a floor that must almost be in the clouds. I knew Las Vegas was bigger than life itself, but nothing could have prepared me for the sights of the strip as we drove here, or for the lavish hotel that we're currently making our way through.

Zach taps a key card to a little box before pushing the door open.

"Holy fucking shit." My chin drops in shock as I take in the view of the lights down the strip. "I'm not even going to pretend to have a clue as to how much this cost you."

"Probably best you don't. Just enjoy it. I plan on only doing this once in my lifetime, so I might as well make the most of it."

I locate the bedroom once I'm able to rip my eyes away from the view. It's still light out yet it's breath-taking; I can only imagine what it'll be like once night comes with all the neon lights illuminating the sky.

"I need to shower," I shout through to Zach.

"Whatever. Just know that I'm starting without you."

"No fucking chance." Walking out of the room once I've dropped my shirt to the floor, I swipe up the bottle that's sitting in the middle of the coffee table before sloshing a generous measure into the glass waiting for me. "To irrational decisions and shotgun weddings," I say, lifting my drink to tap to his.

"Fuck, that's some good shit," Zach groans, looking at his now empty glass like it holds the answers to all the world's problems.

"Don't drink it all before I get back. I need some more of that after the day I've had."

Zach eyes me suspiciously but allows me to retreat instead of grilling me on why my day with his sister was so draining.

Stripping out of the rest of my clothes, I push through

the door in the bedroom to find the biggest bathroom I've ever seen, let alone been in. It takes me a few seconds to figure out how to put the shower on, but once I do, water shoots from every direction imaginable.

"Whoa," I mutter, standing in the torrent of water. The electric shower that constantly cuts out on us at home is going to be a shock to the system after this, that's for sure.

Tipping my head back, I let the water run over me while thinking over the events of today, or more so the sass that's fallen from Danni's mouth. Every single time she comes back at me, it makes my dick hard.

My semi bobs between my legs, taunting me. It would be so easy to wrap my hand around it and bring myself the release I've craved since the moment I found her in the lounge earlier. But I already know that it won't be enough. I need more.

I need *her*.

I make use of the complimentary shower gel before stepping out and wrapping a humongous white fluffy towel around myself. The image of Danni, dripping wet and standing right here wrapped in it fills my mind.

Fuck, that woman is messing with my head.

Despite the fact that she's spent all the time we've had together trying to prove that she doesn't like or want me, it's easy to see why we got on so well until reality was thrown into the mix. She's exactly what I've been looking for. Sass wrapped in a hot little package. She's not the kind of person to just allow me to do whatever. She's the type of woman who will challenge me at every turn, and although she'll probably be a massive pain in my arse, no day will ever be boring with her beside me.

After pulling on a clean set of clothes, I head out to

join Zach. He pours me a new drink as I walk towards him and passes it over after I fall onto the sofa opposite him.

"So, what did she do to get you so wound up?"

"I'm not wound up."

"Titch, I know you too well for you to try to bullshit me. We know you met before you discovered she was my sister. Time to spill, bro. Then I can decide if I need to hurt you or not."

I down my whiskey, wondering exactly how I'm meant to tell him the truth without ending up with a broken nose. We both know that I could overpower him. I might not have got in a ring for a while, but that doesn't mean fighting's not like riding a bike for me. But, I'm the one in the wrong here. I'm the one who slept with his sister, even if it was before I knew who she was. It still breaks the unspoken rules between us.

"Titch?" Zach warns, leaning forward and placing his elbows on his knees. His blue eyes drill into me, and I swallow nervously. This isn't going to go down well.

"Firstly, can I just point out that because you kept your family away from business, I had no hope in hell of knowing she was related to you in any way." His brows rise, although I'm unsure if it's in impatience or amusement at my trying to shift the blame.

"Go on."

"Ugh. So got myself back on online dating—"

"Why? You hate that shit?"

"I know. I was just looking for someone... different. Spike said it was a stupid idea, but I used Logan's picture and said I was a banker."

He laughs as the ball of dread grows in the pit of my stomach.

"Anyway, I met this girl. Intelligent, funny, hot as fu—" My words falter when Zach's eyes darken. "Err... really pretty, beautiful. We got on so well, and to be honest, I forgot that I was meant to be pretending to be someone more..."

"More?"

I shrug, not wanting to look insecure. "Posh, intelligent."

"Titch," he says on a sigh, but I cut him off.

"This isn't about me. Just let me finish, okay?" He nods and gestures for me to do so. "She suggested we meet. I was fucking terrified. She thought I was this suave suited guy, and there I was going to be with messy hair and covered in tats. I'm not sure I've ever been so nervous in my fucking life. I nearly bailed," I admit. "I was sitting there scrolling through our previous chat, knowing that no matter how terrified I was to admit the truth to her that I needed to see her, talk to her in person. Then there she was. Standing in the middle of the place, totally breathtaking and I damn near lost my mind. She was just everything. I walked up to her and..."

"And?" Zach asks, sounding way to invested in this story when he already knows it's about his sister.

"She opened her mouth and basically ripped me a new one for tricking her, and before I knew my head from my arse she'd walked out."

His laugh echoes around the room.

"It's not fucking funny," I sulk.

"Mate, it's hilarious. I've been on the wrong end of that mouth a time or two, I know what it's like."

I stare at him with a blank expression. "She's fucking relentless."

"So that's it, then. You met, she chewed you out, and then you ended up on a plane together here?"

"Err... yes and no."

I laugh as he leans forward and pours himself a new drink. I think he's going to need it.

10

Danni

"You let him screw you on my sofa?" Biff screeches at me, her eyes wide in shock.

"Maybe. Think of it as karma for fucking my brother while I was asleep in the next room."

"Hmph." Lifting her champagne glass, she tips it to her lips. "He's a really good guy. You should probably give him a break."

"He tricked me into thinking he was someone else, B. I can't just forget that."

"I get it. But it's hardly the crime of the century. If there's chemistry there, don't you think you owe it to yourself to find out if it could be something?"

"He's not my type." I wave her off, going for my own much-needed drink.

"Dan," she says on a sigh. "Sometimes the things we need the most aren't the things we think we want. Would it be such a hardship to give him the benefit of the doubt and see if it really is something?"

I think of the way his body moved against mine, and my cheeks flush red.

"No, I didn't think so."

"It probably doesn't matter anyway. The second Zach finds out, he'll probably kill him."

"That could very well be the case. He'd better not to do it today though, he needs a best man."

"So yeah... about this shotgun wedding..."

"He proposed on the beach in LA. It was..." She gets this dreamy look in her eyes and a little green monster rears its ugly head inside me. "So romantic."

"Zach? Romantic?"

"Yeah. I was so shocked. We'd not talked about any kind of future aside from our living arrangements, so I really didn't see it coming."

"And this?" I ask, gesturing to the Vegas hotel we're currently in.

"Neither of us wants a show. I'm not interested in months of my mother giving me stress about the size of the table arrangements and what flowers should be in my bouquet."

"That's if she even agreed to you marrying him," I mutter and watch as she pales. "Don't tell me that you're about to marry him and you've not even introduced him to your parents."

"Guilty," she admits with a wince.

"They're going to fucking kill you."

"Meh, what are they really going to do? Take away my trust fund and my flat? I think I'll cope. We already agreed that I was going to fully move into his place when we got back, and he's offered me a full-time job."

"You really want to work full-time as a receptionist forever?" I ask sceptically.

"Receptionist, no. Artist? Yes."

My chin drops as I put two and two together. "You're..."

"Zach's going to train me up. I'm so excited."

"Your parents really are going to kill you."

"I know. Isn't it great?" The smile that spreads across her face is infectious. "Seriously though, I need you to know that I'm not just doing this to piss off my parents. That's just an added bonus. I really love him, Dan."

I smile at her as emotion burns the backs of my eyes. "I know you do. You don't need to tell me. I see it every time you look at each other, every time you talk about him. It's sickening."

"Oh, shut it. You're just jealous."

"Fucking right I am."

"So what are you waiting for? Your perfect guy could be inside this hotel right now. You just need to stop giving him grief and give him the chance you told me he keeps begging for."

"I guess crazier things have happened in Vegas."

"And if it all goes Pete Tong, it can just be another of those disasters that stays in Vegas and we never have to mention it again, aside from the fact you're about to become my sister-in-law and the man in question is your brother's best friend. I'm sure it'll all be fine."

"Fucking hell," I mutter, having finished off my glass. "What were the chances of this happening?"

"Pretty bloody slim, I'd say."

"More champagne?"

"Yes," Biff says eagerly as I get up to get us both a refill.

Her eyes burn into my fluffy robe-clad back as I walk

away. Her words about crazy things happening in Vegas spin around in my head. Could I throw caution to the wind and just enjoy what he has to offer for the time we're here before going back to my normal life, sans tattooed bad boy, once we return?

My core aches as I think about the fun we could have if I just let go a little. It would sure help ease the tension he's caused within me since appearing in that lounge earlier today. Jesus, was that today?

"So, enough about me. Tell me about this wedding."

"The plan is... pampering, hair and make-up, and then we're heading to a little chapel off the strip for a service this evening. Then anything from there is up for discussion."

"Just a little different to the last wedding we attended."

"Yes, and for very good reason."

I nod at her, totally understanding both her and Zach's need to do it this way. I'm just grateful they invited me. I'd have been gutted to miss it, much like our parents are going to be.

"So have you got a dress?"

"I have. I got a dress for you, too."

"Can I trust you not to have got me a frilly monstrosity?"

"You'll just have to wait and find out. You like ruffles though, right?"

"Ha, you're funny. So what do I have to look forward to here? You booked us in for the full works?"

"Only the best for the bride and maid of honour," Biff says with a smile.

"Awesome."

"It should give you enough time to decide what to do about Titch."

"Great," I mutter.

"Although, that decision might be out of your hands when he sees you in your dress." She winks, and my stomach drops. What the hell is she expecting me to wear? She must notice my concern. "Trust me, Dan. I know what suits you."

We don't leave the spa until not only every inch of our bodies has been scrubbed, polished and waxed to perfection, but our hair and make-up is flawless.

I follow Biff to the lift and stand aside as she hits the number for our floor.

"Right, this is you." She lifts a key card to unlock the door before slipping it into my robe pocket, seeing as my hands are laden with bags. "And hopefully our dresses should be— ah, right here." I come to a stop behind her to find a rail with two dress bags hanging in the centre of the living area.

"You booked me into a suite? Bit much, isn't it?"

"We wanted to treat you," is all she says, walking over to peek inside her dress bag. "You ready to do this? The guys are meeting us at the chapel in just over an hour."

"Sounds good." She takes the two bags before walking towards an open door which I assume goes to the bedroom.

I follow, taking in my lavish surroundings as I go, wondering what I did to deserve all this treatment. With the sun setting, all the lights of the strip in the distance are starting to come to life.

"This place is impressive. Zach must really love you," I say with a laugh.

"He just booked it. I had no idea until we got here that he'd done all this. I was pretty blown away."

When I join her in the room, she's just revealed her dress from the bag. "Biff, that's gorgeous." My eyes run over all the ivory lace billowing from the unzipped bag. "Is it short?"

"It is. And," she says turning to pick up a box, "look at the shoes!" She lifts the lid and reveals the most beautiful pair of multi-coloured sequined Louboutins.

"Whoa," I say, reaching out for one when she lifts them from the box.

"Right, and that leads me onto your dress."

Placing the box gently on the bed, she reveals what's hiding in the other dress bag.

"Err... it's stunning, but I think they left half of it behind," I joke, looking over the small scrap of sequin fabric she's holding up.

"You're funny. I might have an almost traditional dress, but don't forget this is a Vegas wedding, baby."

"Jesus, what has my brother done to you?"

"Now, there's a bottle of bubbles chilling over there waiting for the top to be popped, and then soon there will be two guys expecting us at the chapel. We wouldn't want to disappoint either now, would we?"

I groan. Thoughts of Carter already weren't too far from my mind—I really don't need the reminder.

"You can't tell Zach about what happened," I say, passing her a new glass of champagne.

"You really think you're going to get through your time here without him noticing?"

I shrug, hoping Zach will be too distracted by his soon-to-be bride to notice what we're up to. It's a long shot.

"Just chill out, yeah? Zach will be fine. Tonight is about enjoying ourselves, so put your worries aside and go with the flow." She lifts her brows, and I hate that I'm making this about me when it should be about her and Zach.

"Yeah. Right..." I take a sip of my drink, the bubbles exploding on my tongue, helping to ignite some excitement within me. I'm about to witness my best friend and brother get married. That needs to be my only focus right now. "Let's get you in that dress."

11

Carter

By some miracle, when I leave the hotel dressed in the smart trousers and shirt Zach had previously selected for me, I'm not accessorising it with a black eye or a split lip.

I could see his frustration growing as I explained about discovering Danni that night in Biff's flat and then not realising that she was his sister until his birthday meal, but I also told him quite frankly that it wasn't going to stop me. His eyes widened in shock as I expressed my desire to go after her. After knocking back his fresh glass of whiskey, he stood before me and held out his hand.

Pride oozed from his eyes as he wished me good luck in trying to tame his little sister. I could see the tension pulling at his muscles as he did it, but I appreciated that he was trying to be the bigger man about it.

"It could be worse, you know," I'd said to him once he'd retaken his seat.

"How so? You wanna bang my little sister." He made a gagging gesture as he said it, making me chuckle.

"It could be Spike after her."

"Oh fucking hell. There's not enough whiskey in the world for that situation."

The two of us stand at the entrance to the chapel Biff had chosen for the ceremony, and my usually relaxed and laidback best friend and boss paces back and forth in front of me.

"Please don't tell me you're worried that she'll bail."

"She'll be here," he states, his confidence in Biff not wavering one bit.

"So what's with the nerves?"

"I'm getting married, T. I'm allowed to be a little apprehensive."

"You're sure about this, aren't you?" I don't mean it as a threat, but he stops pacing and is standing right in front of me in a second.

His blue eyes stare down into mine. "Yes, I'm fucking sure. She's mine. Was from the second D offered her a job."

"I know, man. I know. I was just saying. Jeez. Chill your tits."

His eyes bounce between mine for a few seconds before he relaxes a little and stands down. He doesn't go back to pacing; instead he falls down onto one of the seats and drops his head into his hands.

"What's taking them so long?"

"I don—" My words falter when I look out of the tinted windows. A cab's just pulled up, and the pair of legs that's revealed makes my breath catch.

My mouth waters and I fight to swallow as I wait for the rest of her to appear.

"Holy fuck."

"What is it?"

"Shit," I bark, not realising that I said anything aloud. "We... uh... need to go in."

"Fuck. Are they here?"

"Yeah. Come on, let's go."

Regretfully, I turn my back on Danni and usher Zach towards the double doors we were instructed to use when we first arrived and Zach explained what they wanted for the service.

We come to a stop in front of the officiant and wait. Zach alternates between staring at his feet and looking up at the ceiling. I can only imagine how he feels right now, because my nerves are shot and I'm not the one getting married.

After what seems like the longest wait of my life, the doors at the back of the room are pushed open and the music changes.

Zach's body goes ramrod straight, but he doesn't look around. I, on the other hand, can't keep my eyes away.

With their arms linked, Biff and Danni make their way to us. Biff's got the widest smile on her face. Her joy melts my heart, but I can't focus on Biff, because without instruction from my brain, my eyes find her. Danniella Abbot. My best friend's sister and the one woman on the planet I shouldn't go anywhere near. But it's pointless even trying to stay away, because I'm drawn to her like no other.

Her dark hair has been styled and pulled away from her face, but a few locks hang down, making my fingers itch to reach out for one. Her eyes pop and her red lips call to me like a moth to a fucking flame.

Then I get down to the dress. I fight a groan because Zach doesn't need to hear me drowning in lust for his sister at this exact movement, but fuck me, the dress is killer.

It's a silver, barely-there thing that I'm sure isn't what most bridesmaids expect to be wearing to their best friend's wedding, but it looks phenomenal. I also have a feeling that it's going to look even better on my bedroom floor later tonight, because after getting Zach's approval—or at least not a point-blank refusal—I intend on doing everything I possibly can to make her mine. To show her just how good we can be if she were just to give us a chance.

It's not until they're right beside us that Zach turns. I'm so glad I manage to rip my eyes from Danni to see his reaction to his bride, because it's priceless, and I'm sure it would bring a tear to the eye of even the coldest arsehole.

"Holy shit," he mutters, running his eyes over her.

"Fucking hell, put a ring on it before you strip her naked, man. Ow," I complain when his palm connects with the back of my head.

Standing aside, I allow Biff to take my place beside her soon-to-be husband and step up to Danni.

She tenses the second my shirt-covered arm brushes her bare one.

"Do you have any idea what that dress is doing to me?"

"Nothing, I would hope. I am, however, expecting it to help me pull tonight."

"I can guaran-fucking-tee that you're getting lucky tonight, doll."

For the first time since she walked in, she looks at me. Her breath catches as she does so, and I can't help but smirk at her. She's as affected by me as I am by her. Excitement for what this night might hold for us stirs in my stomach, and my cock swells as ideas of being inside her once again fill my head.

She bites her bottom lip, and I'm just about to say something about it being mine to bite on when the officiant begins the service.

I'm forced to sit beside Danni while our best friends say their vows and tie the knot with her scent making my mouth water and knowing I can't touch her. Her bare thigh almost touches mine, and the temptation to reach out and trail my fingertips up it to discover just how soft her skin is almost becomes too much.

"You're meant to be watching the wedding," she whispers when there's a break in proceedings.

"How am I meant to do that when you're sitting beside me showing this much skin?"

"You're like teenage boy, you know that?"

"Can't help myself around you, doll."

Zach glances over, and I shut my mouth. We're here for them; I need to be thinking with my head, not my cock right now.

As they each say their vows, Danni sniffles beside me. A smile curls at my lips that she's such a romantic at heart, even though she tries to appear anything but.

Lifting my arm, I drop it over the back of the bench behind us and wrap it around her shoulders. She tenses, her skin erupting in goosebumps as I brush my thumb over her arm in support.

She glances up at me, but I don't take my eyes from the couple before us. I don't need to look at her to know that her eyes are darker and her breaths have increased from my simple touch alone. I feel it.

Sadly, the second the service is over, she's up out of the seat and hugging both Biff and Zach in congratulations before we make our way back out to reception.

Danni and I both take some photos of the happy couple to remember their big day before we all find ourselves in the back of a cab and heading towards the strip.

Zach and Biff sit opposite Danni and I with huge smiles on their faces, unable to take their hands off each other. As happy as I am for them, I'm equally jealous as fuck, because I'd give my right ball to be able to touch the woman sitting beside me right now, but any attempt I've made since she was crying in the chapel has been thwarted. I'm pretty sure she's not doing it to drive me crazy with need, but that's the effect she's having right now. This 'I can look but not touch' rule she seems to have set is not something I agreed to.

I'm expecting to head to some fancy arse restaurant for a meal, so when burgers are mentioned for their wedding breakfast, my chin almost hits the floor of the car.

"You for real?" I ask the two of them.

"Sure, why not?" Biff says with a shrug, looking up at Zach like he just hung the fucking moon. I hope the motherfucker knows just how lucky he is to be able to officially call that woman his now.

"Burgers and beer, and then we're hitting the strip. Good with you two?"

"Sounds perfect, man."

"Whatever you two want," Danni says, although with much less enthusiasm.

No one even bats an eyelid as we walk into the burger place. It's easy for us to think that this is a little weird, but we seem to be forgetting that we're in the home of crazy. Everyone here has seen everything at least once. Us turning up from a shotgun wedding is probably an everyday occurrence for these people.

"Congratulations," the waitress sings as she comes over to hand us menus and to take our drink orders.

Zach and Biff beam at her while I take advantage of the table covering us from the waist down and place my hand on Danni's bare thigh. She jumps a fucking mile, but thankfully both Biff and Zach are too distracted by the waitress to notice.

"What the fuck are you doing?" Danni spits, trying to push my hand away.

"Nothing," I say, attempting to sound innocent. "If you didn't want my attention then you should have worn a different dress. Or a hazmat suit," I quickly add, because I'm not sure a bigger dress would have made all that much of a difference. I'd still desperately want her out of it.

"How many times, Carter? I'm not interested. Even less so with my brother only feet away."

I lean forward so only she can hear my words. "He's fine with it, doll. I got us the all clear."

"You... you told him about..." She trails off, her voice rising an octave in shock.

"Yeah. I told him how I fucked up but explained that I'm intending on proving myself to you. He's happy. I even came out of it without any bodily damage."

"Don't worry. I can still cause you some if you keep touching me."

Moving so close that my lips brush her ear, I whisper, "Stop trying to deny what you want. I know you're wet as fuck for me right now, and I have every intention of proving that too." She gasps as I slide my palm higher.

"Carter," she squeals, now earning us the attention of everyone within a ten-foot radius.

I allow her to push my hand away, for now, while she blushes bright red and everyone wonders what's wrong with her.

"I'm sorry. Is there any chance I could get a dry white wine, please?"

The waitress startles a little at her sudden demand but quickly recovers and writes it down.

"Same for me," Biff adds, "and beer for you guys?"

Zach and I agree before she leaves us to look at the menus.

The girls both pull theirs closer and look down at them, but Zach's eyes remain on me.

"What?" I ask innocently, but his eyes narrow. He knows exactly what kind of game I'm playing.

"I might have let you off easy earlier, but things can change, Titch. Fast."

"Loud and clear, boss. Loud and clear." I lift my hands from my lap in surrender and to prove that I'm not currently knuckle-deep in his sister. Chance would be a fine thing.

"If the waitress comes back, please can you order me a bun-less chicken burger and a side salad. I'm just going to use the bathroom."

"A bun-less burger. What the fuck is that?" Zach asks, looking like the idea of it totally offends him.

"I'm going to go and check she's okay," Biff says, pushing her seat back.

"No," I bark, a little harsher than intended if Biff's wide eyes are anything to go by. "You two don't need to get in the middle of our drama. Just enjoy yourselves. I'll make sure she's okay."

"Don't do anything in the fucking toilets."

"Z, man. I'm not a fucking animal."

"I've seen evidence of the contrary in the past, my friend."

"The past is the past. We've all seen things that don't need talking about, eh boss?" He shifts uncomfortably in his seat before nodding and turns to smile at his bride.

"I don't even want to know," she says, leaning forward to kiss him.

Zach winks at me before accepting her kiss, and I walk away from the happy couple to give them some privacy.

12

Danni

Closing the door behind me, I fall back against it and tilt my face to the ceiling as I pray for the strength I need to get through the rest of tonight.

The heat of his palm is still burning into my thigh. I shouldn't want him, yet after just one look he's all I can think about. Add his touch to that, and he's damn near consumed my entire body.

I suck in a deep breath before blowing it out through pursed lips. Biff's words from earlier come back to me. I start wondering if we could pull off the quickest holiday fling ever. I can't deny that what she said was right. What happens in Vegas should stay in Vegas.

My stomach clenches as the idea of this being possible starts to build. I've had many nights of meaningless sex with guys and never wanted more afterwards. Surely, I could spend this time getting what I need from him and then move on from it the second we step foot back on English soil. Right?

A little voice in my head reminds me that I wasn't able to forget after the last time, but I push it down. It's easier to ignore than it probably should be due to the amount of alcohol racing through my body and the emotions still raging within me after watching Biff and Zach tie the knot.

Telling myself that I can do this, that I can see what happens, enjoy myself and then move on to what I really want from life, I push from the door and step towards the single toilet in this small, slightly dark bathroom.

A click from behind me has my heart jumping into my throat. I locked it. Didn't I?

I soon realise the answer because the light from the brighter corridor outside fills the room. As he shuts the door, I swear he takes all the air with it.

He's a pretty big presence at the best of times, but right now, standing before me in this small bathroom, he practically takes up every available bit of space.

"Danni, I–" he starts, but I don't allow him to say any more. My body takes over, and in seconds, I've closed the space between us, my fingers are in his hair, and my lips are reaching up for his. "Fuck," he groans as I press my entire body against his.

He stumbles back in surprise, hitting the door I was leaning against not so long ago as his hands find my waist and his lips part, accepting my kiss.

My tongue sweeps into his mouth and immediately finds his. His taste, the exact one I've craved, although with the added hint of beer, hits me and my knees buckle.

Dropping his palms to my arse, he squeezes, successfully forcing me even harder against him. The unmistakable shape of his growing erection is obvious against my stomach, and I can't help the rush of heat heading to my core, knowing that I affect him so much from just a kiss alone.

"Jesus. Fuck. Danni." His voice is no more than a growl as he spins us and pins me against the door.

He takes my wrists in his hands and lifts them above my head. The slight cowl neck to my dress falls forward, showing him just how little I'm wearing beneath, and the already short hemline lifts.

"This dress. Fuck," he barks, his eyes frantically running over every inch of me.

My chest heaves, my nipples brushing against the loose fabric of my dress, and my knickers are already soaked for him. I have no choice but to stand there and allow him to take his fill.

My blood boils as my skin tingles everywhere he looks.

"If the point of this dress was to ensure I saw no other woman tonight, then you've been successful. Although I must admit, you could have worn a bin bag and I'm sure it would have had the same effect on me."

A moan of desire rumbles up my throat. I try to catch it before it escapes, but I can't. The second a smirk appears on Carter's face, I realise it was worth it, because with his long hair hanging in his face as he stares down at me and his dark, lust-filled eyes, it only makes him hotter.

Taking both of my wrists in one hand, he trails one fingertip from the other over my wrist, and, tortuously slowing, he continues down my arm. Every muscle in my body locks up at his touch and the pounding between my legs is the only things I can focus on. My skin pricks with goose bumps and my breathing becomes embarrassingly erratic.

"Oh god," I whisper when he gets to the spaghetti strap on my dress and follows the edge of the fabric towards my breasts. My nipples become painful as he makes his way over the swell of the first one. I arch my back, desperate for him to do something, anything to quash the ache and need he's creating.

He never dips below the fabric and instead continues along to the other side.

"Carter, please," I moan, not caring quite how desperate I sound.

He leans towards me, his scent filling my nose and making my mouth water for more of his kiss. But instead of capturing my lips, he moves to my ear.

"Please, what? I didn't think you wanted me, doll."

His breath caresses the sensitive skin of my neck, and I damn near explode with frustration.

"M-maybe I was wrong."

"I'm sorry, I didn't quite make that out. Could you repeat it?" I don't miss the amusement in his tone. On another day I'd rip him a new one for it, but right now, I don't have it in me.

"Please. Please touch me. Kiss me. Anything," I demand between my heaving breaths.

"Anything?" His fingers brush down over my waist and come to a stop where my dress stops very high on my thigh. He moves it towards where I need him the most. My teeth sink into my bottom lip as I pray that he's going to give me relief from this delicious torture.

He makes it to the edge of my knickers, and then he stops, his eyes finding mine.

All the air that I wasn't aware I was holding in my lungs comes rushing out in one go.

"Carter, come on."

"I think..." he pauses, making me wish I had control of my own hands because I could make use of them right now. "I think we should really get back out there before your brother comes looking for me. Excuse me." He takes a step back, pulling me from the door at the same time, and before I blink, he's gone.

"Carter?" I squeal, standing there with my body not knowing which way is up. "Motherfucker." I race to lock the once again closed door, now needing to put myself back together even more than I did when I first walked in here.

What the fuck was he thinking, storming in here and doing that to me?

"Fuck." I bend slightly and drop my hands to my knees in utter disbelief.

My own movement catches my eye in the mirror beside me, and, when I turn to look at myself, my chin drops. I look like I've just been fucked six ways from Sunday despite the fact that he didn't so much as touch me.

"Fuck. Fuck. Fuck." I start digging into my bag that I thankfully brought in here with me to find my lipstick and to try to do something with the mess staring back at me.

I have no idea how long I've occupied this bathroom. I'm grateful that it can't be the only one, because no one's knocked yet demanding to use the facilities.

With one final fiddle to my now slightly messed-up hair-do, I reach for the door handle and attempt to prepare to walk back out there with my head held high and sit beside him.

All three heads turn to me when the sound of my heels clicking alerts them to my arrival.

"Everything okay?" Zach asks sceptically.

"Uh... yeah. Think I've just had a bit too much excitement for one day."

His brows pull even tighter as he glances between Carter and me, but he doesn't say anything else as I drop into the chair opposite him. Biff, on the other hand, has a shit-eating grin on her face.

"What?" I mouth.

She flicks a look at Carter before wiggling her eyebrows at me.

Picking up the napkin that's sitting in front of me on the table, I throw it at her, much to her amusement.

"Okay, okay."

"What's going on?" Zach asks, still looking concerned as he wraps his arm about his bride's shoulders and kisses her temple. If it weren't so damn cute, I might turn my nose up at his display of affection.

"Nothing. Girl chat."

"You didn't say anything," he points out.

"We don't need words. We just know. Right, Dan?"

"Yep."

"Fucking hell, we don't stand a chance, mate," Zach says with a laugh, turning his eyes to his best friend.

"They're women. We never stand a chance. You probably should have learned that before marrying one, man."

Zach barks out a laugh before our waitress comes over carrying the largest burgers I think I've ever seen.

"Wow, I'm going to look so lady-like in my wedding dress, tucking into his," Biff mutters, her eyes wide as she takes the colossal thing in.

"See, mine doesn't sound so stupid now, does it?" I ask Zach sarcastically when my bun-less burger turns up, the portion size almost achievable. At least without all the carbs I should be able to leave this place without looking like I'm growing a food baby. This dress won't hide any excess, that's for sure.

Silence descends on our table as we all start eating. Thankfully, no one else says anything about my disappearance, but I feel Carter's eyes on me every few seconds as I try to focus on my food and not what happened in that enclosed space down the hallway.

"Fuck. That was good," Carter announces, pushing his empty plate away from him and placing his hands on his still perfectly flat stomach. How do guys do that? If I ate that amount of food, I'd look like I was about to go into labour any moment.

"I can't do it, my dress is going to rip in half," Biff says, copying Carter's move but with a still mostly full plate

"I'm not complaining." Zach looks over at her, his eyes dropping to her tits.

"Ugh. Sister here," I say with a little wave.

"You're going to have to get used to it. Besides, I'm going to have to put up with you two."

"There will be nothing to put up with. There is no us two."

"Riiight. So do you want to tell the truth yet about what happened down there?" Zach gestures over his shoulder towards the bathrooms, and my temperature spikes. "No, I didn't think so. Dessert, anyone?"

"Yes," Carter agrees as Zach reaches for the menu in the middle of the table.

I stare at him in utter disbelief as he weighs up his options.

"What?" he asks, looking over at me.

"Nothing."

"You want to share a sundae with me, doll?"

I open my mouth to tell him where to go, but Zach beats me to it. "Doll? Fucking hell, it's worse than I thought. They've already got pet names for each other." Carter shrugs, not in the least bit bothered by Zach's teasing.

"Yeah, arsehole, dickhead... all the usual ones are up there."

"Oh, mate. Are you sure about this?"

Carter looks from Zach and to me. His eyes soften as they do and something in my chest pulls tight at the sight.

"Yeah," he says with a slight nod to his head. "Yeah, I really am."

A lump crawls up my throat. How can he be so sure about this? I've done nothing but shout at him since he turned back up in my life.

"Well, good luck to you. Don't say I didn't warn you when she cuts your bollocks off when you're sleeping."

"I'll take my chances. Just make sure you fondle them good first, yeah, doll?"

My cheeks heat once more as Zach's lips press into a thin line.

"Would any of you like anything else?" the waitress asks, distracting us all from the weird tension that's fallen around us.

"Yes, me and the lil' lady will share the chocolate sundae, please," Carter says politely before she turns to Zach and Biff.

"We'll do the same."

"But," Biff argues.

"It's our wedding night, kitten. Indulge a bit."

"I fully intend to later." I can't watch as she proceeds to check out my brother like he's already naked before her.

Glancing to my side, I find Carter's eyes firmly fixed on me.

"What?" I snap, just about done with him holding all the cards where my body is concerned. He's played me right into the palm of his hands, and his smug-as-fuck smile tells me that he's very aware of it.

"Aw, a little frustrated, doll?"

"Fuck you."

"All in good time. All in good time."

"I'm not sleeping with you tonight, so you can get any of those ideas out of your head."

He leans forward so only I can hear his next words, although the other two are now preoccupied if the lip smacking is anything to go by. "Now, now. We both know how desperate you are for my cock." I gasp, shocked by his bluntness when we have company, no matter how quietly he whispers it.

"There are plenty of other ways to get what I need, Carter. I don't need, nor want, your cock."

"I think we both know that you're only lying to yourself. But, by all means, do it your own way. I just ask one thing."

"Oh yeah, what's that?"

He pauses for a second and pulls back so I have no choice but to look into his deep green eyes. "Let me watch."

"So you can see what you could have had? Yeah, maybe I will, just so you know exactly what you're missing out on."

He groans as if in pain. "Oh, doll. You're killing me." He has my wrist in his hand before I know it, and he's placing my palm over his crotch. My breath catches as I feel his length behind the fabric. "You feel what you do to me. We're both taking what we need tonight. You can deny it all you like—it's a fun game, I'm quite enjoying it—but we both know how tonight ends, and that's with me as deep inside you as physically possible."

My mouth goes dry as the image of our bodies intertwined once again pops into my head. My body remembers how good he felt when he slid inside of me, and I can't deny that I want to experience that again.

"We'll see. My willpower is stronger than you like to believe."

He chuckles, and it pisses me off. "Let's face it: had I have touched you in that bathroom, you'd have already come all over my fingers."

My body sags in the seat, knowing that the motherfucker is dead right.

"Whatever," I mutter flippantly. "Oh, look, dessert is here."

I smile at the waitress, who places the giant sundae between us, and pick up a spoon. I might not be hungry, but fuck if I don't need something to distract me from wanting a taste of the man sitting beside me.

"Ummm... that's so good," I mutter when the chocolate sauce hits my taste buds.

"It would be better if I could lick it straight from your body."

I don't respond. I don't think I react, but then his chuckle says otherwise as I lift the next spoonful to my mouth.

13

Carter

I'm still hard as fuck after watching Danni lick the ice cream from her spoon. In my head, it wasn't a metal object she was giving that attention to. I know it's wrong with her brother staring daggers at me, but I can't help it.

"Let's get out of here. The slots are calling my name," Zach says, throwing a load of cash down on the table that will more than cover our bill before taking his wife's hand and leading her from the diner.

"After you," I say, pulling Danni's chair out and gesturing for her to go ahead. She does as she's told, for once, and takes off after the others, her arse swaying nicely as I trail behind.

By the time I look up, Zach's already found a taxi that's going to take us back to our hotel.

I watch as he and Biff climb in before Danni goes to do the same.

She bends, the hem of her dress rising enough to reveal exactly what—or not, as the case may be— she's wearing beneath that sinful dress.

"Carter, what the fuck?" she barks, stiffening when I stand right behind her, her arse just happening to fall into my hands.

"Every motherfucker out here is staring at your bare arse right now, doll. I'm doing you a favour."

"I don't give a shit. I'm sure they've all seen an arse beforrrrre," she squeals the last bit as I run my little finger over the damp lace of her underwear. She hops inside the cab faster than I thought possible, but at least she's no longer flashing anyone.

"This dress was a bad idea," Danni sulks to Biff.

"There's nothing bad about that dress, doll. Trust me."

Zach shakes his head at me before leaning forward to tell the driver where we're heading.

Only minutes later, we're climbing back out and walking towards our hotel.

I've seen Las Vegas time and time again on the TV, but even still, it never could have prepared me for what it's like in real life. The sheer size, brightness, and excitement of it all could never be accurately portrayed. It's one of those things that has to be seen to be believed, and I'm so glad I've been able to tick this place off my bucket list.

"Right, boss. You ready to put your money where your mouth is?"

"Yeah, but I ain't listening to any advice from you. I've watched you lose every game of poker we've ever played."

"Cards aren't my game. The roulette wheel, however... that's where I sense I'm going to be lucky."

"Sorry, but I'm not going by your sense. I know how much of that you have, and I'm not putting a penny on it."

"Whatever. We'll just watch you show us how it's done. Ready, doll?" I ask, wrapping my arm around Danni's waist and pulling her to me.

"To watch Zach lose? Hell yeah."

Time seems to speed up as the four of us make our way around the casino. All of us lose money that I'm sure we all need, none more so than Zach, but he's having the time of his life right now with his wife on his arm.

At some point we break apart, Zach and Biff wandering over to the other side of the room.

"So, are you feeling lucky, doll?" I look up at her, her eyes a little glassy from the wine she's been drinking since we arrived, and a sly smile curls at her lips before her eyes drop from mine.

"I'm always lucky, Trick. I just need to find the right guy to help me out." She spins on the spot as if she's looking for someone.

"I can save you the trouble." My hands land on her hips, and I pull her back into my body. I'm already rocking a semi from just watching her in action on the blackjack table not so long ago, so the second her arse connects with it, it swells.

Feeling it, she grinds back against it, making a groan rumble up my throat.

"Let's see. As we both know, I have a thing for suave banker types. Suits, polished shoes, well-educated, and with a respectable job. About my age would be great, although I don't mind a little older, it just ensures he knows what he's doing. But also someone who's not looking for anything serious. I just want a night of fun. Hot. Sweaty. No-holds-barred kind of fun."

My lips land on her neck. I lick up the skin before sucking it into my mouth. She shudders against me, her arse teasing me even more as she moves her hips.

"Or how about..." I whisper, running the tip of my nose around the shell of her ear. "A bad boy with tattoos who can make you scream like no other?"

She groans, and the sound goes straight to my cock. There's no way she can't feel it against her, but she doesn't react other than to step away, allowing the rest of the room to see the tenting of my trousers if they so wished.

She's a few feet away, my eyes locked on her body swaying, when she turns back to me. Her dark eyes sparkle and her lips curl into a wicked smile.

"Are you coming, or should I find—"

"Do not finish that sentence, doll." Catching up to her, I grip onto her hip and direct her towards the roulette table to try our luck.

It's a bad move. We should have gone to the slots, because every time she leans forward to put our chips down, her dress exposes even more thigh. Each time she does it, the temptation to drag her out and up to my suite is getting harder and harder to ignore.

As she places our last two chips down, I reach out and run my fingertips up the back of her leg. She stills with her hand halfway towards the table and looks back over her shoulder. One side of her mouth quirks up, and if I wasn't already sure I was going to get exactly what I needed tonight, then that one look tells me everything I need to know.

Unable to remove my hand, I keep my palm on the top of her thigh and brush my thumb over the swell of her arse.

We watch in silence as the ball is dropped into the

wheel. Everything around me fades. The only thing I can hear and focus on is Danni beside me. I don't need to look over to know her chest is heaving, I can hear her increased breaths.

The ball lands on red and neither of the numbers Danni had selected.

"Apparently it's not my lucky night," she says on a sigh, turning away from the table now we've run out of chips.

"Oh, doll. I can assure you that it's very much your lucky night."

As we walk away from the table, Zach and Biff appear from another direction and join us.

"We're spent out. Fancy hitting the club?"

"Yes," Danni squeals a little too excitedly. "I want to dance." Her voice is a little slurred. I'm not surprised after the amount we've all drunk. The sensible thing would probably be to suggest we head to bed, but this is Vegas. It's not the time or the place to be sensible.

"Let's go then." Zach takes Biff's hand and I do the same to Danni as we follow them out. To my surprise, she doesn't pull away. Although when she wobbles slightly in her heels, I wonder if that's more the reason than wanting to be close to me.

We don't leave the hotel, instead just head for the basement. The bass of the music booms louder and louder as we get closer. My fingers twitch in anticipation of what's to come.

"Drinks then dance," Biff instructs, pushing through the crowd, still proudly wearing her wedding dress.

My excitement wanes slightly at seeing the queue, but the barmen are more effective than I give them credit for, because it's only a few minutes later when another two rounds of tequila appear in front of us.

I glance at Danni, wondering if she's going to be able to stomach another two shots, but it seems she doesn't share my concern because she's the first to reach out and lift the small glass to her lips.

"I'm so ready for this," she says excitedly, going for the second as the rest of us take our first.

I barely blink and my fingers are laced with hers and she's dragging me out into the middle of the dance floor.

The second we come to a stop, she pulls me into her body, rests her head back on my shoulder, and starts moving to the music.

Placing my hands on her hips, I follow her lead, ignoring the burning stare from Zach only a few feet away when I lower my lips and press them to her neck.

One song blurs into another. Danni's movements don't falter, and with her body crushed up against mine, I shut the world out and move with her.

My head spins with the alcohol and the excitement of what the rest of the night might hold.

The song ends. I'm only aware because, as the music drops out slightly, Danni spins in my arms. Her hands skim up my chest before locking behind my neck. She looks into my eyes for the briefest moment, and I swear I can see everything I want looking back at me.

The thought rocks me, threatens to buckle my knees right here in the middle of a Vegas dance floor, but the second her lips meet mine, everything vanishes from my head. The only thing I can focus on is the woman in my arms. My hands side around to her arse, pulling her tighter to me as her tongue slips past my lips, seeking out my own.

The outside world ceases to exist. The fact that her brother is standing feet away and probably about to take my head off doesn't even register. The only thing I'm aware of is her and proving to her that I'm the man she needs. Fuck the expensive suit and the slicked-back hair. I'm it. I'm the one, and I intended on rocking her world so far off its axis tonight that I'm the only one she'll think about ever again.

Time stands still, but our kiss gets dirtier, more desperate. With her leg up around my waist, I grind my steel length against her core, making a moan vibrate up her throat.

"Fuck, I need to be inside you," I groan. I don't expect her to hear me, but by some miracle with the music pounding around us she does, because her hold gets tighter, her nails digging into my back.

Fuck, my need to carry her out of here and fuck her on the nearest available surface is painful.

Sadly, any more thoughts of doing just that are squashed the second another hand lands on my shoulder. It squeezes painfully, and I don't need to look up to know who it belongs to.

"If this were any night but my wedding night, things would be different, but my priority is my wife, not you two." He looks between us. Our chests heave, and I can only imagine that our eyes are wild with desire. I should not be looking into my best friend's eyes right now while my cock is weeping to be inside his sister. "But," he adds when I think he's finished, "if you fucking hurt so much as a hair on her head, I'm fucking coming for you. Best friend or not."

"You've got nothing to worry about," I say with much more confidence than I probably should have. The one thing I'm good at in life is screwing shit up, so I don't know why this thing with Danni would be any different. Danni tenses in my arms, but I keep my eyes on Zach, needing him to know how serious I am about this.

He nods, accepting my words before Biff stands between us.

"You finished with the big brother speech?" she shouts in amusement.

"Yeah. We're out of here. Got plans, if you know what I mean." He winks, and both Biff and Danni groan.

"You go and consummate the shit out of your marriage."

"Oh I intend to. We'll see you guys in the morning, yeah? Assuming she can walk," he says with a smile, chancing a look at Biff, whose cheeks are beetroot.

"Yeah, man." Releasing Danni, I pull him in for a man hug and whisper my congratulations once again in his ear. I hope he knows that he's won the fucking lottery with Biff. She's one of a kind.

I give Biff a quick hug before she embraces Danni. They have a very brief chat. I think most of their conversation is silent. After a few seconds they hug again, and, with one more warning glance from Zach, they disappear through the crowd.

"And then there were two. What do you want to do with the rest of the night then, doll?"

"I've got a few ideas."

14

Danni

As I attempt to move, what feels like a lead weight presses me into the mattress. Staying put, I try to figure out exactly where I am and how I got here.

My brain pounds in my head. It feels like it's too big and trying to escape through my temples.

I crack one eye open, and at the sight of the hotel room things start coming back to me.

Zach and Biff getting married.

Giant burgers and diner bathrooms.

The casino.

Tequila. Lots of tequila.

Dancing. And then... nothing.

Suddenly realising who I'm in bed with, I flip over despite his arm wrapped tightly around me so I can look up at him for confirmation. Not that I need it.

My body aches, my core sore from just this small amount of movement alone. There's no denying what might have gone on in this bed last night.

A flashback of his lips against my collarbone hits me, and my nipples pebble.

I expect to find him sleeping, but when I look up, my eyes lock with his tired green ones.

"Morning, doll." His rough, sleepy voice does things to me, but sadly another issue makes itself known.

"I'm gonna be sick." Pushing from the bed, I race towards the en suite and drop to my knees over the toilet before last night's tequila makes a reappearance.

Sitting back against the wall, the underfloor heating warms my bum as I tip my head back and squeeze my eyes shut, begging for the pain to stop.

"Well, I must say that's the first time anyone has reacted that way to finding me in bed with them." Carter's amused voice comes from the doorway.

"Stop," I beg, not feeling at all strong enough to deal with the alcohol-fuelled mistake I made last night.

I don't look at him. I don't even open my eyes. I know I'm sitting here naked while he stares at me, and I don't need to know what the look in his eyes right now is saying.

"You need to leave," I demand.

"Actually, we need to go and meet Zach and Biff. We're going to be late."

Groaning, I drag my broken body from the floor, knowing that he's right.

My muscles pull, and my stomach turns over again, but thankfully it settles itself this time.

Standing in front of the basin, I rest my palms on the cool porcelain and wait a few seconds before glancing up.

When I do, I'm nowhere near prepared for what I find. My hair is a mess, my face smeared with the remains of last night's makeup. But none of that is the most obvious. It's the red marks littering my neck and chest that hold my attention and fuel my anger. It doesn't stop the vague memory of him putting them there, though.

Glancing up, I find him over my shoulder, still standing in the doorway. Our eyes connect, and an image pops into my head of him looking up at me from between my thighs.

Fuck.

"You need to leave," I spit. When he does nothing to look like he's following orders, I spin on the balls of my feet. "No-ow." The word cracks when I find his naked body staring back at me, his ink on full display, his semi-hard cock pointing at me from below the deep V lines travelling towards it.

Heat stirs in my belly as a vague memory of rubbing my tongue over those exact lines comes back to me. Colour stains my cheeks as I continue staring at him. I bite down on my bottom lip, having a feeling that we were very up close and personal last night.

"There's no point getting embarrassed now, doll. Not after last night."

My mouth opens and then shuts again when I realise that I don't even know where to start with what could have happened between us. In the end, I go with my most pressing question, seeing as my body is telling me that whatever did happen went on for a considerable amount of time. I know I've not been with anyone since our last rendezvous on Biff's sofa, but the tenderness between my legs is certainly not from a quick drunken fuck to end the night.

"You... uh... you remember what happened last night?" I ask.

His eyes drop down my exposed body. My arms are desperate to cover myself up, but I stand strong, appearing confident when all I want to do is curl up in a ball and sleep away this hangover from hell.

His now fully erect, bobbing cock catches my eye, and damn if it doesn't make my mouth water. I bite down on my cheek and try to conjure up a memory of how he might have tasted if I did have him in my mouth, but there's nothing other than a very strong suspicion that it happened.

"It's kinda hazy, but all the important parts are there." His eyes roam my body once again, and it heats, knowing that it's a body he's now very familiar with.

"Oh god," I groan, equally embarrassed and annoyed by what I might have done that have I no recollection of. Although if the heat in his eyes tells me anything, it's that it was a good night.

"You did call for him a lot. But I'm pretty sure it was me who answered your prayers, doll."

"You need to leave. We need to get dressed to meet Zach and Biff."

He nods, taking a step back. "We do. You're right. But this isn't over, doll. Not by a long stretch."

"Great," I groan. I can't help but question my irritation with him when he turns and I get to watch his sculpted arse walk away from me.

He scoops up a few items of clothing and his phone from the bedside table before walking for the door.

"Wait, you can't go out there like that. You'll give some old lady the fright of her life," I say in a panic, rushing after him.

"Aw, you jealous, doll? You want this all to yourself?" He holds the clothes from his body to show me everything once again. Not that I need to see it; the image of him standing naked and proud is now burned into my brain.

"Ugh, do you know what? Do what you want. Get yourself thrown out for indecent exposure. See if I care."

He laughs before pulling the door open to reveal the pristine living area beyond. But when he starts walking through the space, he doesn't go towards the exit but through a door opposite mine.

Realisation hits me at the same time his hand wraps around the handle.

"You've got to be fucking kidding me," I moan.

"What? Zach might be treating us to this luxury, but even his wealth has limits. You thought he got you a suite to yourself? We're roommates, doll. And I'm right across the hall for the taking, whenever you want me."

"Keep dreaming, Trick. Oh, is that how this happened? Did you trick me into bed? Make up some bullshit story about it being your last living day on earth so I'd feel sorry for you and give you a pity shag?"

"Oh doll, there was nothing pitiful about last night." He winks before slipping inside his room. "You've got twenty minutes," he calls before kicking the door closed behind him.

I cry out in frustration and storm back into my own room.

It didn't even occur to me yesterday that he might be in the same suite. I feel stupid for not thinking it. It makes total sense now.

"Fuck," I shout into my empty but very messy room. The bed is a mess, the sheets twisted and upside down, a sure sign of a good night, and my stomach clenches. I'm irritated with myself, but I'm not sure if it's more because I allowed it to happen in the first place or if it's because I don't remember what was clearly an eventful night.

Ignoring the state of the room, I go back to the bathroom and turn the shower on before pulling my toothbrush from the holder in the hope that freshening my mouth will help towards me feeling almost human once again.

The steam billows from the shower by the time I'm done, and I step straight under it. The heat burns my skin, but I don't turn the temperature down. Instead, I welcome the slight burn, use it as punishment for drinking so much that I don't remember what happened last night.

By the time I step from the room, my face is clear of make-up, exposing the dark circles under my eyes and my slightly green complexion. I've not been sick again since I first woke, but my stomach's still churning like it's still a real possibility.

I'm wearing a pair of skinny jeans and a Ralph Lauren jumper as I walk into the bright light of our living space. Carter is sitting on the edge of the sofa, waiting for me. His hair is wet from his own shower and swept back from his face, and he's wearing his standard slim t-shirt and pair of well-worn and ripped jeans. His tattoos are on display, and even from here I know he smells too tempting. Damn him for being so hot and oh-so-wrong for me.

"Let's go." I march past him, and he chuckles.

By the time I'm at the door, he's caught up with me. "You know, I might be offended that you don't want to spend time with me if it weren't for my memory of you clawing at my back last night like you couldn't get enough."

My skin heats at his words before I die a little inside, realising that I've no way of knowing if that's actually true or not.

"All talk of last night needs to not happen until I've had at least five coffees, and even that might not be enough."

Pulling the door open, I storm towards the lift in the hope I can leave him behind. Obviously, that's just wishful thinking, because no sooner have I pressed the button for the ground floor is he stepping inside and taking all the air from the enclosed space.

As the lift starts to descend, the only thing I can focus on is his scent and the sound of his breathing. My skin tingles, teasing me as to what last night could have been like when he had his hands on me. Although tender, my core aches to remember how he felt filling me until I fell over the edge.

"What?" I bark, not looking over at him but knowing he's staring at me.

"You need a reminder, don't you? You need a play by play of what happened inside your room last night, and this morning. You're too much of a control freak not to know, and it's—I'm—driving you crazy."

"All I feel is regret. It shouldn't have happened, and I'm mortified with myself for allowing it to."

"You didn't allow anything, doll. It was inevitable. We both knew that from the second I found you in the lounge yesterday."

Yesterday? How the fuck was that only yesterday?

My muscles ache with exhaustion. A long-haul flight followed by the events of yesterday and then a night of very little sleep is not what I needed after the week I've already had.

"It wasn't inevitable. It was stupidity on my part."

"Wow, you really know how to make a guy feel special."

"Sorry, your feelings aren't really top of my priority list right now, Trick. My sanity is more important."

Thankfully, the lift dings, announcing our arrival, and the doors open. I step out before Carter has a chance to and head for the restaurant we agreed to meet Zach and Biff in.

They're both sitting at a table over by the windows when I walk in. I mutter something about meeting friends to the guy welcoming diners and march past him. Carter's trailing behind me. I don't need to look to know he's there. I feel him. It annoys the shit out of me.

I come to a stop, putting the bright sunlight burning my eyeballs to my back and pulling out the seat opposite Biff, dropping down into it as Carter does the same beside me.

"Well, aren't you two a sight for sore eyes," Biff says with a laugh, her eyes bouncing between us. "Have a good night after we left you, then?"

"Can we not talk about it?" My voice is bordering on begging. The last thing I want to admit is that I'm pretty sure I spent hours shagging my brother's best friend and don't remember a thing.

Reaching out, I wrap my fingers around her mug of coffee and steal it from right under her nose. She looks much more put together than I feel right now. I need it more than her.

I'm just about to lift it to my lips when her words stop me. "Wait, what's this?" she asks, staring down at my hand. "Is that a fucking wedding ring?"

My eyes fly down to where she's staring, and it's like

my entire world falls from beneath me as I focus on the thin silver band wrapped around my ring finger.

"Oh fuck," falls from my lips as I continue staring, praying that I'm seeing things. But when I look up and find everyone looking at my hand, mouths agape and eyes wide, I soon realise that this is real. This is very real.

My heart races and my stomach turns over, once again threatening to make me experience that tequila I now regret even more than when I first woke up.

Reaching over, I pull Carter's hand from where it's resting in his lap, and the sight has my heart falling into my stomach.

"Oh my god. Oh my god," I chant, unable to believe what I'm seeing.

This cannot be happening.

No.

This is a joke.

I start laughing uncontrollably. Tears fill my eyes as the others all stare at me like I've lost my mind. "Why are you all looking so concerned? This is quite clearly a joke, right?" I turn to look at Carter, who's not amused in the slightest. "This is your idea of punishing me for how I've treated you. It's another trick. Right?" My eyes beg him to tell me yes, that it's just a joke.

"No, Danni. This is very much real. Don't you remem—"

"No. No, I don't fucking remember," I shout, louder than necessary if the heads turning in our direction are anything to go by. "I don't remember leaving the club. I don't remember returning to the hotel, or my room. I don't remember this," I spit, lifting my hand to him, "and... I don't remember fucking you afterwards." A couple of gasps sound out around us, telling me that our audience is bigger than I'd like. "This is a fucking nightmare."

I stand, pushing the chair out behind me so forcefully that it topples over and crashes to the ground, ensuring even more heads turn this way.

"You," I spit, poking Carter in the chest with my finger, "you need to fix this." In a rush, I pull the thin band of metal from my finger and slam it down on the table before marching from the room.

I can't deal with this.

"Danni, wait," both Biff and Carter call behind me, but my steps don't falter. I need to get away from this shit show, and the sooner the better.

15

Carter

"You married my fucking sister?" Zach barks before another thought hits him. "On my own wedding day." His eyes are wide and in total shock about what's just transpired in front of him.

"Technically it was after midnight, so..."

"Not the fucking point."

I fall back into my chair, staring down at the ring on my hand. *I'm fucking married.* The realisation isn't as much as a shock to me as it was to Danni just now, because I felt the foreign object on my finger the second I woke up. My brain was just too fuzzy and filled with the images of her naked body to really focus on it. Sitting here now, though, memories start to hit me.

The three of us sit in silence as my new reality settles into my head. I'm married, and my wife just slammed her ring down on the table and stormed off. So, I'm not just married... I'm married to a woman who hates me.

Something inside me sinks. This is far from the worst thing that's ever happened to me. In fact, it could be one of the best. I knew there was something special about Danni from the moment I saw her profile online. As far as I was concerned, something happening between us was inevitable. I never could have imagined this, but I'm not exactly panicking that this is now our life.

Reaching forward, I pluck her ring from the table. I hold it between my thumb and finger and flick it back and forth as I try to drag up as much as I can remember from last night. From the moment I made her mine.

A smile curls up at my lips, my chest aching with something as I remember the look in her eyes as she stared up at me. We were both drunk as fuck, but still, I knew that wasn't all it was about. There was more. I'd put money on it.

Feeling two sets of eyes burning into the top of my head, I risk a glance up. Both Biff and Zach's foreheads are creased in concern as they stare at me.

"I should go and see her," I mutter, unsure of what else to say in this fucked-up situation.

"No," Biff says, surprising me. "Leave her for a bit. She needs time to process. Trust me, I know how she works. If you go up there now, you're likely to come out of it with an injury."

The waitress comes over, interrupting anything I was going to say in response. So with a nod at a still very concerned looking Biff, I reach for the menu.

I ask for the first thing I see. "Could we also order something to take up for someone else after we've finished?" I ask the waitress. When she agrees, I turn to

Biff, because as much as I hate to admit it, I don't really know my wife. Well, aside from knowing how to make her scream. Biff's eyes soften at my thoughtfulness before telling the waitress what she thinks Danni might like.

"Softening the blow with pancakes might really help in your favour," Biff says once we're alone again.

I reach for the coffee the waitress poured and take a sip of the red-hot liquid. It burns my lips, but I hardly feel it. I'm too distracted by the unexpected turn my life has taken in the last eight hours or so.

"So now what?" Zach asks, staring at me like what he really wants to do is kick my arse.

"Mate, I've no fucking clue. None of this was planned."

"Good to know." He sucks in a calming breath, and Biff places her hand on his forearm. He relaxes immediately at her touch, and the sight melts my heart. Zach never would have admitted it, he spent all his time trying not to get attached to anyone, but Biff is exactly what he needed. He was already pretty awesome, but she's only made him a better person.

"I won't hurt her," I promise, although the second the words are out of my mouth, I regret them. "*Why do you have to make everything so hard?*" My father's voice rings out in my ear. "*You screw everything up.*"

I try to swallow down the pain and rejection I've felt my whole life. Maybe this is the one thing I'm not going to fuck up.

"We know you won't," Biff says softly, nudging Zach to respond at the same time.

"I'm sorry. I just... This is fucked-up. You've just married my fucking sister."

An awkward silence falls over us.

"So..." I say, desperate to crack the tension. "Did you

two have a good night?" I don't really need to ask, it was written all over their faces when we first appeared.

"You could say that, yeah," Zach says with a smile, glancing over at Biff, whose cheeks turn an amusing shade of red.

"When are you guys heading home?" Danni and I are flying back tomorrow morning, according to the ticket Zach emailed to me, but no one's said anything about them.

"Beginning of next week. We've got a few things we want to do here, and I'd like to spend some time at the studio with the guys."

"I need to visit," I say, wondering if I could convince one of them to do me a little artwork while I'm here.

"Oh no, you've got that look in your eye," Zach points out.

"What look?" Biff asks, staring at me, trying to see the same thing Zach is.

"The look he gets when he's about to ask me to ink him."

"Ohhh," she sings amusedly as the waitress returns with our plates full of food.

The coffee had already gone a long way to fixing the hangover that's raging in my body, but the food helps to push the lingering sickness aside.

"You got any space left?" Biff asks, glancing up from her plate.

"Plenty."

"Maybe you'll let me have a go one day." Her voice is so quiet I almost miss it.

"You?"

A sly grin pulls at her lips. "Zach's going to train me up. He reckons I've got what it takes."

"And, as much as I hate to admit this, he's not often wrong with these things."

Biff smiles, her excitement obvious in her eyes. I've seen her artwork. I also know she's good enough.

"Would you like me to bring over the extra breakfast, or would you like it delivered as room service?" the waitress asks when she comes back over to clear our plates. As tempted as I am to let some other poor soul deal with Danni and whatever mood she might be in, I reluctantly tell her that I'll take it—but not before Biff requests the largest cup of coffee they can supply to go with it.

"Wish me luck," I mutter as the lift comes to a stop on our floor.

"You'll be fine. Just... make sure you duck if she lifts her hands." Biff and Zach both laugh like this is the funniest thing they've ever experienced, while my stomach twists with nerves.

I'm confident she's not going to cause me any lasting damage, not physically anyway. My biggest issue is that I'm not freaked out in the slightest about the fact that she's now Mrs. Carter J Wright, yet she's so overjoyed by the prospect that she's locked herself in our suite.

Blowing out a long, slow breath, I prop the tray against the wall and somehow manage to unlock the door and push inside.

As I pretty much expected, the living area is empty, but her bedroom door is shut. Making my way over, I rap my knuckles on the door lightly. I don't really want to wake her if she's asleep, but we also need to talk.

Silence.

"Dan, I brought you breakfast and coffee."

There's a few more seconds of silence before her voice comes through the door. "How big is the coffee?"

I laugh to myself. "The biggest we could get." I bite my tongue from adding something about just how she likes things. I don't think she'll appreciate cock jokes right now.

"Couldn't Biff have delivered it?"

"No, she's got plans with her husband. As do you, doll."

Silence hangs heavy between us once again, but after a couple of long seconds, I hear footsteps and then the door begins to open.

"Coffee?" she demands, putting her hand through the gap.

"No, it's all or nothing."

"And I assume that includes you."

"Sure does."

"For fuck's sake."

"Me and pancakes."

"I want one of those things, so I guess I don't have a choice."

"Aw, see, I know you wanted me really."

She stands aside and pulls the door open so I can see her. She's still dressed as she was when we went for breakfast, but there are unmistakable signs that she's been crying that weren't there earlier.

"Dann—"

"Don't. Don't 'Danni' me. We wouldn't be in this mess if it weren't for you," she spits, spinning on her heels and storming to the bed. She sits herself against the headboard and keeps her eyes to the other side of the room.

"Me? I'm sorry, doll, but in case you hadn't realised, it

takes two to tango. I didn't drag you to the chapel last night and force you to marry me."

"No? Because I don't remember a fucking thing. You could have done anything."

"Jesus, do you not know me at all?"

"No, Carter. No, I don't, and that is most of the fucking problem. I got drunk and married some randomer in Vegas. Fucking hell. How is this my life?" She drops her head into her hands and breathes in a few deep breaths.

Placing the tray on the bedside table, I sit on the edge of the bed and reach out. My fingers gently wrap around her wrists, and I pull her hands away. Amazingly, she allows me, but she keeps her eyes averted.

"Danni?" My voice is barely a whisper, and even I can hear the emotion in it.

Dropping one of her hands, I lift my fingers to her cheek before wrapping them around the back of her neck and brushing over the smooth, tear-stained skin with my thumb.

After blinking and swallowing down whatever it is she's trying to keep hidden, she turns to look at me. Her eyes are pooled with tears that are going to spill any second. The sight makes my chest ache. I don't want to be the reason for her sadness.

"You know me, Danni. More than you think you do, and more than anyone else in the world. We may not have spent a lot of time together face to face, but everything I said via message was true. You were talking to me, the real me. Not the man I was pretending to be to find something, someone meaningful. Not the showman act I put on to hide everything that I try to keep beneath the surface. I was just me, and I was totally honest, more so than I've ever been. So please, please just give this... us, a chance."

One tear drops, and I catch it with my thumb. A sob rumbles up her throat, making me wish I could take all of this away, but it's too late. The deed has been done... quite literally.

Leaning forward, I rest my forehead against hers. What I really want to do is press my lips to hers, but I'm not sure she'd appreciate that right now.

Our eyes lock, unspoken promises and warnings passing between us. She's afraid of being hurt, I can read that much in them. Fuck knows what she sees in mine. Maybe it's my weakness, my need to find the kind of connection I know we could have if she allows it. My fear? I've no idea, but when she blinks, cutting us off after a few seconds, all I know is that I feel totally lost.

I'd hoped that the day I found myself married to the woman of my dreams, my insecurities buried might settle at last, but it seems my reality is very different from what I always hoped it would be.

"Your coffee is getting cold," I whisper, pulling back and giving her the space I think she's desperate for.

She nods, sitting up straighter and accepting the tray when I move it over to her lap.

"Thank you for this," she says softly.

"Anything." Her head snaps up, and she blinks a couple of times as she looks at me. It's as if she's looking at a ghost and not sure if it's her imagination or not. After a few seconds, she shakes her head and turns her attention to her breakfast.

16

Danni

I got drunk and married in Vegas. I'm such a fucking cliché.

My lungs burn by the time I run up the unthinkable number of stairs to the suite. I went for the lift, but as I approached a huge crowd moved into it, and the last thing I wanted was to be surrounded by people while balancing on the thin line of sanity I was so close to falling off of.

The second I make it to the main door, I crash through and immediately race to my bedroom before slamming the door behind me. It makes no difference—no one is here to hear my frustration, but I do feel slightly better for letting just a little bit of it out.

I drop my head into my hands as I desperately try to drag up any memories of the night before. The last thing I remember was dancing with Carter in the hotel's nightclub. I certainly do not remember any mention of getting married or a journey to a chapel. I don't even know what I wore.

A sob rips from my throat. None of this was how it was meant to be. I wanted to find a nice, respectable man with a good job that I could date for a while. Marriage and kids have always been a part of my life plan, but not yet, and certainly not like this.

I look down at my bare finger. How hadn't I noticed it when I got up? The continuous pounding at my temples is all the answer I really need for that question. And this new reality sure isn't helping me recover from the world's worst hangover.

I fall down onto the end of my bed and allow the tears I was holding in to fall. What the hell is going on with me? I've been known to be spontaneous in the past, sure. I'll say yes to most experiences in life. But this? I've never done something so life-changing before without giving it some serious thought. The decision to go back to uni to do my masters while I worked took me months. Yet it seems I just got married on a whim. And to a guy I don't know.

I think back to the parts of last night that I do remember. The way he looked at me with heat in his eyes. The way his body moved so perfectly with mine while we were on the dancefloor. His husky promises in the bathroom of the burger place.

He's not a bad guy, that I'm sure of. I don't need his friendship with my brother to tell me that. I sense it. But husband material? The kind of man I take home to meet my parents and introduce as the one I'm planning on spending my life with? I've no fucking clue.

My head spins. My tears fall. Yet I'm no closer to remembering any of it or figuring out what I'm meant to do now. I can't go home married. Not when we only came here so Biff and Zach could tie the knot. Fucking hell, I'm the world's worst sister and best friend. That thought only makes my tears come faster.

I fall back onto the bed and stare at the ceiling through blurry eyes.

I'm someone's wife!

Thoughts about what I could do now are on repeat in my mind. I'm surprised any of them allowed me this time. I really thought one of them would have followed, Carter especially. I'm glad they didn't. I needed these few minutes to try to get my thoughts together, not that I'm any closer to having a clue as to what I want to happen next.

I'm in two minds when the knock does come at my door. I want to keep him out, pretend that none of this is really happening, but the lure of coffee is too much, and I break down and allow him in.

I regret it the second I look into his green eyes. There's hope in there, the hope I've constantly been trying to squash every time he so much as mentions a future between us.

Why is he so confident that he wants me? He barely knows me, and the little bit of time he has spent with me I've been nothing but a raging bitch.

The huge cup of coffee and the pancakes go a long way to making me feel almost human once again, but the second I put the tray to the side and look up at Carter, everything comes crashing back.

"I... uh..." He shifts to the side slightly so he can push his hand into his pocket. "Picked this up for you." He uncurls his fist and reveals my wedding ring. My stomach twists uncomfortably as I stare at it. The slight tremble in his hand makes me feel somewhat better that I'm not the only one struggling with this right now.

Hesitantly, I reach out and pick it up. It looks tiny in his palm.

"You deserve more than that one, just so you know," he says as I stare down at it.

"It's a perfectly nice ring, Carter. It's just... I'm not sure I should have it."

"I've been rejected a few times in my life, but less than twelve hours after saying 'I do' is a new one, I must say." He puts humour into his tone, but as his eyes darken, I wonder if there's more truth to those words than he'd like me to know.

"This is so fucked-up."

"Spend the day with me. No pretence, no bullshit, no Mr and Mrs. Just us, just hanging out. I told Zach and Biff that we'd meet them later for dinner."

I stare at him. I guess there are worse ways to spend my day than discovering a little bit of Vegas with him.

"O-okay."

"Yeah?" The way his face lights up at my agreement tells me that it's the right decision. No matter how things turn out for us, we're going to need to get along for Biff and Zach's sake, so I guess we may as well at least attempt to be friends.

"On one condition."

"Which is?"

"I need more coffee, and at least thirty minutes to do my hair and make-up before walking out of this room."

"Consider it done, although it's really not necessary. You look beautiful already."

I smile at him. "Thank you for trying, but I'm well aware that I look about as hungover as I feel right now."

He opens his mouth to say more but decides against it. Instead, he stands from the bed and walks to the door. "I'll order you a coffee. I'll be ready whenever you are."

Pulling the door closed behind him, he leaves me alone with my new wedding band. I stare down at it, hoping its presence will bring back memories of me getting it, but still, there's nothing.

A loud sigh falls from my lips as Carter's deep voice ordering my coffee filters through the door.

Not allowing myself to think in circles, I push from the bed and set about getting ready to grace other humans with my presence. I know this is Vegas and everyone and their wife is probably regretting the night before in some way, but I'd prefer not to look like I do as well.

I place my wedding ring down on the dresser, but I quickly pick it back up again when it feels wrong abandoning it like that only hours after receiving it. Or maybe I even chose it in the first place, who knows.

I glance around, wondering what to do with it, before my necklace catches my eye. Flipping my hair out of the way, I undo the chain and slip the ring over it. I ensure it's hidden behind my jumper before plugging my curling wand in and attempting to do something with my frizzy disaster hair.

I'm halfway through taming my mane when Carter knocks. "Coffee delivery," he calls through the door.

"It's safe to enter," I laugh.

I keep my eyes on the mirror before me and look over my shoulder. I watch him take up almost all of the doorway. He's not wearing anything special, just a t-shirt and jeans, but shit, I'm not sure I've ever seen a guy rock the look quite so well. His hair is all over the place, probably thanks to me and this situation we've found ourselves in.

A cocky smile appears on his lips when he realises that I'm checking him out. He stalks into the room and comes to a stop right behind me.

"Here's your coffee, wife."

My breath catches at his name for me.

"Shit, sorry. Is it too soon for jokes?"

"It might forever be too soon."

"Oookay." His face drops as he backs away from me.

"Shit, Carter. I just…"

"It's okay. I know this isn't what you want. I just thought that maybe you'd…"

"Maybe I'd what?" I ask when he trails off, staring down at his feet like he regrets opening his mouth.

He sucks in a breath before he brings his green eyes up to meet mine. They're dark and full of emotion. It doesn't matter that I can't get a proper read of how he's feeling about all of this, because it hits me in the chest nonetheless.

"Maybe that you'd give this a chance. I know it wasn't planned or whatever, but—"

"Yes," I say, interrupting whatever it was he was going to continue with.

"Yes?" His cheeks start to lift with a smile.

"Like you said earlier, let's just hang out. We've got plenty of time to figure out what to do about this mess when we get home. Let's just enjoy Vegas while we have the chance."

"I'll be waiting." He winks and backs out of the room to allow me the time to finish what I'm doing.

I make quick work of putting on some make-up to

brighten my complexion before drinking my coffee and finding some shoes.

When I pull the door open, the sound of Carter's deep, rumbling voice fills my ears, and goosebumps prick my skin at the sound. I wish I could remember last night. The aches in my body tell me that it was a really good one.

I bite down on my lip as I think about our first time. I wonder if last night was as hot? I sigh. Maybe I should see about a replay...

I'm expecting to find him on the phone when I enter the living area. Instead of it being at his ear, he's talking into it, but the second he spots me, he locks the screen and drops it into his pocket.

"You ready to go?"

"Yeah, but if you're in the middle of something, I can wait," I offer.

"No, it's fine. Let's go. I've got plans."

"Oh yeah?"

"Come on, I'm going to show you that spending time with me isn't all that bad."

"I never said..." I trail off, knowing that I've not been all that welcoming to his company since the first moment we met. "Maybe we should just start over." I stop before the door that will lead up from our suite. "Hi, I'm Danni. Operations Manager for my family's antique business, five foot two, coffee lover, wine connoisseur, looking for something a little more serious," I say, rattling off my online dating profile.

He looks me up and down, assessing the goods, and I can't help tinges of desire erupting in my belly.

"Carter, friends call me Titch. Tattoo artist, some might say comedian, your husband."

"Comedian?" I ask, ignoring his final point.

"I like to think so."

Shaking my head. "Why do I get the idea that you're the only one who does?"

He shrugs and I laugh, following him into the lift.

"So what's the plan?"

"You'll have to wait and see."

As the lift descends, the tension in the small space becomes heavy. We're standing side by side, the heat of his body burning my arm. My fingers twitch with my need to do something, but I fight it. Although, when we come to a stop and the doors start to open, it becomes apparent that maybe I wasn't the only one with the same thoughts, because no sooner have I taken a step than his fingers are linked with mine. He glances at me when I still for a second before he smiles as I continue forward.

He walks straight up to an awaiting taxi, and after quietly muttering our destination to him, we climb in and set off.

It's a short journey down the strip before the car comes to a stop in front of The Venetian.

"Why here?" It's not that I don't want to see it, I'll happily follow him anywhere to soak up a little bit of Vegas, but I'm curious as to why this was his first choice.

"Seems like a good place. Venice is meant to be…" He leans towards me, his breath tickling my ear. "Romantic."

"Oh, so this is a move?"

"Yes and no. I always thought it was kinda cool, and I hoped you might too."

"Lucky for you, I do."

"Awesome, let's go then."

We both thank the driver and hop out of the car.

"Wow, it's stunning," I muse as we walk around, looking at the architecture.

With our hands interlocked, we dodge other holiday makers and enjoy the sights this Venice replica has to offer. We head into an art gallery when a painting in the window catches Carter's eye. He follows me into a couple of the shops, but neither of us spends any money aside from the coffee and cake we stop for.

"You fancy a ride?" Carter asks as we stand on one of the many bridges, watching the gondolas going up and down the Grand Canal.

"No, it's okay," I say with a laugh.

"Yes. Come on. Let me give you a memory you might look back on fondly once this trip is over." His voice has a sadness to it that tugs at my heartstrings. I haven't meant to make him feel like I don't enjoy spending time with him. I've discovered he's actually a really great guy, now I've dropped my walls slightly. Although, it still doesn't mean I'm all that thrilled about our drunken wedding.

He takes my hand once more and drags me down to where people have been getting on and off. Thankfully, it's not all that busy, and after only a few short minutes we're at the front of the queue.

"After you, m'lady."

"Why thank you, sir." I take his outstretched hand and allow him to help me step onto the very wobbly boat.

My stomach tumbles the second I'm basically standing on water. It might be a makeshift river, but still, I already feel a little sick.

I keep my eyes on Carter as he climbs aboard and sits down with him.

"Are you okay?"

"I get a little seasick."

"And you didn't want to mention that before now." He glances at me, amusement in his eyes.

"I didn't have much of a chance, did I?"

"I'll keep you safe, doll."

"I'm not worried about going over the edge. It's probably only two foot of water beneath us. I'm concerned about puking my pancakes on your shoes."

"It'll be a smooth ride," the gondolier says with a laugh.

"Great," I mutter at having both of them laughing at me.

Carter's strong arm wraps around my shoulders and he pulls me into his warm body. His scent fills my nose, and my body immediately relaxes. The heat of his lips almost burns the top of my head as he drops a chaste kiss there.

"Tell me if you feel too sick. We'll get off."

Suddenly, I don't even realise we're floating. I'm too lost in him, to his tenderness, his thoughtfulness.

"I'm good." He stills when I snake my arm around his waist, but my need to connect with him is too strong in that moment. My fingers brush over his abs, and I swear he shudders. A smile of achievement spreads across my face, knowing that my touch affects him so much.

"There we go, lovebirds," the gondolier says with a smile. It's only when I look up that I find he's brought us to a stop at the edge of the river where more people are waiting to get on.

"Oh wow, I don't feel sick at all." My cheeks heat as I look over at the very still water surrounding us.

"At least I know never to take you on a cruise," Carter mutters as I climb out of the boat.

"Was that something you were planning?" I ask with a laugh.

"Who knows, doll. It wouldn't be the craziest thing we've done."

"True," I say, a little sadness creeping into my tone.

"So what's next?" Carter asks, changing the subject.

"I thought you had everything planned."

"Not everything." He glances around before his eyes land on something. "Fancy some gelato?"

"Are you serious?"

"Deadly, why?"

"Because I've already had pancakes and cake today."

"So?"

"I've not worked out all week."

"Doll, I can assure you, we did plenty of exercise last night." My cheeks burn as my imagination begins to run away with me. "Your body is perfect," he whispers into my ear, making my skin prick with goosebumps.

"Okay, but I'm having salad for dinner."

"Eat your heart out."

With our hands once again entwined, we make our way over to order tubs of gelato. We find ourselves a bench and enjoy it while watching everyone roam around us.

"I could sit here all day, people watching."

"You ever try to imagine what their lives might be like?"

"All the time."

"Like, those two over there." He nods to an older couple probably in their seventies. They're standing looking over the river, their hands connected. "You think they're childhood sweethearts, or do you think they're new lovers?"

My brows draw together, and I look at him out of the corner of my eye.

"I'm not being a creep. I'm just wondering, or more hoping that their love still burns that strong."

I stare at the couple to see if I can work it out. The man turns to the woman as she says something, and lines appear on his face as he laughs at whatever it was. They look so relaxed together. "Childhood sweethearts, definitely."

"Why?"

"Look at the way he's staring at her. That's not something new. That's years of love and adoration right there."

"You think they know how lucky they are?"

"I sure hope so."

"So what's your dating history? Any exes I should know about?" Carter asks before I get to point out his obvious romantic side.

I blow out a sigh. "Nope. I've got nothing of any excitement. Few short-term boyfriends. None that were worthy of any longer."

"Ruthless."

"Not really. Things just... ran out of steam, I guess. What about you?"

"Same. I'm usually seen as the one-night bad boy." He shrugs, and I laugh.

"Such third world problems. All the women just want your body."

"Hey," he says, attempting to pout but failing miserably. "It was fun to begin with, but it got old pretty quick for me."

"So what do you want now?"

"Everything I said online. I wasn't looking for marriage." He lifts his hand that still displays his wedding ring and laughs. "Just someone who's not going to expect me to leave once she's got what she wanted."

A long sigh falls from my lips. "How much do you remember from last night?" I ask, dreading the answer already. If he remembers everything I don't, I'm going to feel awful. I should have more than just a few flashbacks of his hands and lips on me.

He's silent a few moments and I assume he's thinking back. "It's sketchy," he admits.

"So we might not actually be married?" His head snaps to mine—I can only assume it's the hope in my voice that shocks him.

"No, we definitely are. I've got the paperwork to prove it."

"But it could—"

"No," he snaps. "We really did. I remember that much."

"So how did we get there?"

He shrugs. "Like I said, it's sketchy."

"Great. Well, at least it's not just me," I mutter.

"I knew you were drunk. But I didn't release you were that drunk. I need you to know that I didn't take—"

"I know," I say, stopping him mid-sentence. It hadn't occurred to me until that point that he could be worried about what went down last night. What I thought of him, seeing as I how don't remember it.

"When we got back to the hotel you were fully on board with consummating our marriage." My cheeks heat, and I drop my head into my hands. "No need to be embarrassed, doll. It was sexy as fuck hearing my wife demand I fuck her."

"Oh my god, oh my god."

"Then watching you ride me."

I groan. "Of course it's that part that you remember in great detail."

"There's no way I could forget any moment when you're naked."

My entire body heats at his words. The deep rumble caresses every one of my senses and has desire pooling in my lower belly.

"I'm sorry," I whisper, emotion clogging my throat that I don't remember what should have been the biggest event of my life.

Carter's arm wraps around my shoulders, and he pulls me to his body. His lips once again press against my hair.

"You've got nothing to apologise for," he murmurs against me. "We were both as drunk and as crazy as each other."

"I guess so," I say on a sigh, enjoying the warmth of his body once again.

"I'd like to do one more crazy thing before we head back, if you're up for it."

17

Carter

"I guess that all depends on what it is," Danni says, her body tensing against mine.

"I want to go and visit the Vegas studio." She relaxes for a second before she thinks of something.

"Wait, you're not suggesting that I get a tattoo, are you?"

"Only if you want one. I was more going for me, to be honest."

"Thank God for that. You're not getting a needle within ten feet of me."

"Is that right?"

"Yeah, so don't be getting any crazy ideas about inking me."

"Oh, doll. I had those ideas from the moment I discovered you're a virgin."

"Well, you can think again. I'm more than happy to

watch someone cause you pain, but no one is touching me."

Dropping my lips to her ear, I whisper, "Can I touch you?"

Jumping up from the bench, she turns her narrowed but heated eyes on me. "I think it's time to go."

"You just want to watch someone hurt me."

"Yep, that's exactly it."

"Sadist."

Her lips curl into a smile before a soft laugh passes them. My own lips twitch up and something squeezes in my chest.

"What?" she asks when she finds me staring at her.

"You're really beautiful."

"Oh stop it. Compliments aren't going to get you back into my bed. You're going to have to try harder than that."

"I have a few *tricks* up my sleeve."

"Ha, funny. Come on, I want to see you squirm."

"You do know that tattoos don't really hurt, right?"

"I'll just imagine that they're torturing you, then."

Shaking my head at her, I thread my fingers through hers and together we walk through the masses of people and back out to the strip.

"Aren't we getting a cab?" Danni asks when I turn her left and continue walking.

"Nope, it's not far."

It's only a few minutes before the very familiar pink neon of the Rebel Ink sign comes into view.

"I can't believe my idiot brother has done all this."

"I get where you're coming from, but the reality is, he's anything but an idiot."

"Yeah, I'm starting to see that."

"I can't believe he kept it a secret all this time. I mean, it's epic."

"I understand why he did it—families are complicated beasts—but that doesn't mean I didn't tell him time and time again to come clean."

"I wish he had. He received so much stick from our family about how he lived his life, mainly from Harrison. I don't really understand why he didn't ever throw it back in his face."

"He just wanted his own life. I think he felt like more of an outcast than he ever really let on."

"I guess. Turns out he was right to feel that way," Danni says, clearly thinking of her newly acquired half-sister, Kas.

"Have you spoken to her much?" I ask, assuming she'll know who I'm talking about.

"We message every now and then. I think she feels awkward. We're a fully-fledged family, and she's just her."

"It must be hard."

"Yeah, and I get the impression she's as stubborn as Zach."

"And that won't make it any easier," I say with a laugh.

"So what about your family? I'm assuming from your previous comment that yours is just as complicated."

A bitter laugh falls from my lips. "Yeah, you could say that. Rain check?" I ask as we come to a stop outside the studio.

"Sure, but don't think I won't ask again."

"Why does that not surprise me?"

Pushing the heavy door open, I lead Danni into the studio reception.

The woman who greets us looks exactly as I was expecting from the brief conversations we've had on the phone. Dark hair, even darker make-up, and covered in ink and piercings. Although she's younger, and hotter, than I was expecting, I must be honest.

"Good afternoon, how can we help?"

"Megs!" I say, marching over and pulling the horrified woman into my arms.

"Err... do I know you?" Her words are muffled against my chest, and I can't help laughing.

"You've never met me in person."

"Wait..." She pulls back and looks at me. "British accent, Londoner... I'm assuming..." I nod as she continues looking me over. "Titch!"

"The one and only."

This time she's the one pulling me in for a hug. "It's so good to meet you."

When she finally releases me, I stand back and gesture for Danni to join us. As I glance back at her, I find her staring daggers into me as her eyes flick between the two of us. Her lips are pressed into a thin line, and her brows are drawn together.

"This is Danni, boss man's little sister."

"Hey," Megs says, giving Danni a double take, probably as confused by her expression as I am.

"I'm assuming he's been here already."

"Yep, his first port of call," Megs says with a laugh. "Can't believe he got married."

"Crazy shit, huh?"

"So... did you just turn up to see me in the flesh, or did you want something?"

"Oh, I most definitely want something." Danni scoffs behind me, and when I turn to look at her, she looks as shocked that she made the noise as I am. Her little show is telling me everything I need to know right now, and I can't help but keep it up.

"You want me, or one of the other guys? They're all busy, but I think they've got time later."

"Why would I want them when I could have you?" I wink at her, but she doesn't see because she's too busy studying Danni over my shoulder.

"Aw, always such a smooth talker. Come on then, you can show me the goods."

Megs takes a step towards an archway that leads to more doors, and I turn to Danni. "You coming?"

"Yes," she states firmly, and I can't help but smile.

"I'm quite liking this current look on you. It's sexy," I whisper in her ear when she steps up to me.

"What look?"

"Jealousy."

"What?" she blanches. "I'm not jealous."

"Whatever you say, doll." I smile at her and turn back to follow Megs.

The second we're in her room, I pull my shirt off, much to both Danni and Megs' delight, if their widened eyes are anything to go by.

"Whoa, you don't waste any time, do you?"

Shoving my jeans and boxers down enough to reveal the bit of skin she's going to need, I hop up on her bed. Danni gets herself comfortable on the chair a few feet away, but at no point does she take her eyes from me.

"What's the point when I know what I want?" Squeezing my hand into my pocket, I pull out a creased piece of paper with my design on. It's nothing complicated, more a memento of our time than an actual piece of art.

Megs stares at it for a few moments. I can almost see the cogs turning in her brain as she works it out.

"I thought you were going to at least give me a challenge," she mutters, getting her kit ready.

"Next time I want something bigger, I'll let you know."

"You ready?"

"Always."

The buzz that I've missed even in the few hours it's been since I last laid down some ink fills the small room. I glance at Danni as she tenses.

"You sure you don't want a go? I'm sure I could convince Megs to lend me her machine."

"You can have anything you want, sweet cheeks," she teases.

"Not a chance. Make sure that hurts, won't you?" Danni says to Megs, making me laugh.

The first touch of the needle makes me wince a little, but after a second the feeling is like second nature, therapeutic almost.

I keep my eyes on Megs as she works, but, feeling eyes burning into me, I look up. Danni stares at my naked skin as Megs' delicate inked fingers work away. Her hands are curled into fists and her lips are pursed in frustration.

When she notices that she's got an audience, I blow her a kiss. She shakes her head, but if it's meant to be a warning, it falls very short of the mark.

With our eyes holding, it's not long before Megs announces that she's done and allows me to see her masterpiece.

"Perfect. Thank you."

"You are more than welcome. You want any more, you know where to come."

"You got it. Just don't tell Zach, he'll be pissed I let someone else at this work of art."

"My lips are sealed. I—"

"Can I see?" Danni asks, cutting off whatever Megs was about to say.

"Nope."

"Wrap me up, baby." I wink at Megs as Danni fumes in her seat. She mutters something under her breath a second later before pushing from the chair and storming out of the room.

"Please, do tell," Megs encourages as she covers up my new ink.

I bark out a laugh. "I don't even know where to start."

"Okay, well… I really hope you're tapping that, because she's seriously hot for you."

"You reckon?"

"I know. Although, I can't imagine boss man would be too thrilled. She looks like a good little girl, and even from all these miles away, I know you've got a rep."

"Brilliant," I mutter, not all that thrilled that my reputation precedes me.

"So correct me if I'm wrong, but with that," she nods to my new ink, "combined with the ring on your finger and the jealous woman, I'm assuming you've had an eventful time in Vegas so far."

I laugh, a full-on belly laugh at her assumption, and it feels so damn good. "Megs, you have no fucking idea."

"I see the aftermath of plenty of these situations. Let me let you in to a little secret…" I nod for her to continue. "The ring, the tat, they don't mean anything. It's what's in here that counts." She pokes her index finger into my chest, harder than truly necessary if you ask me.

"Ow," I complain, her long ass talon digging into my skin.

"Oh, don't be a pussy. You want her?" She tilts her chin towards where Danni left a few moments ago. "Then you fucking follow her and prove it. Flirting with me and making her jealous is going to get you nowhere but in the fucking doghouse, you got it?"

I nod, my lips twitching into a smile. "I got it." Standing from her bed, I pull my jeans back up and drag my shirt over my head. "Thanks for this."

"Anytime. It was good to see you in real life."

After pulling Megs in for a hug, I rush out of the studio to find my wife.

She's nowhere to be seen. I set off running, hoping that it'll catch up with her, but I never do.

I'm trying to catch my breath as I push through the hotel entrance and race towards the lifts.

"Whoa, Titch. What the hell is going on?" Zach says, suddenly appearing in front of me.

"Huh? What? Nothing."

"Then why are you running through the hotel like a mad man?"

"Just trying to catch up with Danni."

"Why? What have you done?"

"N-nothing," I stutter, not wanting to admit to him that I might have already hurt her.

"Day one and you've already fucked it up. Nice going, man."

"Fuck you," I spit, much to his surprise if his raised eyebrows are anything to go by.

"No wonder she's run, if you're in such a good mood."

"Whatever. I'll see you later for dinner."

I push him aside and continue in the direction I was going. Two of the lift doors close just as I get there.

"Fuck's sake." Taking off in the direction of the stairs, I run up those instead, although by the time I'm halfway to our floor, which now feels like it's in the fucking clouds, I seriously regret it.

By the time I all but fall through the door to our suite, I'm fucking exhausted. The living area is empty, but her bedroom door is shut. I stumble over and don't bother knocking, knowing that she'd only try to keep me out if I did.

"Where'd you go?" I demand the second I find her sitting on her bed.

"I left."

"No fucking shit," I fume, my anger starting to boil over.

18

Danni

I've never been a jealous person, or not that I was aware of, but sitting there watching her with her hands on Carter and having to endure the blatant flirtation between the two of them had the green-eyed monster emerging within me faster than I could control. Then the knowledge that she knew exactly what she'd just inked on his skin and he refused to show me just tipped me over the edge. It was childish to storm out, but I just couldn't cope, watching her fingers brush against his skin. It was all kinds of wrong, because although technically we're currently man and wife, I've got no claim on him. He's not mine as much as I'm not his. *So why in that moment did you want him to be just that?*

I shake the thoughts away and lean back against the headboard with my eyes closed. I try to push the image of her working on his skin aside, but it won't leave me.

Before too long, the sound I'm expecting rings out around the suite. I should have gone somewhere else, but I had no idea where, and when I knocked on Biff and Zach's door, there was no answer. My only option really was to come back here.

I expect him to be pissed and to ignore me. What I'm not anticipating is for him to come barrelling into my room with his chest heaving and his green eyes alight with anger.

"Where'd you go?"

"I left," I sass, unable to keep the sarcasm from my tone.

"No fucking shit."

He storms towards me, his nostrils flaring and his fist clenched tightly. To some it might be intimidating, but that's far from how I'm feeling right now.

Not wanting him to tower over me, I push from the bed. Of course, he still stands well over a foot above me, but I don't feel as small as I would if I were sitting.

"What are you going to—" My words are cut off the second his lips slam down on mine. His fingers thread into my hair and grip almost painfully as he tilts my head to the side so he can deepen the kiss. I should resist. I should pull back. But when his tongue teases along my bottom lip, I'm powerless.

Dropping one of his hands, he brushes the side of my breast with his knuckles before flicking his thumb over my nipple and making me gasp, but it's not just from pleasure, because a memory slams into me of him licking and sucking at my breasts last night.

My body heats as I picture his lips on my naked skin, and my body reacts as if he's doing it right now. My core clenches and floods with heat as I picture him kissing down my stomach until he's found my centre.

"Oh god," rips from my lips as he trails his down my neck, pulling my jumper down so he can kiss across my collarbone. "Carter, please."

"I thought you were pissed at me," he says, his own anger dissipated, replaced by amusement.

"I am."

His fingers grip the hem of my jumper before he pulls it up and over my head.

"Why?" he asks, his eyes taking in my black lace-covered breasts.

"Because you're a prick."

He laughs and lifts one finger so he can run it around the swell of my breast. My eyes shutter, desperate to close so I can focus on the sensation. But the second he stops, they open once more.

"That might be true, but I'm going to need more than that. Why did you run?"

"Because I did." My stubborn streak knows no bounds. He's going to need to work harder than this to break it.

"Not what I'm looking for, doll."

His finger drops to the lace trim of my bra. My skin erupts in goose bumps as he teases me closer to where I need his touch. My nipples pebble behind the lace, but the padding isn't thick enough to hide them from him.

"Give me what I need, and you'll get what you want."

"I…" I swallow, my mouth suddenly dry. "I don't want anything."

"Hmmm…" He leans forward, just enough that his lips brush the sensitive bit of skin beneath my ear. "I think you're lying. You want me to take those hard little nipples into my mouth and suck. Just like I did last night. You want me to keep going until you're soaked for me and begging for more."

A groan rips from my throat at his words.

"See. You can't even deny it. Now... why did you run?"

"She..."

"She what?" He pulls the cup of my bra down. Cool air races over my breast, making my nipple pebble almost painfully hard. He blows a stream of air across it, and every muscle in my body locks up.

"S-she was touching you." I look to the other side of the room, mortified that he's getting this out of me.

"I see. Anything else?"

He repeats his earlier action until both of my breasts are spilling from my bra, only this time, he lifts his hands and pinches both nipples once before pulling back.

"Carter," I moan.

"Come on, Danni. Tell me what you're really thinking, what you're really feeling, what you really want."

"You wouldn't show me, and I..."

"And you?"

"Damn it, Carter," I snap. "She knew what it was, and I didn't, and I—" His lips find mine once again, his hands wrapping around my hips, and we're moving. After a beat, my back hits the softness of the sheets and he crawls over me.

"Now that wasn't so hard, was it?" he asks against my lips.

"Fuck you."

"Oh, doll. I fully intend to."

His lips take mine once more, cutting off anything I could have to say back to that. His hands brush up from my waist until he palms both my breasts, pinching my nipples and making my back arch for more.

His lips trail across my jaw, down my neck, and, eventually, he gives me what I need. What I crave. His hot lips wrap around one nipple, and he sucks it deep into his mouth. His teeth sink into it gently, giving the pleasure the perfect bite of pain.

"Carter," I moan, pushing up higher and offering more of myself to him.

"Mmm," he groans, the vibration shooting straight to my core. My denim-covered legs wrap around his waist, and I attempt to pull him down, anything to get some friction where I need it most. "Feeling a little desperate, doll?"

"I need... ah," I cry when he bites down on me once more. "I need you to remind me."

His eyes come up to mine. They're dark, possibly darker than I've ever seen. "Remind you of what?" He lifts a brow in amusement.

"I need to remember last night. Bits keep coming back to me, but I need—yesss," I hiss when his fingers make quick work of the button on my waistband.

"You need?"

"To experience it. Force it back to me. Please, Carter. Please."

"You don't need to ask me twice, doll."

He sits up and pulls the fabric from my legs before discarding it on the floor. Remaining on his knees, he runs his eyes up the length of my underwear-clad body.

One side of his mouth curls up in delight.

"Like what you see?" I ask, propping myself up on my elbows.

"Like you wouldn't believe."

"I might, but you're still fully clothed."

"Huh, so I am," he mutters, looking down at himself.

"Maybe you should do something about that."

"Me?" I ask, pushing myself so I'm sitting before him.

"Yeah. You." His eyes bore into mine, daring me. Not that I need it.

Reaching out, I lift the fabric of his t-shirt and drag it up his sculpted torso. "Arms," I demand before pushing up on my knees and pulling it over his head. My breasts brush against his chest, and we both sigh in pleasure.

The second his arms are free, he reaches around my back and unclasps my bra. He pulls the fabric away from my body teasingly slowly, drawing out the frustration that's already running rampant around my body.

"Much better."

He drops his hands to my thighs and flips me backwards. I bounce on the mattress and laugh—that is, until I look up and find him dropping both his jeans and boxers. His hard length springs free, and my mouth waters. My teeth sink into my bottom lip as I wonder what he might taste like.

"You forgotten that too?" he asks, stroking his length slowly.

"Did I..."

"Rock my fucking world? Yeah, just a little."

Achievement blooms in my chest as I look up into his eyes and then back down again. I move to sit, but he places his knee on the edge of the bed and stops me.

"Not right now. I can wait."

My chin drops to argue, but his fingers wrap around the lace at my hips and all thoughts leave my head.

They're thrown over his shoulder before he drops to the floor and drags my arse to the edge of the bed.

"This... this is what I need right now." He wastes no time in parting me and diving straight in.

My head falls back as the sensation of his tongue circling my clit engulfs me. I cry out in delight as he circles my entrance with his finger.

"Carter, yes. Yes," I beg, needing him filling me, stretching me and pushing me over the edge.

Sliding two fingers deep inside me, he bends them and grazes the exact spot I need.

Desire pools in my lower stomach as he licks and fucks me into a frenzy.

My fingers dive into his long hair and I grip on, keeping him in place to ensure he gives me the release I so badly need.

I need him to banish the jealously that erupted within me in that studio. I need him to shatter the frustration that's pulling my muscles tight.

"Yes, yes," I chant over and over as my body climbs higher and higher.

"Come for me," he murmurs against my pussy, and that along with one more graze of his fingers has something shattering inside me.

"Fuuuuuck," I cry as my muscles clamp down on him and my body convulses violently on the bed.

"I could watch you coming all day long. So fucking sexy."

Despite the fact that his tongue has only just left my clit and his fingers are still stroking deep inside me, my cheeks heat at his words.

"Oh, doll. Your juices are all over my face. Too late to go all shy on me."

"Shut up," I mutter, averting my gaze. But he doesn't allow it.

Removing himself from me, igniting a round of aftershocks from my core, he climbs up my body. His fingers connect with my cheek and he turns my head so I've no choice but to look at him.

"You're fucking incredible, you know that?"

I shrug, not feeling totally comfortable with this sudden show of emotions. Easy sex I can handle. I can tell myself that it's just a Vegas thing, and that it'll be over when we step off of the plane, but having him looking down at me with so much longing and hope in his eyes? That's something I can't leave on the aircraft and hope it stays there.

"Can we not?"

"Can we not what? Because I think we already started."

"Can we not with this." I gesture between the two of us. "The words, the things we'll regret once the moment has passed."

He thinks for a minute. "I won't regret—"

"Stop." I press my fingers to his lips. "The whole trip was a disaster from the get-go. What I need is to be able to get back to my normal life once we're home and not be worrying about feelings or whatever is developing here when they shouldn't."

He stares at me, his eyes narrowing in confusion. "You fucking serious right now?"

He sits up and lifts his hands to his hair, pulling harshly.

"Carter," I sigh. "I just think it's better that we remember what this is."

"And what is that, exactly?"

"Well, it started with lies and it turned into a drunken mistake. Not exactly the thing dreams are made of." It pains me to say it, but I can't have him looking at me like he is. Like this might be something.

He's up and off the bed faster than I can blink. He turns his back on me and slams his palms down on the wall, making me jump. My eyes drop to his newly-wrapped ink, but I don't get a chance to focus on it.

"I've clearly got you all wrong. I actually thought there might be something here." The hurt in his voice guts me, but I need to stay strong. It's not exactly been my speciality since meeting him. It's time I learnt some self-restraint.

"When did I ever make you think there might be something?" As far as I remember, all I've done is tell him that he's not my type and that I wasn't interested.

"Oh, I don't know. Maybe when you asked me to marry you."

"I did not," I argue, pushing from the bed and putting my hands on my hips, owning the fact that I'm naked.

"How would you know? You don't remember."

"That's not fair."

"Is it not? You need to stop pretending there's nothing here."

"There is nothing," I cry back, my voice starting to get louder with my frustration and desperation to keep him at arm's-length.

"Really? So that's why your wedding ring only made it as far as your necklace. You want me to believe that you don't feel this, then you're going to need to try harder."

With one last perusal of my body, he rips the door open and storms through it.

"Fuck you, Carter. Fuck. You."

"You had the fucking chance," he calls back. Running to my still-open door, I slam it shut. The loud bang echoes around my room, and for all of two seconds it makes me feel better.

19

Carter

What the fuck just happened?

I fall down onto the edge of my bed and lower my head. She was putty in my hands. I was seconds from sliding into her hot, tight pussy, and she just freaked the fuck out.

I told her how incredible I thought she was. So what? She is. She's this sassy, feisty, intelligent, sexy woman who's kept me on my toes from the first moment I saw her online, yet it seems she's going to do anything to keep me at arm's-length even when her body screams for me to take her, to make her mine.

"Fuck's sake." I slam my hand down on the mattress, but it doesn't have the impact I was hoping it would. What I really need is a fucking punching bag to take my frustration out on.

Instead of heading out to find one, I turn to grab my phone.

"Motherfucker," I bark when I realise I left everything in her room.

I sit there for a few seconds, debating what to do. I don't really need it. Spike probably doesn't give a shit about my drama and will tell me to pull my panties up and take what I want, but those are my only pair of jeans and I really need those if I'm going to meet Zach and Biff for dinner in a couple of hours.

"Fucking hell, pain in the arse woman," I mutter, pushing from the bed and walking back through the empty living area. In a heartbeat, I'm standing in front of her door once again.

This time, I knock. I wait, but there's no response. My need to make sure she's okay has me pushing through her door even if she doesn't want me.

The room beyond is empty and exactly as I left it, with our clothes scattered over the floor. I look to the bed where she was laid out and practically begging for me before I opened my stupid mouth and ruined everything.

The sound of water running fills the room, and I look to the slightly ajar door on the other side. My fingers curl with my desire to walk in and show her exactly what I need and how fucking infuriating she is. My teeth grind as I try to tell myself to do the right thing, to swipe my clothes from the floor and leave as quickly as I entered. Only when my feet move, it's not in the direction of my bedroom.

Pushing the door open, I spot her immediately behind the glass screen, standing under the rainfall shower. She's turned away from me, and I get a full two seconds to watch the water stream down her back and over the curve of her arse. My cock swells as I step closer, but my movement must catch her eye.

"Carter, what the fuck are you doing?" Her eyes are wide as she turns and stares at me, but I've made a decision now, and nothing is going to stop me.

Taking her wrists in my hands, I lift them above her head as I gently push her back against the wall. She gasps when the cold tiles connect with her heated skin, and I use it as my opportunity. I press my lips to her and plunge my tongue into her mouth. She tries to pull her arms free, but I hold tight.

"Tell me you don't want me."

"I..."

"Tell me no, and I'll walk straight back out and never touch you again."

Her chest heaves as she stares at me, the water cascading around us while I wait.

"Danni?"

"Yes, yes. Okay? I want you. I fucking want—" My lips find hers once more now I've got the answer I need. I take both of her hands in one of mine and drop the other to her breast. Pinching her nipple between my fingers, I delight in her arching from the wall to get more of my touch.

"You ready for more, doll?"

"Yes, yes. Please, Carter."

Dropping my arm, I hitch her leg up around my waist so my cock can tease her entrance, but high enough to miss my new ink.

"Carter," she moans, thrusting her hips forward to try to get more of me.

"So impatient," I mutter against the sensitive skin under her ear. "Were you in here wishing I'd join you?"

She groans as my fingers graze her clit.

"Were you considering giving yourself another release?"

"No. You…"

"Good girl. This is mine now." She's about to argue—her entire body tenses with whatever is about to fall from her lips—but I push my fingers farther back and plunge two inside her. All that falls from her lips then is a moan of desire as her walls ripple around me, desperately trying to drag me deeper. Her hips thrust when I don't move in an attempt to get herself some friction. "Fuuuck, that's hot."

I lick, suck and nip at the skin on her neck as she continues to ride my fingers.

"Carter, please," she begs, making my cock impossibly hard for her.

"Please what, doll?"

"Fuck me, please."

"As you wish." I pull my fingers from her heat and release her other arm. She squeals as I lift her and wraps her arms around my neck. "I won't drop you." She eyes me curiously but releases her hold slightly.

With my hips pinning her against the wall, I drop one hand and guide myself to her entrance.

"Oh god," she cries as I slowly push inside her. "Oh god, oh god."

"Careful, doll. I'm going to start getting jealous soon if you keep calling someone else's name."

She laughs, and it does delicious things around my cock. "Christ, Dan," I groan, dropping my lips to hers.

My tongue plunges into her mouth as my cock slides deeper inside her. The sensation of her combined with the torrent of water running down my back is fucking mind-blowing.

I lift her higher and slide her back down the tiles until she's forced to rip her lips from mine when she cries out in pleasure.

Sucking the soft skin of her neck into my mouth, I trail kisses across any part of her body I can reach as I continue to piston in and out of her.

"Oh, god, Carter. Carter." Her chest heaves as her cries get louder.

"That's it, doll. Come for me. Show me exactly what I do to you."

"Fuck. Fuck." Her nails dig into my shoulders and her thighs clamp tightly around my waist as she falls over the edge. Her pussy ripples around my length, pulling me even deeper as she rides out her release.

"Jesus. Fuck, Danni. Fuck." I push her into the wall as my body goes lax with my own release, my lungs burning as I fight to drag in the air I need.

We stay frozen in place for long seconds, the only noise that can be heard over the water behind us is our increased breaths as we come down from our highs.

"That was—"

"Mind-blowing," I add.

"I was going to say unexpected, but yeah, that works."

She wriggles in my hold, and I reluctantly pull out of her and allow her feet to touch the floor once more.

Standing before me, sopping wet and with her wide, dark eyes staring up at me, all I want to do is take her in my arms and never let go again.

"I'm... I'm sorry I freaked out."

Reaching out, I take her hand and pull her so her breasts press against my chest. "You think I'm not freaking out here?" I brush a lock of wet hair from her face and tuck it behind her ear.

"No. You seem totally happy with this situation. It's almost like you planned it."

I laugh. "I can assure you that I didn't. I may have a little more of a memory of our wedding night than you, but I can't honestly say it was as much a surprise to me."

"Did I really ask you?"

"You really did, doll."

"Will you tell me about it?"

"Yeah," I say before falling quiet.

"Well, go on then."

"Oh, you mean now? No. I'm not telling you now."

"What? Why?"

"I want to see if you remember it first." She huffs in frustration, and I feel bad for not telling her the truth. The real reason that I don't want to give her the details of our wedding is because I have a feeling that once we touch back down on English soil, she's going to go running back to her old life and try to forget this ever happened. She might think twice if she still has no idea how it went down.

Am I tricking her to keep her close? Maybe. I just have to hope it'll be worth it.

"Now, let's clean you up before we have to go for dinner." I reach for her shower gel and squeeze a generous amount into my palm before running my hands over every inch of her.

By the time I'm done, my cock is hard once again, and I'm desperate for a second round.

Looking down, she stares at it. "Again?"

"Always. Now, it's your turn." I pass her the bottle and wait for her to return the favour.

I see the moment she realises that it's her chance to look at my ink, and she eagerly takes the bottle. I expect her to start elsewhere and not look too keen, but her impatience gets the better of her and it's the first part of my body she goes to.

I know the second she realises what it is, because a loud gasp fills the room.

"Carter, you didn't?"

"I want to remember it."

She looks up at me, a mix of horror, shock, and bewilderment in her eyes.

"But... it was a mistake. A drunken one at that."

"Maybe so, but that doesn't mean I want to forget about it. About you."

"Fucking hell," she mutters, staring at the design I sketched out when she was getting ready this morning. It's roman numerals of our wedding date wrapped in forget-me-not flowers like the ones that filled the chapel. Simple and to the point.

"One day, I'll put it on you," I say, my voice full of confidence I don't really feel, but I need her to know that I'm really fighting for this, that I'm serious about us.

"Oh no, no, no. That is not happening."

"Why? Don't you believe in us, doll?"

"It's not that, I'm scared of needles."

"I promise that when you've got my hands on your body, you'll barely notice."

"Whatever you say. You are aware that you're totally crazy, right?"

I shrug, wrapping my fingers around her wrist and encouraging her to start washing. I need her touch right now more than my next breath.

We finish up and wrap ourselves in the fluffy towels

sitting on the side before I leave her to it. The second I removed contact from her, it was like she immediately shut down. Feeling like I've probably already pushed her too much for one day, I leave her with her thoughts.

"Hey, man. How's it going?" Spike says when he picks up his phone. I've sent him a few messages since we arrived yesterday but not yet explained what's going on. I sent him a picture of Zach and Biff tying the knot as he requested, because he 'needed to see Zach being pinned down with his own eyes'. He's asked about Danni—obviously, he's intrigued as fuck as to how things are going to go between us—but I've yet to tell him the whole truth.

"It's... interesting."

He laughs. "She giving you that much of a hard time?"

"Yeah, you could say that."

"She not putting out?"

"You say that like she'd be able to resist me, man."

"Many women are able to. Me, on the other hand? Fucking pussy magnet, mate."

"Shut the fuck up."

"So to what do I owe the pleasure of this call?"

"We got married." Whatever he just took a sip of sprays from his mouth.

"Fuck, my fucking computer." The sound of his chair being pushed back sounds out before he barks, "Hang on. Do not go fucking anywhere."

I wait while he mops up what I assume is his work desk.

"You only ruined like, two sketches that I've spent hours working on."

"Sorry," I say with a wince.

"Whatever. What you've got to say sounds way more interesting. Hit me with it."

I give him the basics. I don't tell him anything that Danni doesn't know, because when she does either remember or I tell her, then it's just going to be between us.

"She married you and has no memory of it. Titch, that's fucking epic, even for you."

"I know," I mutter. This is just another fuck-up in a whole long line of them.

"Your parents are going to have a fucking field day with this."

"They'd need to talk to me to find out first."

"True," he agrees sadly. "Anyway, you don't need them now."

"How'd you figure that?"

"You're making your own family. How long until you knock her up?"

"Knowing my luck, I probably already have and it's quadruplets."

He barks out a laugh before thankfully changing the subject and asking me about Vegas, or more specifically, Megs. He's got some weird kind of crush on her, which mostly means he stalks her Instagram and gets himself off to her photographs.

By the time Spike stops chatting, I'm late for dinner. I'm half into a clean pair of boxers when a knock sounds out and Danni pokes her head around my door.

"Shit. Sorry," she says, disappearing once again.

"S'all good, doll. It all belongs to you," I call out.

"I'll just meet you in the restaurant."

"Which one is it?"

"I don't know. Zach texted us with the name. Just look at that."

I blow out a frustrated breath as the main door to our

suite opens and closes, signalling that she left quite happily. I'd kind of hoped she'd refuse and wait for me so we could go together.

I grab my phone from where I threw it on my bed after my conversation with Spike and pull up my messages. As always, there are loads of unread ones. I do notice that none of them are from my parents checking to see if I'm still alive. I do however have some photographs from my brother showing off. Standard.

I find Zach's name and stare at the restaurant. The letters start to swirl before my eyes in a way I'm all too used to. I give up after a couple of seconds and make my phone speak it to me.

Zodiac Bar and Grill.

I'm more frustrated than I should be by the time I step from the suite. I don't even bother trying to look at the list of everything inside this hotel that's pinned up in the lift —I already know it's pointless. Instead, I head straight for reception and ask one of the ladies behind the desk for directions. It's so much fucking easier and a hell of a lot quicker.

By the time I arrive, they all have drinks and are happily chatting away. I almost consider turning around and going back to my room to have a pity party for one, but Biff spots me before I get a chance to run.

"Titch, over here," she calls, waving me over. "We've already got you a beer, just waiting for you to order."

"Oh... um..." I grab the menu as if I'm actually going to read the thing. Zach's eyes burn into the top of my head. He knows exactly what I'm doing. "I'll just have the steak."

"So, have you two kissed and made up?" he asks.

"You want the real answer to that?" I ask with a smug-as-fuck grin on my face. I can't help but laugh when he pales.

"Everything is fine," Danni says coldly.

"So, I visited Rebel earlier."

"Oh yeah? What did you think?"

"Home from home, man. You've done a great job."

He smiles proudly as if I'm talking about his first born. "Who'd have thought that when I bought it a couple of years ago all the Abbot kids would end up married in this very place."

"Do you have to?" Danni asks.

"Just stating facts, sis."

"Yeah, well, if you could refrain I'd be more than grateful."

"Fucking hell. I don't want to get involved, but if she's still this uptight then you clearly didn't do your husbandly duties correctly earlier, mate."

"I didn't think you wanted the details."

"I don't. But I also want to make sure my baby sister is being looked after."

"Shut the fuck up, Zach," Danni barks. "Could I have another, please?" she asks a passing waitress, holding her now empty glass out to her.

"Sure. Anyone else?" She looks around the table, but seeing three still-full drinks she backs away.

"Careful, you don't want two drunken mistakes in as many nights," I say, looking at her hard-set face. Her walls are up so high right now that I've got no chance of getting inside them.

"Ah, so now you agree that last night was a mistake."

"Whatever, Dan. Drink yourself into oblivion, but be careful, because I might not be there to carry you over the threshold tonight."

"Is it wrong to be glad that they're having their first marital fight before us?" Biff whispers loudly to Zach.

When the waitress returns with Danni's drink, we all order food and talk about the night ahead. Danni sits there, silently fuming the entire time. I want to say something, but I don't bother, because I have a feeling it'll only end up with my head being bitten off.

The night is so different to the one that went before. Yes, the food is incredible, and we drink way too much, but that's where the similarities end. Danni gives me the cold shoulder almost all night. If I didn't know that I hadn't dreamed our time together in her shower, then I would be starting to worry that it didn't actually happen. I know I was concerned about how she would deal with the situation that is us when she got home, but I was at least hoping she'd embrace it while we were here. At least give me a chance to prove to her that I'm worthy of her, despite her first impressions.

When we get to the club Biff chose for the night, there is no bumping and grinding. She doesn't even go as far as giving me a chaste kiss before she disappears into her bedroom when we get back to our suite sometime before sunrise.

The room spins when I lie down alone in my bed. Knowing she's right across the living room and slightly intoxicated is a temptation that I don't need. I can still vividly remember her allowing her wild side to take the lead last night when we got back. It was sexy as fuck, watching her strip out of her makeshift wedding dress and take control. It was her confidence about what she wanted that made me think she knew what she was doing. I never would have thought she'd wake up the next morning with very little memory of the night before. It clearly didn't rock her world as much as it had mine.

With a sad sigh, I roll over and try to come up with a plan. A plan to prove to her that there could be something meaningful here. I know I'm not what she thinks she wants. If she could just drop her unrealistic expectations and see what's right in front of her, I could be the one she's been looking for. I'm just wrapped in tats instead of a fancy designer suit.

20

Danni

My head throbs as I sit silently beside Carter, waiting for our gate to open to start our journey home.

I rest my head back against the wall and shut my eyes. There's a large family with overly loud children sitting opposite us. I pray to God they're not going to be flying first class, because I'm not sure my head could take this noise for hours on end in a confined space.

"Don't they just make you never want to have kids?" I mutter, not opening my eyes to see if he realises I'm talking to him.

"They're just enjoying themselves."

"No, they're being little shits is what they are."

"How would you know? Your eyes are shut."

"I have ears, Carter."

"Yeah, so they're a little loud, but they're just playing a

game. If you really paid attention, you'd hear them laughing. They're happy. They're not getting in anyone's way. They're just passing the time without complaining. Unlike someone I know."

"Well," I huff, "they should read a book or something. Anything that's quiet."

"Maybe they can't read."

"Really? Their parents can afford for the entire family to fly to Vegas, but the kids can't read. I highly doubt that."

He doesn't respond, forcing me to turn to look at him.

"What?" I ask when I see his brows drawn together in concern.

"Nothing. I just wasn't expecting you to be such a judgemental bitch."

His words hurt, but as I think back over what I just said, I can't really argue. There could be a million reasons why those kids aren't reading a book right now, and who am I to judge?

"You're right. I'm sorry. It's the hangover."

"I feel like shit too, but I'm not picking holes in anyone."

"Oh, so you're not judging me right now?"

"You're my wife. I'm allowed."

"I don't remember that being in the vows."

"Funny, because I didn't think you remembered any of them."

His word hit exactly where he intends, and I snap my lips shut. As much as I might enjoy this teasing banter with him, I'm exhausted. I've no idea what time it was when we eventually got back to the suite last night, all I know is that I've not had anywhere near enough sleep to deal with this.

I've had a few more hazy flashbacks from the night in

question, but nothing of any significance. I have an image of a jewellers in my head, and for some reason I keep thinking of blue forget-me-nots. It could be a coincidence, my mind playing tricks on me, but something tells me it's real.

I could ask about it, but he seems set on withholding details of that night from me, so it stops me.

"I'm assuming you don't want kids, then?" Carter asks out of the blue after being quiet for a number of minutes.

"What makes you say that?" It's a stupid question, and I regret it instantly. "I do, actually. Not yet, but one day in the future."

"As long as they don't make any noise in an airport," he deadpans.

"I'll just warn them to stay away from hungover people."

Thankfully, we're invited to board not long after, which puts an end to any further conversation about how I see my future.

I had such a clear picture of what I thought I wanted. But since I walked into that restaurant and found him waiting for me, everything has got a little blurry. I hate the unknown, the confusion. I like my life to be like business: organised, planned, and to the point. But suddenly I'm weaving about all over the place, and my head and heart are constantly warring, not knowing which way is up.

It's all his fault. All of it. If he hadn't have tricked me into thinking he was someone else, then none of this would have happened. If I met the Carter I believed I was meant to be meeting that night, I might now be in the beginnings of a serious relationship, not at the start of an unplanned shotgun Vegas wedding that can only end in disaster.

The second we're able to rest our seats back, I put my ear buds in and close my eyes. If I can sleep this entire journey, then maybe things won't seem quite so bad when we touch down in London.

A girl can only dream.

I lift my hand to the wedding ring still hanging around my neck. I went to take it off this morning, but I found I just couldn't do it. Not yet.

There's plenty of time to rehash my drunken mistake once I'm back and alone in my flat, and I can shove this thing in a drawer and pretend it never happened.

By the time we touch down at Heathrow, I'm feeling much more refreshed thanks to the hours of extra sleep I was so desperate for and the healthy breakfast I was served.

"So I guess this is it, then," I say to Carter when we emerge from arrivals and out into the damp English weather. I was hoping Carter might have headed home as soon as we disembarked, but then I guess, knowing him like I do now, I shouldn't have been surprised when he insisted on coming with me to collect my luggage and walking out together.

"You really are trying to get rid of me, aren't you?"

I shrug. "I'm sure you've got loads of stuff to do. It's not like our trip was planned. Real life awaits."

"What if I don't want it to?" he asks, a little hope filtering into his voice.

"Carter," I sigh. "This little trip was... interesting. But I've got a life to get back to. A job. I can't just continue to party with you and pretend none of that exists."

"Did I say anything about pretending? Something big happened while we were in Vegas, doll, and I'm not prepared to forget about that just yet. Forget about you." He steps up to me, his scent filling my nose, and his hand lifts to tuck a lock of my curly hair behind my ear. "I'm not ready to forget any of it. I'd hoped I might have proved to you that I want this. I want to see where it goes. We can push the husband and wife thing to the side for now and just go back to the beginning. I just want to give this the time it deserves."

I stare at him. The honesty in his words makes my heart ache. It desperately wants to agree, to throw caution to the wind and see where this thing could take us. But my head? That's a very different story. It's screaming at me to turn and run as fast as I can, because whatever this is, is only going to end in heartache. Carter isn't the kind of guy who does a happily ever after. *Or is he?*

Fuck. My head is so messed up.

"I..." His eyes brighten that he might be about to get the response he wants. It kills me not to be able to give it to him. "I need some time, Carter. I need to go home, get back to reality, and then see how I feel. I'm not making any decisions after a few days of drinking in Vegas and a long-haul flight."

His shoulders drop, and I hate myself that little bit more for doing this to him. But it's right. I can't get carried away with this. I need a plan.

"So what? I call you in a few days and find out if you want me in your life or not?"

I wince. It sounds so harsh when he says it like that. "Please, don't be like that."

"Why not? That's exactly what you're saying. And if you decide that you don't, then what? Can I expect divorce papers through my door in a few weeks' time?"

"I don't know, Carter," I all but cry. "This situation is way beyond anything I've dealt with before. "Just call me in a few days and we'll talk. That's all I can offer right now." I know I'm taking the pussy way out, but I don't know how else to deal with this. What I really need is to talk to someone who might be able to make me see straight. Biff wasn't a lot of help while we were in Vegas, and rightly so—she was in newly wedded bliss.

What I really want is a hug from my mum and for her to tell me that everything will be okay, only I'm terrified to admit what's happened in the last three days. It's going to be bad enough that Zach planned a Vegas wedding without them. But Mum's going be heartbroken when I admit what I've done.

"Danni," Carter begs as I walk towards an awaiting taxi.

"Just give me some time." Every muscle in my body demands for me to turn, but I'm petrified of what I might find looking back at me.

Stiffening my spine, I speak to the driver before allowing him to put my case in the boot and climbing into the back of his car. At no point do I look back, but it's not until we turn away from the taxi bay that we lose his attention. My skin cools immediately, and the huge weight of regret fills my stomach.

I shouldn't have left things like that. He deserves more from me.

"Fuck," I bark, slouching back in the seat. The driver's eyes meet mine in the mirror for a beat, but thankfully he doesn't say anything, just allows me to be miserable in peace.

I should be feeling relieved that I can go home and

continue with my normal life, so why is it that as I sit here, I'm already starting to miss him? I don't know why, but I was beginning to get used to his annoying banter.

I let out a sigh and try to switch my mind off as we make our way through the city. Going over everything again and again isn't going to get me anywhere. I'm still married to a guy who turns me on more than anyone I've ever met but is nothing like I've always said I wanted.

Does that matter? a little voice shouts in my head, but I ignore her.

The second I get inside my flat, I turn on my coffee machine before dumping my case on my bed and running myself a bath. The five-star chair-come-bed on the plane was pretty comfortable, but still my muscles are pulled tight with the stress of the past seventy-two hours.

With a steaming mug of coffee resting on the side, I step into the hot water. It burns, but I welcome the sting of pain as I sink down lower. I rest my head back and will everything to float away.

By the time I get out, the water is uncomfortably cold and my coffee has long disappeared. My phone's been vibrating against the unit I put it on in my bedroom before I stripped off; I dread to look. As far as I know, he doesn't have my number, but I'm sure it would take him minutes to get hold of it.

With my little bit of relaxation ruined, I wrap myself in towels and go and see who wants me.

I breathe a sigh of relief when I find it's just Biff wanting to know if I got home safely and to make sure I didn't throw Carter off the plane.

I reply that we're both back in London safe, but I don't go into any more details. I'm sure that once she's back she'll thoroughly grill me on everything that's happened.

It's still early, and even though it's a Saturday morning, I'm seriously tempted to go into work to catch up with what I missed the last few days as a way of distracting myself from reality, but when my phone starts ringing, I lie back on the bed and forget all about it.

"Hey, how's it going?" Lauren asks. We've only exchanged a few messages since the night of Zach's birthday a couple of weekends ago.

"Um…" I hesitate.

"Wow, that good?"

"You've no fucking idea. Are you sitting down?"

"Hang on." I hear her open a door, and then the sound of birds singing rings through the phone. "Okay, shoot."

I give her the basics, much to her horror.

"You got fucking married in Vegas, and to someone you don't even like?" she screeches.

"Yeah. I mean, I don't really not like him. He's not like, horrible or anything. He's just not…"

"Your ideal man," she finishes for me. Although Lauren and I have drifted apart over the past few years as our lives have taken different turns, she's still the one who knows me best. We met when we were sixteen, we started adulthood together and leant on each other as we made the biggest decisions of our lives, most of which involved a lot more planning and brainpower than my smart arse move to get married.

"No. He's a tattoo artist, he's covered in ink, he's got a foul mouth, he's…"

"Just like Zach and Ben."

"Err…"

"Both of whom are pretty great guys, don't you think? So what, he's not a banker, or lawyer? They're all pretentious jobs anyway. I'm not sure any banker has ever thrown his girl over his shoulder and carried her caveman-style to the bedroom."

"Who says I want that?"

"Oh, come off it, Dan. You've been spending too much time with your parents' friends. Does this guy give you the feels? You know, *the tingles*," she whispers.

I think back to the night on Biff's sofa and then in the shower last night. Oh yeah, there's tingles.

"I'll take your silence as a yes, then."

I huff.

"What's the worst that could happen? Your parents won't care, they've always told you they'd support you as long as you're happy. They're not like Biff's. He might turn out to be the exact bit of rough you need."

I sigh.

"Come on, out with it."

"What if he hurts me?"

"And what if he doesn't? What if he's the most incredible husband and the one person who can really make you happy?"

Her words are still spinning around in my head long after we cut off the call. Deciding that going into work is kinda sad after a few days living it up in Vegas, I put on a pair of yoga pants and a sports bra and head out for a run. The drizzle from when we first arrived has cleared, replaced by warm spring sun. It could be the exact medicine I need to clear my head.

Slipping my phone into my pocket, I put my earbuds in and set off on my normal route.

When I descend the steps to my basement flat almost an hour later with a takeout coffee and cupcake in hand, the last thing I expect to find is someone waiting for me. Someone with a daunting looking suitcase.

Now what?

21

Carter

Pushing through the door to our flat, I startle a little when I find Spike awake and sitting on the sofa, staring down at his phone and clutching a coffee.

"Morning," I grunt.

"Ah, here he is. Mr. Danniella Abbot."

"Please, don't," I groan, dropping my small case where I am and launching myself at the other sofa.

"Uh oh, trouble in paradise already?"

"There hasn't been any paradise, only trouble," I mutter.

"But I thought you said you'd got your dick wet? That must have been getting pretty close to paradise."

"Jesus, that's my wife you're talking about."

"Exactly. Which leads me to my next point." I look up at him, wondering what mind-blowing statement is going to fall from his lips next. "Why are you here? Shouldn't you be shacking up with your little lady?"

I open my mouth to respond, but he beats me to it.

"Do not tell me that you're here to kick me out so she can move in. This is my gaff, and you know it."

"You think I'd want to move her into this shithole? She actually has some standards."

"Fuck you, arsehole. I'll have you know this place was cleaned yesterday."

"Of course it fucking was. Ann comes every fucking Friday."

"Right, so what's you point? It's a great flat."

"To you it is. It's right between a strip club and a load of bars."

"Fucking right, my man. What else does a single guy need? Anyway, anyway, you're distracting me. She's not moving in here, yet you're here. So... what gives?"

"Nothing fucking gives. She left me at Heathrow like a forgotten fucking toy, telling me that she'd ring me in a few days once she's got her head straight or some fucking bullshit."

"And you're letting that happen?"

"What the fuck am I meant to do?"

"Force her hand a little."

"I'm not forcing her to do anything. I've already fucked things up enough for her. In case you'd forgotten, I tricked her into thinking I was my brother to get a date in the first place, then I went on to marry her while we were both drunk."

"And doesn't that just prove the lengths you'll go to for this chick?"

"That's one way of looking at it. Unfortunately, it's not her way of looking at it."

"Make her."

"How?" I ask again, hoping his idea might be a little more eloquent than anything else he's said since I got back.

"Repack that case and get your arse to her flat. Tell her you're moving in with your wife. Make her get to know you. Make her realise that she can't live without you."

"That's crazy, you know that, right?"

"Maybe. But it's not out of the question. I can see that you're considering it."

And fuck if he's not right. I told her that I'd prove to her by the end of our few days together that she should give me a chance, and she's run as fast as she could. Maybe it is time to do things on my terms and not allow her to hide back inside her comfort zone. That place is for fucking chumps, and no wife of mine is one of those.

I push up from the sofa, my muscles set with determination.

"Yes, man. Make her fucking yours."

I'm making my way past the kitchen when a wine glass catches my eye. "Am I about to stumble across a half-naked woman?" It wouldn't be the first time I walked into the bathroom, hell, even the hallway, to find one of Spike's conquests flaunting everything she's got.

"Nah, she already left."

I guess that explains why he's up so early.

I dump my bag on my bed and hit the shower before repacking with some clean clothes and going to do exactly what Spike suggested.

I never thought I'd be taking relationship advice from the king of fuck 'em and chuck 'em, but it seems he was right when he tried convincing me not to lie on my dating profile. He told me time and time again that I was enough and that the right one would turn up. He was proved right when the one girl I found turned her back on me the second she saw who I really was. It was only luck that she turned out to be Zach's sister and that I was able to fight for a second chance. So maybe he's more knowledgeable than I ever gave him credit for.

After all, what's the worst that could happen? She could slam the door in my face, and I come back here with my tail between my legs.

"Hey, man. You get back okay?" Zach asks when our call connects.

"Yeah, great. Listen, I need a huge favour."

"Go on," Zach says with a groan.

"I need her address. She got in a taxi the second we arrived back and I've no way of finding her."

"Do you think that maybe she did that on purpose?"

"Honestly, I don't give a shit. If it were Biff, what would you do?"

We both know the answer. He'd go to the ends of the earth to find her. "I'm fucking serious, you hurt her and I'll—"

"Hurt me, yeah. I got that memo. Just tell me."

"Fine," he grunts, clearly unhappy with it but knowing it's the only way to deter me. "How do you want it?"

"Just tell me. I'll remember."

He rattles off an address for the fanciest end of Kensington, and I wince. It's a huge reminder of why I'm not the kind of man Danni was looking for. She was after successful businessman, not an artist with more issues than money.

Refusing to think of all the reasons we're so wrong for each other, I hang up and grab my bag once more.

Spike's in the kitchen when I pass.

"Wish me luck."

"You don't need it. Sweep her off your feet with your charm."

"I think we both know I don't have a lot of that."

"Fine. Show her your tats and rock her world, she won't be able to refuse after that."

"I'll do my best," I say with a laugh as I leave him to the washing up.

I order a car as I descend the stairs to our building, and after only a two-minute wait standing on the pavement, my driver appears. The street is pretty quiet, that's not really a surprise. What I said about our flat earlier is true. We might live over a bakery, but a few doors down to our left is Pulse, one of the city's best strip clubs, and we're surrounded by all other kinds of bars. It's been amazing over the years. We can fall from our front door and directly into a place full of drink and often women. It's no wonder Spike is as big a dog as he is. He just can't resist temptation.

The second we enter Kensington, the obvious differences from where I just left make themselves known, the architecture becoming fancier, more detailed. There are more people about, jogging, meeting friends, and what they're wearing is markedly different to the few hungover people who were on our street.

Before I've even got out of the car, I feel totally out of place.

I stare at the house I'm about to walk towards. It's huge. There's a giant black front door with chrome fittings, and the windows are massive, I'd imagine letting loads of light into the vast rooms beyond. I can't even comprehend just how much money it must be worth.

After I walk through the front gate, I turn left towards

a set of stairs that descend to the basement flat, although I have a feeling it's not going to be like any dark and dingy basement flat I've ever been in before.

Unlike upstairs, the front door down here is bright pink. I can't imagine Danni and Zach's older brother was all that thrilled about that decision, but I guess at least you can't see it from the street. There are thriving plant pots surrounding the small space and a bistro set that's already in the beam of sun from above. It might only be a small bit of outside space, but it's perfect, and weirdly, I can already imagine myself drinking a morning coffee out here.

I ring the bell, trying to push down my apprehension about how she's going to react, but it never comes because the door doesn't open and I'm not met with my fiery wife.

Glancing in through the window, I find a spotless kitchen, but other than a mug sitting on this side, I see no sign of life.

Not wanting to give up so easily, I pull out one of the chairs and take a seat, prepared to wait for her. There's a good chance she's just upstairs with her brother and his family, but like fuck am I knocking on their front door, looking for my new wife. I chuckle to myself when an image of her angry face pops into my head. My cock swells slightly. I do love her when she's angry.

Not all that much time passes before I hear footsteps heading my way, but my arse is numb from the metal seat and I'm dying for a coffee. If I knew she'd keep me waiting like this, I'd have stopped to pick one up.

As I keep my eyes on the stairs, a pair of pink trainers and then a set of sculpted legs wrapped in a floral pair of yoga pants emerges. I watch her body as it's revealed to me, my mouth watering as I take in all her perfectly displayed curves and the light sheen of sweat that covers her skin.

She's clutching the exact thing I want when all of her emerges: a coffee, and something that can only be delicious inside a paper bag.

She doesn't notice me straight away, so I get to witness her shock when I stand.

"Jesus, fuck, Carter. What the hell are you doing here?" The little paper bag lifts to her chest in shock, and my hand twitches to reach out to save it.

As I take a step forward, her eyes land on something behind me.

"W-why have you brought a suitcase?"

"I'm moving in," I state.

"Um… you're fucking what?"

"Moving in. I think it's only right that as man and wife we live together."

"Carter," she says on a sigh. "We're not man and wife, we're a massive drunken mistake." Her frustration is obvious, and I can't help but push her buttons.

"I've got a wedding certificate that says differently. We're connected now, doll. It's time you accept it."

"Nothing to accept. You're not moving in here. This is my home."

"What's yours is mine now, doll."

She blows out a breath, her body tense as we stand, locked in our stare. She might not know all that much about me yet, but she's about to learn that when I want something, I don't stop until I get it.

"You're infuriating."

"And you're hot. Especially when you get that look in your eye where I'm not sure if you want to fuck me or kill me."

"I'd put your money on the latter of the two."

"Forty-eight hours in Vegas and you've become a gambling expert, who'd have thought it."

"I might have already been an expert, how would you know?" Her hand drops to her waist as her hip pops out. She has no idea, but she's just laid down the ultimate challenge.

"Doll, I watched you at the tables. You are most definitely not an expert."

"Whatever. Are you going to get out of the way yet so I can go in?"

"Sure, lead the way."

"You're not moving in here."

"I beg to differ." I stand aside and gesture towards her door. "I think we also might need to discuss the colour of this."

"Read my lips: you are not moving in, and you are certainly not changing the colour of this door."

"Hmmm."

"What?" she snaps.

"Interesting to know you're more concerned about the door than me moving in."

"You're impossible." With a huff, she plucks her front door key from its really novel hiding place under a plant pot and pushes it into the lock.

"That was there the whole time," I mutter. "I could have unpacked by now."

Without saying a word, she marches through the door before swinging it as hard as she can behind her. Thankfully, I see it coming and get my foot inside just in time.

"Now that wasn't very welcoming to your new housemate, was it?"

She doesn't stop. She marches straight through the open-plan living area and towards the back of the flat, to what I discover is a seriously impressive master bedroom.

"I've gotta say, this place is nicer than what I'm used to. I think I'm going to really enjoy it here."

"You're not staying," she barks, pulling a door open and disappearing inside.

I take a seat on the end of her bed and wait.

"Why are you still here?" she asks when she emerges with a couple of items of clothing draped over her arm.

"Because I live here."

Her face starts to turn bright red as she stares at me. Her little fists clench, and I can't help but laugh. It's going to take a little more than that to intimidate me. I've fought and broken guys twice my size, a five-foot nothing brunette woman is less than scary.

"Come on then. Come and hit me if it'll make you feel better. Get rid of that anger."

She drops the clothes in a pile on the floor and storms over.

"I'm not going to hit you."

"Why? Are you too good for that? I forgot you're the little posh girl who only wants a fancy banker on her arm to make her look good." Her lips purse in frustration, and her eyes darken. I'm definitely touching a nerve.

"That's not—"

"Hitting me because you're angry won't bring you down a notch, doll. I won't tell anyone. It can be our dirty little secret. Just like our marriage."

Her arm lifts, her small fist amusing as she moves for my chest. Only, she gets nowhere near. My own arm shoots out and my fingers wrap around my wrist.

She stares at our connection as if she can't believe it's

really there. She's got a lot to learn about me, my reaction times only one of them.

While she's distracted, I take her other wrist and walk her backwards until she's pressed up against the wall.

I lift her arms and pin them above her head. Her chest heaves and her lips part as she stares at me. Anger still pours from her in waves, but it's quickly being overtaken by desire.

"You won't win any fight with a pathetic attempt like that."

"I-I don't want to win. I just want you to leave."

I lean in towards her ear and smile when my breath makes her shudder. "Are you really sure about that?"

I step closer and press the length of my body to hers. A moan falls from her lips, but from the way she stills immediately after, it's obvious that it wasn't intentional.

"Let me show you just how good it could be, having me as a housemate. I've got some tricks you've not even discovered yet."

"Carter, I—"

This time I don't give her a chance to argue. I've had enough with words, it's time to let our bodies do the talking.

My tongue delves between her open lips and teases hers. She resists for a few seconds longer than I'd like, but I know it's more out of defiance than it is lack of interest.

Her body sags against mine as she accepts the kiss. She lifts one leg and curls it around my hip, lining us up perfectly. I growl as her heat surrounds my hardening length.

"See, you're already reaping the benefits of this situation."

I kiss across her jaw and down her neck.

"There is no situation," she breathes, her argument now weak at best as her desire takes over.

Releasing her hands, I kiss down her chest and along the edge of her sports bra. Not seeing how to easily remove it, I continue down.

Her leg drops from around me, and as I kiss down her bare stomach, I hook my fingers into her leggings and pull.

I slip her trainers off and then pull the fabric from her feet before placing one hand behind her knee and pushing it wide and high, opening her up for me.

"Carter, I just went for a run," she warns.

"You're mine, doll. I call the shots."

She starts to argue, but the second I fix my lips around her clit and stroke it with my tongue, she loses her train of thought.

"Fuck, fuck, fuck." Her hands dive into my hair. She pulls me closer and refuses to let go. Just how it should be.

"Carter," she cries when I slide two fingers inside her as deep as they'll go before bending them and searching out her g-spot.

Her walls ripple around my fingers, her body trembling as she stands on one leg, approaching her release.

"Come, doll," I mumble against her centre, and she does exactly that.

She cries out my name as her grip on my hair gets impossibly tight.

I slow my movements until she's spent, then I lower her leg back to the floor and lift her into my arms.

Her arms wrap around my neck and her legs around my waist. Her lips search out mine, and she groans when she tastes herself on my lips.

"This. Off," I mutter against her lips, tugging at the insanely tight fabric containing her tits.

She releases my shoulders and successfully pulls it up and over her head in one smooth move.

Lifting her higher, I take one of her nipples in my mouth and then the other. I watch as her head falls back in pleasure before I throw her down on the bed.

Dragging my shirt over my head, I make quick work of removing every other item of clothing I'm wearing before taking her hips in my hands and flipping her to her front.

I drag her to her knees at the end of the bed before lining myself up with her entrance and thrusting straight into her.

"Fuck," she cries, her body jolting forward at my invasion, but I don't allow her to move. My fingertips dig into her hips and I pull out and slam inside her once again, feeling more at home than the few moments I spent inside my flat earlier.

"This," I say on a thrust. "This. Is. Why. You. Need. Me. Here."

"I did just fine before. I've got a vibrator in that drawer that does a perfectly good job."

"Oh yeah. Maybe one day you can show me and we can compare." I'm about as intimidated by her threat as I was by her fists. There's no way a small battery-operated device could come close to this right now. The connection. The passion. The wild need. It's unrivalled.

"Fuck you." I'm assuming she wants it to be a threat, but it just comes out as a moan of pleasure.

"Oh, doll. I am, and I can tell you for nothing that it won't be the last time, either."

One hand releases her hip in favour of running up her stomach to find her full, needy breasts. I squeeze them before pinching her nipples. Each time I do, her pussy squeezes me so tight I almost come without warning.

Her back arches further, ensuring I hit her even deeper.

Fuck.

Tingles erupt at the base of my spine as my balls start to draw up. I skim my hand back down her stomach until I find her clit. I pinch it hard and she crashes over the edge, followed only a second later by me.

We both cry out as pleasure races through our bodies. Her legs give out, and she flops forward onto the bed. I follow close behind, my weight pressing her into the mattress.

"Are you trying to kill me?" she asks once she's caught her breath.

"No, just stopping you running away."

"This is my house, I'm not going anywhere."

"Nor am I. So I suggest you get used to the idea. I could use a shower, you?"

Her lips part, but she doesn't say anything as she watches me climb from the bed and poke my head into the open door she disappeared into not so long ago.

"Fucking hell," I mutter, seeing a massive walk-in wardrobe. "I guess I shouldn't be worried that you don't have space for my stuff."

"I'm not worried, because it doesn't need to be here."

I glance over my shoulder to find her quite happily staring at my arse. She might try to tell me that she doesn't want me, but unfortunately for her, her actions speak louder.

Moving away from that door, I push the other one open to find a luxurious bathroom, complete with walk-in shower and a free-standing bath.

"Carter, what are you—"

I ignore her and turn the shower on. The water drowns out her complaining.

I know the moment she joins me. I feel her angry stare burning into my back.

"Come and join me, doll. The water's lovely."

I turn to find her standing naked in the doorway. "Make yourself at home, why don't you?"

"That was the plan." I reach out for her shower gel. It's got Love Hearts all over it. I pop the top and take a sniff. "Hmm... so this is why you taste so sweet," I muse, squeezing a generous amount into the palm of my hand before making a show of rubbing it over my chest and abs. "You want a taste yet?"

She crosses her arms over her chest. It makes her cleavage look incredible as she watches the movement of my hands.

When she gets down to my cock that's still sporting a semi, she sucks her bottom lip into her mouth. Her eyes defy her. She's seriously considering it.

My length hardens, remembering how hot her mouth was the last time she sucked me deep. She doesn't remember it, but fuck, that's not something I'm ever going to forget.

"Come on, doll. Stop denying yourself."

Shaking her head, she steps towards me and right under the spray of water. "I'm not doing this because I want you. I'm doing it because I need a shower."

"Sure."

Squeezing another blob of shower gel into my hand, I rub them together before lifting them to her breasts. She jumps, but the second I brush her nipples she caves.

"Now, isn't this better than doing it alone?"

"Meh." She shrugs as I continue trailing my soapy hands around her body before I reach for the shampoo. My fingers massage her scalp as she moans quietly.

"See, I told you, doll. Tricks."

"You have no food," I say in horror as I shut her fridge and start on her cupboards.

"In case you'd forgotten, I've not been here for a few days," she says, walking through to join me now dressed in a cute summer dress. If she wasn't still trying to get rid of me, I'd start to think she chose it for my benefit.

"On second thoughts, I've found something else I want to eat more."

"No," she says holding her hand up. "You promised me lunch. The fact I'm even considering this is crazy, so you need to seriously sweeten the deal if I've got to put up with you."

A smile curls at my lips. I fucking knew I'd win her over eventually.

"Okay, how's this. I take you out for lunch, and then we hit the supermarket to sort this dire situation out. You've not even got any dried pasta in the cupboard."

"I don't really cook a lot." I quirk a brow. "Okay, or ever."

"Get ready to go. I'll get dressed." I swipe the towel from my waist as I leave the room.

"Clothes are a requirement in this house," comes from behind me. I chuckle in response. I'm confident I can turn her to my way of thinking with that, too.

She joins me in the bedroom as I'm pulling a shirt over my head. She squirts some stuff on her hands before scrunching it in her hair. It instantly tames her previously slightly wild curls.

"What?" she asks when she catches my eye in the mirror over her shoulder.

"N-nothing." She stares at me a while longer, but I keep my lips sealed. I can't play all my cards in the first couple of hours. Plus, I don't want to appear desperate. Well, any more than I'm sure I already am.

"Ready?" I ask when she seems to have finished.

"Yes. Let's go."

22

Danni

I shake my head as I follow him from *my* house. I'm equally amused by his audacity as I am pissed off that I wasn't able to get rid of him. That's because deep down, I don't *want* to get rid of him. I enjoy him being around more than I can admit, but I also know this is a disaster waiting to happen. For some insane reason, he expects me to embark on a life as a married couple when really, we've never even dated. I know hardly anything about the man. For us to suddenly live together in my one-bed flat is insane.

"Come on. I've got a car waiting."

I lock up and climb the stairs to catch up with him. He's not told me where we're going, and I've decided to attempt to ignore my inner control freak and go with the flow.

"So do you just not cook for one, or can't you cook?"

he asks me after confirming our destination with the driver.

"Bit of both. I don't enjoy it, so I've never really taken the time to learn. I spend too much time at work, and the last thing I want to do when I get home is cook."

"Fair enough."

"What about you? I'm assuming you can."

"A little. I find it relaxing."

"Well, I hope you packed your apron."

"Of course. I like to cook naked, so it's important to keep the goods covered." My chin drops as I imagine him walking around my kitchen in nothing but a frilly apron like my nan used to wear, his arse on full display. Shockingly, it's an image I'm interested in experiencing. "See, now you're interested, right?"

"In having your flaccid cock near my dinner? No, that's not overly appealing," I lie.

"What if I covered it in frosting?" My mouth waters. Damn him. "I'll add frosting to my list. Chocolate sauce, too, in case you like to experiment."

"What?" I ask in shock. "I never said I wanted—"

"It's all in your eyes, doll. I can practically see your thoughts."

"The only thing in my head is how to get you out of my flat."

"After you've licked my frosting, I hope."

I growl, my back teeth grinding in frustration.

"Can I see the list, please?"

"I don't have one."

"So how do you know what you want to buy?"

"It's all up here." He taps his temple.

"Huh."

"What's that meant to mean?"

"Nothing. I've just never met anyone with that good of a memory."

"That's because you've never met anyone quite like me before."

"You've got that right," I mutter, making him laugh.

The rest of the short journey is in silence as I stare out of the window, trying to figure out where he's taking me. I'm not sure I've ever been to this part of town before.

The car pulls to a stop beside a row of shops, and my brows pull together when I don't see anywhere to eat.

"Thanks, man," Carter says to the driver before pushing the door open and climbing out. I join him on the pavement. My confusion must be written all over my face, because he looks at me and smiles. "Trust me."

Nodding, I accept his words, and when he twists his fingers with mine, I don't pull my hand away. It feels quite comforting.

I'm shocked when he pulls me to a stop outside of a nondescript looking door. It looks like anything but a restaurant.

I remain silent as he pushes the door open, my eyes darting around everywhere, trying to figure this out.

We descend a set of stairs, and that's when the dining area comes into view. My eyes almost bug out of my head. "Wow. I was not expecting this."

"Impressive, right?"

"I'll say. What is it?"

"Purple Peas is an award-winning low carb restaurant."

I can't help but smile. He's noticed that I try to eat low carb. "Carter," I sigh.

"See, I know more than you think."

"Good afternoon, table for two?" the waiter asks when he comes over to greet us.

"Yes please." He grabs two menus before directing us to a small table over in the corner of the basement dining room.

The decor down here is incredible. Everything is purple, chrome and glass. I've never seen a restaurant like it.

"This is something else. How didn't I know about it?"

"It's fairly new, but it's getting more and more popular."

"And how do you know about it?"

"The guy who just brought us over here. He's a client of mine."

"Why didn't he say anything?"

"Because we're on a date." My heart pounds at his assumption.

"I'm not sure…" His brow rises, and I trail off.

"We're on a date, doll. Now, take your pick. Everything is either low or no carb, so you can eat your heart out and not worry."

I stare down at the menu for a few moments, not knowing what to look at first. "Everything looks so good. I don't know how I'll choose."

"What's your favourite food?" he asks, looking genuinely interested.

"Aside from all the carbs I try really hard not to eat?" I ask, thinking of the bread, pasta, cake and chocolate that I cheat with occasionally. Usually when I'm with Biff. I like to tell her that she's a bad influence, but it's not like I really put up much of a fight.

"Yeah."

"Salmon, cheese of any kind, spicy chicken wings."

He nods, taking it all in.

We order drinks and, soon after, food, once I've managed to choose. I've not tasted the food yet, and I already know that I want to come back here.

The meal is incredible and reminds me why I try to eat the way I do. I'm so full after three courses, but I'm not bloated like I know I would be if I had all the carbs that usually come with a big meal. Having said that, the thought of having to go shopping now doesn't fill me with delight.

"I think I'm too full to walk around a supermarket," I complain when we emerge after well over two hours in the restaurant.

"That's the best way to go. Stops you making hungry impulse purchases."

"It's like you want to ruin all my fun," I joke.

"We've already had plenty of fun today, don't you think?" His hand brushes across the small of my back, and I shudder at his touch.

His fingers wrap around my waist and he pulls me into his side. I'm too content with a full belly and his hot body against mine, so I stay put.

"So what's your usual supermarket?"

I call us another Uber, and in only a few minutes we're on our way to the store that's closest to my flat.

With me pushing a trolley, Carter takes charge in filling it with everything he thinks we need, all the while asking my preference about all kinds of food.

"Strawberries or raspberries?" he asks as we stand at the fruit section.

"Both?"

He nods, picking up a punnet of each.

I watch as he collects all kinds of meats, vegetables,

herbs and spices. I've got no clue what he's planning, but it seems like he's got it all under control.

"Make sure you pick up anything you need or want."

"Gee, thanks," I say with a laugh. I don't want to tell him that he's already filled the trolley with about four times the amount of food I buy on a weekly basis. I pick up a few things, including some more coffee, just to make it look like I actually need something.

When we get to the checkout, we've got a conveyer belt full of food. I feel like a kid again, shopping with my mum when she used to buy almost everything in the shop. With two older brothers who were always hungry, she was forever restocking our kitchen.

"I was going to suggest we walk back, but I'm not sure that's such a wise idea," I say, looking at the trolley full of bags as we walk out towards the car park.

"I've already got a car waiting." I turn to him in shock. "When did you do that?"

"You'd wandered off to find something. I knew we'd need one, so..."

"You're just a little bit too efficient." I hate to admit it, because I always thought I was on top of things, but he's taking it to another level.

"Why don't you go and chill out. I'll find a home for all this. Plus, I want to prep something for dinner tonight."

I place the bags in my hand on the counter and turn to him. "I can help, you know."

"I know, but I'm saying you don't have to. Go and watch TV or something. I'll come and join you once I'm done."

I narrow my eyes at him slightly. I can't figure out if he's trying too hard to make this work or if this is just who he is. "Oookay. I'm not sure I'm going to want dinner though," I admit. I'm still so full from lunch.

"Then we can have it tomorrow. It's no problem."

He continues emptying the bags onto the counter, and I hesitate to leave. It feels weird to allow him to sort all of this out when it's my flat.

"Go," he says, pressing his hands against my arse and squeezing lightly.

Not wanting to sit on the sofa watching him work, I grab my laptop from the side and go through to my bedroom. I keep the door ajar so I can hear him but close it enough so that he won't be a distraction.

I pull up my emails and get to work, catching up on everything I missed last week. Carter crashes about in the kitchen, and after a while the most incredible scent starts to filter down. He wasn't lying. He really can cook. Maybe having him around won't be so bad.

I've no idea how much time passes. I lose myself in work and barely register the noises he makes. It's not until the door opens and he walks in that I really remember he's here.

"You didn't need to run away," he says, reaching behind his head and pulling his shirt off in one swift move. I'm powerless but to drop my eyes to his bare, inked skin. My fingers twitch to trace the artwork, to really discover what's there and to find out the meaning behind it.

"W-what are you doing?" I stutter, feeling stupid that he's able to make me forget myself by only removing his shirt.

"I splashed marinade on my shirt." Bending over, he pulls another from his small case and pulls it on.

"Marinade?" I echo.

"Yeah, you know—sauce that you put meat into make it taste good."

"I know what marinade is," I say with a huff. I might not be a culinary genius, but I'm not an idiot.

The bed bounces as he launches himself onto it.

"Hey," I complain, gripping on to my laptop to stop it flying from the bed.

"Hey! Whatcha doing?"

"Work."

"Wow, sounds riveting. Fancy telling me what it is you do exactly?"

"I already have."

"No, you told me you were an Operations Manager. I've since discovered you work for the Abbot family business that Zach ran away from, but that's the extent of my knowledge. Care to fill me in?"

I blow out a breath and close the lid of my computer. "I'm in charge of the day-to-day running of the company. I oversee staffing, budgets, and expansion, amongst other things." When I see his brows are drawn together in confusion, I summarise. "Together, Harrison and I run the company. We've spent the past few years taking everything over from our father and his associates. Harrison is the antiques expert, and I'm the businesswoman. Perfect team."

"You don't like antiques?" he asks.

"You've seen my flat, what do you think?"

"I'm assuming not."

"I don't hate them; most are just a little old-fashioned for my taste. I love the business, the money-making side. I find it all fascinating. Challenging." I pause for a few minutes. "So what about you? Did you always want to be an artist?"

"Yeah," he says with an unamused laugh. "It's the only thing I'm good at."

"I don't think that's true for a second."

"Drawing has always been my escape. I could never imagine doing anything else."

"Did you go to art school or something?"

"Nah, I started working in the studio straight from school. I was lucky to find a place willing to give me a chance. I learnt on the job."

23

Carter

My stomach twists with the way she looks at me. It's similar to the look I've received all my adult life from my family when they think about my lack of education and qualifications.

It's bullshit. Utter fucking bullshit. Whoever said you had to sit in a classroom and succeed to do well in life needs fucking shooting.

"So no, I didn't go to college or university. I've not got the qualifications I'm sure you require of most of your dates." I don't mean for the words to come out quite so spitefully, but the memories she's dragging up within me have poison filling my veins.

"What? No, that's not even close to what I was thinking."

"Really?" I ask, climbing from the bed, turning my back on her. My muscles tighten and my fists clench. My usual reaction to feeling like this is to fight, but that's not exactly an option right now.

Instead, I blow out a long breath and try to push down the feelings of not being good enough. This isn't the side of me I want her to see this early on in whatever this is—or ever, if I have an option.

"Carter," she breathes. The bed creaks behind me and still I flinch when she places her hand on my forearm. "Qualifications don't define us. I have no requirements for such things in the men I date. All I want is someone successful with motivation and drive to continue to improve. And I mean that in whatever sector they are in. I won't cover up the fact I'm always pushing for more, for better. I can't be with someone who isn't the same. We'd clash. End of."

I force myself to swallow down the emotion this conversation drags up before moving away from her touch and back out to the living room.

"Carter," she calls, her footsteps racing behind me. "I really don't care. You're incredibly talented. There is so much more to life than education. I—"

"I know. I believe you," I say, cutting her off. "I just need to get some fresh air. I'll be back in a bit."

Before she has time to say anything, I march towards the front door and pull my trainers on.

I leave everything behind in my need to outrun my demons. The second the front door shuts, I take off running. I'd usually head to the gym and unleash my frustration out on a punching bag, or better, someone's face. But I'm the wrong side of town for that, and I need this release now.

My feet pound against the pavement as I pick up pace. I've no idea where I am or where I'm going, but I'm fairly confident that I'll find my way back when I'm ready.

I run until my heart thunders in my chest and my lungs heave for the air I need. I slow to a walk, my muscles screaming at me to stop, but I can't. Not yet. Those feelings of uselessness are still clutching at me, and I need them gone. I'm no longer that boy anymore. I need to let him go.

I end up taking two wrong turns before I stumble upon a familiar street and jog down towards where I now live.

The whole thing suddenly feels ridiculous, but that still doesn't stop me from taking the stairs down to Danni's flat and pushing through the front door.

"I'm sorry, I've got to go." Her soft voice filters down to me before I walk through to find her dropping her phone, pushing from the sofa and walking my way. She comes to a stop right in front of me and stares into my eyes.

"Are you okay?"

"Yeah, I'm good, doll. I'm just going to shower and then I'll finish off dinner, if you'd like it."

"Yeah. That would be nice."

I nod and step around her towards the bathroom.

"Your phone's been going off."

"Who was it?"

"I don't know. I didn't look."

"I've got nothing to hide," I call back.

I turn the shower on and then undress.

"It's Spike," she says, making me jump. I didn't realise she'd come to stand in the doorway.

"Couldn't resist watching, eh?"

"I wasn't sure if it was important."

"If it's from Spike then probably not. You can read it."

"It's locked."

"Five-five-eight-eight."

"O-oh okay."

"It's just a passcode, doll. Like I said, I've got nothing in there to hide."

"Okay, he wants to know how it's going with the ball and chain. I'm assuming that's me?"

"Ha, yeah, that would be you."

"Shall I reply?"

"Up to you."

She smiles at me coyly before turning and walking from the bathroom, still looking down at my phone.

I chuckle at her, wondering what she's going to say to him. It's not until she's disappeared from sight that I realise just her presence has rid me of the final lingering anger from our earlier conversation and the memories it dragged up.

"I hope you're hungry," I say as I re-join her back in the living area and turn the oven on.

I pull out everything I prepped earlier from the fridge. I put the chicken into the oven once it's up to temperature and begin plating up the salad.

"That smells amazing," Danni says from the sofa where she's scrolling through something on her phone.

"It's one of your favourites," I admit.

"Oh?"

"Just wait and see."

I serve our dinner out on her little bistro set by the front door. It's a warm evening on her quiet street in Kensington. Spike and I could never do this at our place, even if we did have some outside space.

We stay out chatting and drinking until it gets too cold.

"I think it's time for bed," Danni slurs slightly as we make our way inside.

"You go to bed, I'll tidy up."

She looks over her shoulder to the bedroom and then back to me.

"It's okay. I'll sleep on the sofa."

She nods, and my heart drops slightly.

"G-goodnight."

"Sleep well." The earlier lightness to my voice has vanished, replaced with that dejected one I'm so familiar with.

She drops off a pillow and blanket for me as I'm cleaning, and, not half an hour later, I'm stripping down to my boxers and attempting to get comfortable on her sofa.

Her flat is so quiet compared to what I'm used to. Although we can't hear the music from the surrounding clubs and bars, there's always noise of some sort. The only thing here is the soft tick of the clock somewhere behind me that taunts me with every minute I lie here wide awake, wishing I was in bed with her hot body tucked against mine.

I've no idea how much time passes, but at some point the sound of footsteps approaching has me opening my eyes.

There are no lights on, but my eyes have well-adjusted, so I see her as clear as day as she walks towards me in a tiny pair of pyjamas.

I don't say anything. I've no idea if she knows I'm awake or not. She crouches down bedside me.

"Carter." Her voice is so soft. It would never wake me if I were asleep. Her touch, however, when she places her hand against my arm is another story. My body is instantly aware of everything from that second.

"Yeah?"

"I can't sleep with you out here. Come to bed."

"For real?" I pray she can't see as well as I can, because the smile that splits my face is huge.

"Yeah, come on."

She pulls the blanket from me before lacing her fingers with mine. Gently, she pulls me from the sofa, and we walk towards her bedroom where she immediately crawls under the covers. I follow her actions and climb in behind her but still the second I lie down. She might not have wanted me sleeping on the sofa, but that doesn't mean she wants me here doing anything.

Every muscle in my body screams for me to do something, but I'm aware that we've already rushed most elements of this relationship. Although parts of my body might disagree, I'm happy to let her take the lead. For now.

She shifts beside me, her arse brushing against my side, and my body moves without instruction. I roll on to my side, wrap my arm around her waist, and pull her tightly into me. The satin of her pyjamas catches against my rough, calloused hands, but pressed up against my body, it's almost as soft as her skin.

"Good night, Carter."

"Night, doll." I drop a kiss to her bare shoulder and rest my head back on the pillow. Unlike out in the living area, I fall almost immediately asleep. I tell myself it's the comfortable bed, but I know I'm only lying to myself.

When I wake the next morning, I feel refreshed and ready for what she might throw at me. Yesterday was... eventful, and looking back now, seemed like the longest day of my life. It started in a different country and ended up with me living with my wife.

Shaking my head at the craziness that is my life right now, I stretch my body out and turn to the side to find Danni, only her side of the bed is empty.

As I lie quietly, I can just hear the soft beat of music coming from the living room. A smile curls my lips, wondering if she's still wearing the little satin set I fell asleep thinking about.

I'm up and in the bathroom before I've had a chance to blink. I do my thing, ensuring I don't smell like the waking dead, and go in search of my wife.

I find her the second I pull the bedroom door open. She's standing with her back to me, waiting for the coffee machine and staring into the fridge like she's lost something.

She must hear my footsteps, although she doesn't turn to look, but she also doesn't flinch when I slip my hands around her waist and step up behind her.

She's pulled her hair up, exposing her neck, and I can't help but place my lips to the sensitive bit of skin beneath her ear.

I don't hear her moan of pleasure, but it sure vibrates against my lips.

"Good morning. I don't think I got a chance last night to tell you how sexy you look in this." I tug on the hem of her top.

"Oh yeah?" she asks coyly.

"Yeah," I groan, peppering more kisses to her neck, my cock growing against her arse.

I slip my hands under her top, my need to feel her skin against mine all-consuming.

But at the same time I do, she spins in my arms. With the fridge still wide open, I move her to the side so she presses up against the counter when I step closer.

"Carter?" she asks, her desire-filled eyes bouncing between mine.

"You hungry, doll?"

Her eyes drop to my chest and lower before she bites down on her bottom lip. Oh yeah, she's hungry.

Lifting my hand, I press my thumb against her chin and pull her flesh free before taking it in my own mouth. The taste of her and the coffee she's already had mixes with my minty breath.

She sags against the counter as she accepts my kiss. Her hands lift and make their way up my chest, but I help her out by lifting her and sitting her on the edge. Parting her knees, I step between them, ensuring my now fully erect cock presses against her pussy.

"You feel that?" I mumble against her lips.

She nods. Her arms rest over my shoulders as she plays with the hair on my neck, making me shudder with pleasure.

"It's what happens every time I look at you, doll."

"Carter," she moans, her head falling back as I take her breasts in my hands and squeeze gently. Her nipples are pert beneath the fabric, and she gasps when I pinch them. Hard.

"Off," I demand, finding the bottom of the fabric and tugging it up and over her head. The second her breasts are exposed, I drop my lips to them.

"Hmm... So good, doll. So fucking sweet," I say between kisses and licks.

"Oh god," she groans, her fingers curling around the edge of the counter.

"You really wanna meet him?" I ask, quirking my eyebrow.

"W-what?"

I don't respond. Instead, I tap her hips with my fingers, signalling for her to lift. She does so immediately, and in seconds, I have her naked on her kitchen worktop.

"Now that's a breakfast I can't refuse." I drop to my knees, barely even feeling the sting from the tiled floor as I part her lips and find her clit with my tongue.

She cries out, her hips lifting. But with my hands holding her thighs wide, she's not got far she can go.

"Oh fuck. Oh fuck," she chants as I slide two fingers inside her. She's still as tight as I remember, and my cock weeps to feel her gripping it tight.

I look up her body. Her chest is heaving, her nipples rosy and peaked. Her lips are parted, and her eyes are locked on me.

My breath catches as our connection holds. It's like she reaches into my chest and squeezes my damn heart.

"Carter." My name is part warning, part plea, making me realise that I've stopped moving.

"Sorry," I mumble against her and get back to work.

At the point I feel her start to fall, I pull out and back away.

"W-what the... what the fuck are you doing?" she barks, her eyes wide as she stares at me in disbelief.

"Finishing properly."

I push my thumbs into the waistband of my boxers and push them down my thighs. Her eyes drop to my hard length, and she swallows as she stares.

"Well, what are you waiting for?"

"Nothing, doll. Absolutely nothing." I step up to her, wrapping my hands around the back of her knees so I can open her up for me. "Go on," I encourage, nodding down at where my cock is teasing her entrance.

She hesitates to start with, but her hand is soon moving towards my length. A loud growl rumbles up my throat as she wraps her fingers around it and helps to guide me inside her.

We cry out simultaneously as we find a rhythm. With her legs wrapped around my waist, I drop my fingers to her clit and help push her towards the release she lost not so long ago.

"Shit, shit, shit."

"Let go, doll." And she does. She squeezes down on me impossibly tightly as she crashes over the edge, successfully pulling me over with her.

Dropping my head to her neck, I breath her in and try to calm my racing heart.

"Well, that wasn't quite what I had in mind for breakfast."

"Walk about in tiny things like that and you might find it happening more often."

"You like me in satin, huh?"

"I like you in nothing more." I pinch her nipple and she yelps in surprise.

"Carter," she warns, although if the way her pussy rippled is anything to go by then she doesn't really want me to stop. "We need to eat, then I'm going for a run."

"No, you're not."

"I'm not?" she asks in shock as I allow her down from the counter.

"No. I've got something better in mind."

"Should I be worried?"

"I guess that all depends on how hard you want me to go on you."

"Hard, Carter. Always hard." She winks and then sashays naked from the room.

"Fucking hell," I mutter, watching her arse sway, my cock hardening once again at the sight.

24

Danni

After having a quick shower, Carter leaves me to do my thing in the bathroom. I watch him walk out with a towel wrapped around his waist, feeling a little disappointed. He might have just taken me on the kitchen counter but I was slightly hopeful for a second round.

Those thoughts are soon squashed when the scent of breakfast cooking filters in. I hate to admit it, but Carter being here so far has a lot more pros than cons. The orgasms, the food, the banter. I might think he's a bit of an idiot, but I must admit that I'm really coming around to his brand of idiot. I think back to how he acted yesterday when we started talking about qualifications. It was immediately oblivious that it was a subject he wasn't happy discussing, but I'll stand by what I said. I don't care if he has no qualifications; it's work ethic, drive, and passion I want. I couldn't care less how book smart anyone is. I really wasn't expecting him to disappear off to clear his head. It left me with so many questions, but I don't feel like I should ask. We're just getting to know each other, and I don't want to bring up any subject that causes him to react like that.

I shake the thoughts from my head, pull on my running clothes, and tie my hair up before going to see what he's putting together in the kitchen.

"Perfect timing, breakfast is served."

"Whoa, that looks incredible."

"It's just eggs, bacon and avocado, a side of toast for me, and a smoothie."

"It's way above the standard of my usual breakfast."

He pulls my chair out for me as I approach the table, and I can't help swooning. Who is this amazing guy, and how did he end up with the title of my husband? And isn't that the million-dollar question, because while I might not be asking about his meltdown yesterday, I'm equally not asking about the truth from that night.

I sigh, and he doesn't miss it.

"You like it all, right?"

"Yes, yes. It's perfect." The smile that curls up at his lips would knock me on my arse if I were standing.

The second I'm settled, I grab my knife and fork and tuck in to prove that this is beyond anything I was expecting.

"So where are we going?" I ask as I follow him from the flat. He's wearing a pair of shorts that are hanging low on his hips, and a fitted shirt. It's even more mouth-watering than the breakfast, but I'm not telling him that.

"We're going to work out my way. I'm all for a jog

around the park, but I prefer something a little more whole body."

Now I'm intrigued. A car pulls up in front of the curb and we climb in.

"This isn't quite what I had in mind," I admit, relaxing in the back of the Uber.

"I don't want to wear you out before you even get there."

I watch London go past as we travel across the city to yet another part I've never been to before. It's full of warehouses, some still in use, some which seem derelict.

As Carter climbs from the car, I've no idea what I should expect.

He joins our fingers and walks me towards one of the derelict looking buildings. "Trust me, the inside is very different."

He pulls the door open. Music and the sound of people instantly fill my ears. We make our way through reception, and I can't believe my eyes. The most incredible boxing gym appears before me. The design is unbelievable. It's like the kind of place you'd see in an old film. Everything is vintage looking.

My eyes dart around, taking it all in as we make our way past the men and women working out. Many acknowledge Carter with a nod or quick wave, but he doesn't stop to talk to anyone.

"Ladies' locker room. Drop your stuff, and I'll meet you back out here. But be prepared. I'm about to put you through your paces."

I look over his shoulder at all the punching, skipping, and weights going on. I'm pretty fit. I run at least three times a week. This shouldn't be so hard. Right?

I drop my gym bag that he made me pack into one of the lockers before lifting my hands behind my neck to remove my necklace. My wedding ring still hangs in the centre. Carter might still proudly wear his, but I'm not at that stage yet. I'm still trying to get my head around the whole thing while being constantly amazed by the man who gave it to me.

I carefully place it into the small zip section of my bag and close the door to the locker, pinning the key to my sports bra.

He's already outside waiting for me when I pull the door open and step out.

"Right, warm-up first, and then I'm going to show you how to throw a punch properly."

"Who says I can't already?" He stares at me with an eyebrow raised. "Okay fine, so I've no idea and I've never hit anyone."

"Lucky for you, I'm almost an expert at it."

Turns out, I was wrong about being fit, because I'm exhausted from Carter's warm-up alone. My arms and legs now feel like jelly as I stand before him with giant gloves attached to my hands. This must be how babies feel with those scratch mitt things on.

"Remember, use your hips and hit the target as hard as you can."

I do as I'm told, but I'm sure Carter barely even feels the impact of my fist hitting the padded block he's holding up for me.

"Better," he says encouragingly, but I'm sure he's just trying to make me feel good.

I have about five more attempts before someone thankfully comes over to talk to Carter and gives me a reprieve.

"Titch, my man. How's it going?" a loud voice booms across the fast space.

When Carter turns, his face transforms as he takes in the approaching man. "Mickey," he says with a wide smile. "It's been too long, man. How are things?"

"Fucking awesome. The circuit is doing better and better. This place is... well, you can see it. But what about you? You've not fought in how long now?"

"A long time," he says, glancing over at me.

"Well, let's get you in the ring then. What are you waiting for?"

"Nah, man. I'm just here teaching my girl some tricks."

"Wait a goddamn fucking minute. You've got a girl?"

My cheeks heat as the man turns his attention to me. He's older than Carter, by quite a few years I'd say. He's obviously been a fighter, he's got various scars—the most obvious on his bottom lip—and his nose has quite clearly been broken one too many times.

"Hey, I'm Danni."

"My wife," Carter admits proudly.

"Fuck off, someone of this calibre married you," he says, looking between us.

"Nah, she was drunk. Doesn't remember a second of it." Mickey laughs, and I wonder if he thinks Carter is actually joking or not.

"Anyway, as I was saying. I've got a new guy, thinks he's got what it takes. I, on the other hand, think his ego is too big to fit in the fucking ring, let alone to win a fight. You wanna knock him down a peg or two?"

"I dunno, Mick. It's been months since I even had a friendly."

"It's like riding a bike, you know that. Come on, your girl here wants to see you in action, don't you sweetheart?"

I shrug, because I've no idea what to say for the best. Carter might be resisting, but I saw the way he looked at the ring when we first entered and then how he's watched the guys who've been sparring in there.

"Come on, he's right over there." Mickey looks up before shouting, "Xander. Get your arse over here."

The guy in question immediately stops what he's doing and heads over.

"Xand, this is—"

"I know who this is, Mick," the young guy says with a roll of his eyes.

"Good. I'm glad Titch's reputation precedes him. Now get taped up, both of you."

"Wait, you want me to fight him?" A flicker of terror covers the guy's face before he swallows it down and steps into Carter's personal space. A sinister smile curls at his lips as the two men stand toe to toe.

"You keep telling me how good you are, boy. Time to prove your worth to me if you want a shot at the circuit."

I glance to Carter. His face is set, a determination I've not experienced before oozing from him. He might have tried to convince Mickey otherwise, but it's clear that he's fully on board now the challenge has been laid down, and I can't deny that a trickle of excitement races through me at the thought of watching him. I've never been a boxing fan, but then I've ever had someone quite like Carter to watch.

"Fine with me."

"I hope you're smarter than you look," Carter spits down at the boy. "I've eaten bigger guys than you for breakfast."

"Don't you worry about me, old man. I'll run fucking rings around you every day of the week."

"That's enough. Save it for the ring."

Mickey stands between the two and pushes them in opposite directions.

"Come and sit over here. I need to know you're safe." Carter's large hand rests in the small of my back and he guides me over to some seats that are quite a distance from the main ring.

"I won't be able to see."

"That could well be a good thing," he mutters, but it's more to himself than me. I don't get to ask what he means, because he continues. "Stay here, okay? No matter what happens, I need to know you're sitting here out of harm's way."

The serious expression on his face stops me from saying anything.

"Take this." He pulls his shirt over his head and drops it to my lap.

He bends so he can look into my eyes. "No matter what happens," he repeats. "Stay the fuck here." He reaches out and takes my chin in his fingers. I fight to swallow the dread that's formed a giant ball in my throat. His lips press to mine for a quick yet powerful kiss. "Right here," he warns again, pointing at the chair.

"Don't you need gloves?" I ask as he takes a step back.

One side of his mouth quirks up in a smile. "Nah, not that kind of fight, doll."

That dread I was already feeling drops into the pit of my stomach.

Fuck.

I watch with wide eyes as he tapes his knuckles, accepts a slap on the back from Mickey, and steps into the ring. Everyone who was previously working out must have figured out what's going on, because they all start to make their way over. Thankfully—or not, I'm yet to know—no one stands in my way. I've got a perfect view of the ring and whatever's about to happen.

Xander eventually joins Carter. The slight smirk that was previously on his face before is now a full-blown smile, and I understand what Mickey was saying about his ego. He thinks he's God. I can't help but hope that Carter's about to teach him a lesson.

They start bouncing around, sizing each other up before Xander goes for Carter.

I squeal as he throws a punch and squeeze my eyes shut.

It's only the roar of the crowd that makes me realise I can't see anything, and I drag them open once more. Thankfully when I do it's clear, even to a novice like me, that Carter is currently on top.

Fists fly, curses are barked, and people shout at the two fighters as they go at it. The bit of blood that first emerged soon turns into what seems like rivers of it.

The next time Xander starts laying into Carter, I find I can't watch. Getting up from my seat, I all but run towards the women's locker room. I need the image of him covered in his own blood gone from my mind.

This isn't how today was meant to go. We were just going for a workout.

I pace back and forth on the tiled floor as the cheers, ooh and ahhs continue from out in the gym. Every time my breath catches wondering if he's gone down, if Xander is getting the better of him.

"Fuck. Fuck."

My hands tremble and my stomach turns over. A huge part of me wants to know, needs to know that he's still standing and holding his own against the young one, but the other part is terrified I'll watch as he's seriously hurt.

I can't do it. I can't.

I've no idea how much time passes before a roar goes up and then everything goes quiet. My heart pounds as I wait to find out what happened.

I'm just about to leave the safety of my hideout to find out if he's okay when there's an almighty crash. I look up to find a bloody and very angry Carter storming my way.

"What did I tell you?" he barks. His eyes are wild as he stares at me.

"Fucking hell. Are you okay?"

"No. No I'm fucking not. And do you know why? Because you didn't listen. I told you to stay there. I told you not to move."

He continues towards me until I've no choice but to back up.

We eventually come to a stop in the middle of the showers.

"I'm sorry. I just couldn't watch. I—" My words are cut off as his lips crash to mine.

My feet leave the floor, and my legs wrap around his waist. My back hits the wall and he leans forward, crushing me between him and the cold tiles.

"You didn't fucking listen," he mumbles against my lips. "I couldn't find you."

His hands are everywhere, his tongue sweeping into my mouth. The copper taste of his blood fills my mouth, but I don't have it in me to pull back. Not when he clearly needs this so badly. I've no idea if he's hurt, if he won or lost, but none of that is important right now.

He briefly drops me to my feet, but only for long enough to drag my leggings down. The second my bottom half is naked, he has me back against the wall.

Something digs into my back, and at the same time he pushes inside me we're covered in a torrent of water.

It's freezing for a couple of seconds, but my heated body barely notices.

He thrusts up into me violently, his fingertips bruising my arse as he holds tight.

"I. Couldn't. Fucking. Find. You," he mutters between thrusts.

"Carter," I cry, my head falling back as the pleasure begins to get too much to bear.

"I needed you there. I needed to know you were safe."

"I'm fine. I'm fine. I'm fiiiiine," I scream as I fall over the edge.

He drops his head into the crook of my neck and roars out his own release.

Our chests heave against each other's as we fight to catch our breaths.

"Fuck. I'm so sorry."

He pulls me from the wall and away from the now warm water and sits himself on the bench with me astride his lap. His arms circle my waist, holding me tight.

I gasp when he pulls his face back and I get a look at him. A lot of the blood has now washed away, but there's a fresh stream of it coming from both his eyebrow and his lip.

"Carter," I breathe, lifting my hand to wipe it away.

"I'm fine."

"You're bleeding."

"Doll, this is nothing."

"Did you... did you win?"

A smile curls at his lips. "What do you think?"

"I've no idea. I left because I couldn't bear to watch him hit you, and now here you are, angry and covered in blood. I've no idea what I'm meant to think." My eyes search his, trying to read his thoughts.

"Doll, I always win. Why do you think Mickey wanted me to fight the kid?"

"To teach him a lesson," I whisper.

"Exactly. Maybe next time he'll remember this when he starts spouting about him being the best."

"So... you don't box then?"

"Sometimes. I've just always preferred to leave the gloves out of the ring."

"Y-you're a cage fighter?"

"We prefer MMA, doll. Sounds... less vicious."

"Jesus, Carter. You didn't think to tell me any of this?"

"I wasn't hiding it, hence why I brought you here. What I said earlier was true, I've not fought for months. I haven't needed to."

Silence crackles between us for a long minute. "Why did you need to?"

"To escape. To forget my demons for a few minutes."

My brows draw together. I desperately want to ask, but now really isn't the time. We're in the locker room at his gym, having just fucked in the showers, and I'm half naked.

"We need to clean you up."

"I'll be fine. As long as you're okay."

"Nothing was going to happen to me."

"I know. I just needed you to be there when it was over. I needed to see you." My heart damn near breaks in my chest. He leans in towards my ear, and his next words rip me in two. "You're my lucky charm."

A sob rips from my throat.

"Hey, don't cry."

Tears well in my eyes as I think back to him in that ring.

"I'm sorry. It was just scary. I'm glad you won though."

"There was never any doubt."

"And you're worried about the kid's ego." I roll my eyes, the tears thankfully staying put.

"I think we're done here for the day. Get sorted and we'll head home, yeah?"

I want to argue. There's still blood running down his face, but I keep my lips shut and nod. After a couple of seconds, he places me beside him on the bench and stands.

"I'll wait for you outside. Don't go anywhere else."

25

Carter

Fucking Mickey. Despite the fact I've not fought in a long time, he knew I wouldn't back down from a challenge. He also knew I wouldn't lose either, which was the point.

The kid was good. Better than I was expecting after what Mickey said about him. I thought it was going to be a walk in the park. It was not. It was hard fucking work and just proved to me how unprepared I was.

With my family mostly minding their own business and me finally having a life I was enjoying, my need to fight wasn't there, bubbling under the surface, like it had been in the past. Getting in the ring was the wake-up call I needed. I need to step up my game. Not because I intend on fighting again anytime soon, but because I want to know that I can. If for some reason I need to fight and the only guy here is bigger than me, I need to know I can hold my own.

All eyes turn on me as I pull open the women's locker room door and step out. They'll have all seen me race in here in a panic once the fight was over and I made it through the exuberant crowd. It'll be the reason why we weren't disturbed. Smiles spread across most of the faces; they know why I went in there and they know what went down.

I nod before slipping into the men's and walking straight to the showers. I'm already soaking wet from our accidental downpour a few minutes ago. I may as well finish the job.

I strip out of my wet shorts and stand under the hot spray. It stings against my cuts, but I push the pain away. My ribs ache, but I'm confident they're just bruised, not broken, and my jaw smarts where he got a few good solid punches in. But it's noting I can't handle.

Don't get in the ring if you can't handle the pain. Words from my past float down to me. I picture myself in an old warehouse, much like this one but a million times less fancy, as the crowd cheers, hungry to watch some action, to smell the blood.

I remember just how fast my heart was racing that first night. That was before I met Mickey. I was that big-headed, loud-mouthed kid back then. Much like Xander. But Mickey saw something in me, thank fuck. Aside from my art and the studio that had taken a chance on me at only sixteen, Mickey was the only one who thought I was worth something. He didn't give a shit that I'd failed every exam I'd sat. He didn't care that I never went to college or university. He didn't think I was a let-down, a total failure, because I could fight. And fuck, I could fight fucking well.

I don't allow myself to stand there any longer than necessary. I need to get out for Danni.

The look in her eyes when I found her in the middle of the locker room... She was terrified. It might sound awful, but in those seconds, seeing how scared she was for me, it was the fucking happiest moment of my life.

She cared. Despite all her pretences and walls, she fucking cares.

I quickly drag on a pair of sweats and a shirt before shoving my feet in my trainers and rushing from the room. I doubt she'll be ready before me, but I want to be waiting for her when she does emerge.

Mickey spots me the second I step from the room and starts over.

"For someone who hasn't fought in a while, that was epic, man."

"Yeah, well. I needed it." *I had someone to fight for all of a sudden.* The little voice in my head rings out. In the past when I've fought, it's only been for me. Other than a crowd of strangers and fellow fighters, I've never had anyone in my corner cheering me on. And, although that wasn't exactly what she was doing, she was here. For the first time in my life, I had someone who cared if I walked out of that ring or not, and fuck, was I making sure that was the case.

"You should come back, you know. The guys on the circuit would love to see your face again."

"I doubt that," I mutter, knowing that I've beaten most of them.

"We've got a load of newbies, and with your rep, they'd pay me to fight you."

"Always about the money, Mick."

"Fucking right. Don't tell me you don't remember it. You're still my highest earning fighter."

"It was fun while it lasted, man. But I'm done."

"Oh, come on, you can't tease me with that." He gestures toward the ring.

"I can. You saw my girl, I won't put her through that again."

"They all get used to it. We've all seen it before. Hell, give her a few weeks and she'll be up there too."

I can't deny that the idea of her in the ring with another woman doesn't turn me the fuck on, but no. Not happening.

"Never."

Something catches his eye over my shoulder before he looks back to me.

"I'll text you the next location. Consider it an open invitation."

"Is everything okay?" Danni's warm hand slips around my forearm and squeezes.

"Yeah, doll."

"We're just reminiscing about old times."

"Ready to go?" I turn to Danni, ignoring Mickey's attempt to drag me back into this life.

I gave it up for two very good reasons. I need to remember those and focus on what I want right now.

The car journey back is in silence, and I hate it. I've no idea what she's thinking or where her head is.

The second it pulls up in front of her house, she's out of the car and heading for the safety of her flat.

"Danni, wait," I call, jogging in behind her.

She spins on her heels and stares at me. Her eyes are hard, her muscles pulled tight, and for a second I'm afraid that she's about to call time on this, that I'm about to be sent back to Spike with my tail between my legs.

A phone ringing breaks the tension and she digs inside her bag for it. She hesitates for a few seconds before swiping the screen and putting it to her ear.

"Hey," she says, a smile forming on her lips for whoever she's talking to. My stomach twists, knowing that it's not for me. "Uh yeah, that should be fine." Silence. "Yeah, I'll ask him, but he owes me, so it shouldn't be an issue. Text me the time and place. Or did you want to go together?" Silence. "Okay, yeah. That sounds perfect." Silence. "Okay, I'll see you in a couple of days."

She hangs up but continues staring at her phone.

"Danni?"

I take a step forward, but she doesn't react.

"I... That was Biff. She needs us at some charity event her parents are organising on Saturday. She's introducing them to Zach for the first time and needs some support."

"I work Saturdays."

"Well, get it off. Biff needs you. Zach needs you. *I* need you." Her voice cracks, and it damn near breaks my heart.

"Doll," I breathe, closing the space between us and wrapping my arms around her. Her body trembles against me as she sucks in calming breaths. "I'm so sorry. I shouldn't have forced you to watch that. I'm sorry. I'm fine."

When she pulls back and looks at me, there are tearstains down her cheeks and her eyes are flooded with many more.

"Please, don't... don't do that again."

"Okay." I take her cheeks in my hands and stare down into her eyes, needing her to see exactly how serious I am.

"I heard what Mickey said. He wants you to fight again. But I can't... I don't think I can do that, Carter."

"It's okay. You won't have to. Today was a one-off."

"O-okay. I..." She hesitates. "I trust you."

My heart constricts at her words. "Fucking hell, doll. You fucking slay me, you know that, right?"

She shakes her head shyly. "Go and sit on the edge of the bed. I need to clean up your face."

"It's—"

"Don't argue."

Putting my hands up in surrender, I step around her and towards the door. Ripping my shirt off, I throw it towards her washing basket and drop down as instructed while she crashes about in the bathroom.

After a few seconds, she emerges with a bowl of warm water, some cotton balls, and her first aid kit.

"You really don't need—" My words are cut off with one look from her.

"Sit back." I do as I'm told and she straddles my waist after placing everything beside us.

The first touch of the cotton ball against my lip stings, but it's very much sweetened by having her pressed up against me.

"Hmmm... this is nicer than I was expecting." My hands grip onto her arse, and I grind her down against me as she continues to work.

"Carter," she warns.

"Oh, don't play innocent. You didn't sit here because it had the best access."

Her cheeks redden slightly.

"No," she admits. "I sat here as a distraction. I thought this might hurt."

"I don't feel a thing, doll."

"That's because all the blood in your body has rushed south."

I shrug. I can hardly deny it. She can feel it.

My fingers trail over her body as she works. She cleans up the blood before putting a Steri-Strip over the split in my eyebrow. I want to tell her not to bother, that I've had much worse in the past, but I know it'll be pointless, so I keep my mouth shut and enjoy her tending to me.

She squirms on me when I tickle up her ribs.

"Will you stop trying to distract me?"

"Sorry, you're too close. Too tempting."

"Yeah, well, I need to make sure you're okay."

"I'm fine. I keep telling you this."

"But I need to know."

"You know what that means, right?" She looks into my eyes, a line forming between her brows as she tries to figure out what I mean.

"No. What does it mean, ol' wise one?"

I lean forward until my lips brush her ear. "It means that you do actually like me. Some might even say that you care."

She sighs and pulls away slightly, forcing me to find her eyes. They're soft and hold so many things I want to discover. "Of course I like you and care. You think I'd have let you move in here if I didn't?"

I shrug, not wanting to expose my insecurities about how she feels. "I wondered if it was just my kitchen and bedroom tricks that kept me here."

"Carter," she sighs. "All of this. Us. It's been crazy. But..." She trails off, and the hope I was beginning to feel dies a little.

"But," I encourage.

"I-I do like you. I do care. And... I think there might be something here."

I can't fight the smile that finds its way onto my lips.

"Yeah?"

"Don't tell me you don't feel it."

"Oh, doll. I feel it. I felt it from the moment you shouted at me the first time we met."

"Well, what did you expect? You tricked me."

"It got you here, didn't it?" I lift my hips once again and she gasps as my cock brushes her core. Leaning forward, I press open-mouthed kisses down her neck. "And... you know you love my tricks."

She chuckles, and everything in my world suddenly feels right.

"Now, I think it's time you show me just how much you like me, seeing as you were the one who got me in this state. Getting an injured man all aroused, whatever next?"

"Well, if you weren't stupid enough to put yourself in that ring then you wouldn't be injured, would you?"

"I own that ring, doll. For a lot of years, it was the only home I knew."

She opens her mouth to respond, but, not wanting to say more, I use it to my advantage and plunge my tongue into her mouth.

"Fine," she says, her chest heaving once I let her up for air. "Challenge accepted."

Her small hands land on my chest, and she pushes until I fall back on the bed. One side of my lips curls up in delight as she flits her eyes all over my chest and abs.

"Do these hurt?" she asks, her fingers brushing the slight bruising on my ribs.

"A little. I'm hoping you're about to distract me though."

A wicked smirk covers her face before she folds herself over me. Her lips start at my collarbones before slowly making their way down my body. She stops at both of my nipples and runs her tongue around the small discs, making me shudder.

"Danni," I complain, threading my fingers into her hair and gently pushing her lower to where I need her.

"A little impatient, are we?" she jokes, resisting my encouragement and instead trailing her tongue around the indentations of my abs.

"Fuck, doll," I groan when she runs the tip of her tongue along the waistband of my boxers.

My cock jumps in desperation, hoping to get her closer, but instead of doing so she sits up.

Staring down at the bulge in my joggers, she reaches out and run her fingers along the length of me.

My teeth grind as I try to keep control of myself.

"You hungry? I think I might go and make myself some lunch."

She lifts her leg as if she's going to get off the bed, and I panic. Her wrist is in my hand in a second.

"Don't even fucking think about it."

She manages to keep her serious face for all of two seconds before she laughs. "Relax, I wouldn't do that to you."

"Good," I bark. "Now, as you were, please."

"Only because you asked so nicely," she sasses, crawling down my legs and hooking her fingers into the waistband of both my joggers and boxers. She tugs until my cock springs free. Her eyes zero in on it as if she's deciding what she wants to do—either that or just torturing the fuck out of me. I guess I deserve it after making her watch me fight.

After what feels like a year, she moves. She pulls the fabric from my legs before settling between them.

The second she takes me in her hand, I damn near come like a fucking teenage boy getting his first stroke. But that's nothing compared to when she leans forward and licks around the head. My entire body flinches with the sensation, one hand comes up to thread into her hair while the other twists in the sheet.

"Fuuuuck," I growl when she takes me into her mouth. It's hot, wet, and so fucking good. "Danni, fuck. So good. Fuck." I fight to keep my eyes open to watch her, but as my release closes in on me, I lose all control. My eyes slam closed as my balls draw up and pleasure hits me so hard that I swear the fucking world tilts slightly.

When she's finished, she looks up at me and licks her lips. I swear it the most erotic sight I've ever seen.

"You're overdressed," I say, propping myself up on my elbows. "Get it all off and come and ride me."

"But your ribs—"

"Are perfectly fine. Especially if you do all the work."

26

Danni

The rest of our Sunday was spent quietly at home. Carter cooked both lunch and dinner, and both were as incredible as everything else he's made. He seems to amaze me at every turn, and I can't help that I'm enjoying him being here more every minute.

His fight might have been scary as hell, but it taught me something, something I'd been refusing to admit to myself for days, if not longer. I was falling for Carter, and falling hard.

So what he's not what I said I wanted? He doesn't wear a suit to work, and his exercise doesn't involve a calm game of golf. Who cares? He's got so many other things that were on my list. He's dedicated, passionate, hard-working, talented. He's just... him. And my heart is tumbling for him faster than I can control.

I fiddle with my necklace and glance at the clock,

wishing I could go home in an hour or so and spend the evening with him.

Our lives run on totally different schedules. While I usually work eight in the morning until whenever I'm too tired to do so, he works mid-afternoon to often late at night. It's only been five days, but I'm already missing him not being around.

He might insist on getting up with me in the mornings and making me breakfast, but I feel awful because he should be sleeping, then when he comes back after his shift at the studio I'm usually falling asleep on the sofa.

If this is going to work, then we need to figure out how we're going to spend time together. If we're going to make a go of this then I want it to be for real, not a part-time thing where we only manage to fit time together around work.

It's Friday night, and all I want to do is go home and spend the night eating some of Carter's incredible cooking and chilling out on the sofa with a little Netflix, but he's working and he's already warned me that he's going to be late after rescheduling his weekend appointments so we can attend this charity thing for Biff.

Of course, I want to go and support Biff and Zach. Equally, I want to be there to experience her parents' reaction to her new tatted-up husband, because they are going to lose their shit.

I sigh, thinking of my parents. Biff and Zach visited them the day they got back to break the good news. From how Mum sounded on the phone when she called me immediately after, I would say that breaking the news was a suitable description. She sobbed and asked me why her kids feel the need to run away to get married without them. Guilt like I'd never felt hit me like a truck. I didn't have it in me to be anything but supportive. The last thing I wanted to do was shatter her already broken heart. Thank God Zach and Biff kept our drunken nuptials to themselves. For now at least.

As well as making me a healthy breakfast every day, Carter has ensured I have a good lunch too. I have never eaten so well in all my life. I've always tried to curb my snacking habit, but prior to meeting him it was a battle I always faced. Well, no more. He's successfully keeping me filled with healthy, incredibly tasty food every day, and the last thing I want to do is snack.

Thinking that I might cheat tonight, when I push my way through the front door of my flat, I'm fully prepared to pull up the Just Eat app and order something naughty. I've been so good all week; why not?

That is, until I find a note on the side. Finding my name scrawled across the front of the folded piece of paper, I open it up to see what's inside.

I gasp. I thought it was going to be a handwritten note, but what I find is so much more than that. It's instructions for dinner, only they're in sketches, not words.

Following his drawings, I open the fridge and find a foil-wrapped tray waiting for me.

'Cook Me' it says on the top, but the writing is beautiful, showing just how talented an artist he really is.

I follow all the instructions, put the salmon in the oven, and plate up the side salad he's already prepared before going through to my bedroom to change out of my work clothes. I pull my phone from my bag and send him a text.

Thank you so much for dinner. Wish you could join me x

I'm disappointed when he doesn't immediately reply after seeing that he's read it, but I know he's busy. Zach and Biff had already sorted his clients for tomorrow before Biff even called about her parents' thing.

With a sigh, I dish up my dinner. I pour myself a large glass of wine and curl up on the sofa for a night alone.

I end up falling asleep after the wine, and that's where Carter finds me when he eventually gets home later that night. I'm woken when I'm lifted and pressed against his warm body as he carries me to bed. He deposits me in the cold sheets but soon strips down and joins me. His arm wraps around my waist, and he pulls me back into his body.

"Hey," I say the next morning, finding him looking at me.

"Hey, doll. Did you sleep well?"

"Y-yeah. Did you have a good night at work?"

"Meh... I missed you."

I swoon. "I missed you too. I hate that we don't get more time together."

"Careful, people will start thinking we're a married couple, hearing you talk like that."

"Who's listening?" I ask, looking around the room like we might have an audience. "Are you ready for this thing this afternoon?" I have a feeling that he's going to hate it. It's going to be full of rich pretentious people, just like Biff's parents. I'm sure they'll all shit bricks when Zach and Carter turn up, both with tattoos, and Carter still sporting the lingering evidence of his fight last weekend.

"Can't wait. If Biff's parents are as interesting as she

says they are, then I'm sure it'll be heaps of fun." His voice is full of sarcasm.

"They're really going to hate you two, you're aware, right?" I ask, needing him to know that their presence is not going to go down well.

"And you think I give a shit? I spent most of my life in a place where no one wanted me, doll. Biff's parents will be a walk in the park."

"Wha—" My question is cut off when he places his fingers to my lips.

"Not the time. I promise I'll tell you everything but... not today. Let's just deal with Biff's dysfunctional family before we start on mine."

"Okay," I whisper, not all that happy about him keeping things from me, but equally, I understand.

We spend the morning at his boxing gym. It takes a little convincing on his part to get me there and a lot of promising that he won't step into the ring. Helpfully, Mickey isn't there and the others just greet him when they pass. No one even mentions him fighting, which is a relief.

By the time we get home to get ready for Biff and Zach to pick us up, my muscles are aching. I have a long bath before pulling a floral dress from my wardrobe, straightening my hair and applying my makeup in a way I know Biff's parents will approve of. I've attended a couple of events with her in the past when she's needed a buffer, so I know what they expect: nothing short of perfection. It's exhausting, and I'm not even their daughter.

Bang on cue, my phone rings, telling me that they're waiting at the curb.

"Carter, it's time to go," I call from the kitchen.

His footsteps fill my ears, but nothing could prepare me for what I find when I turn around.

His hair is styled in a way I've never seen, he's given his scruffy face a good trim, and he's wearing a crisp white shirt with the sleeves rolled up, exposing his tattooed and muscular forearms, with a slim pair of black trousers that hug his thighs in the most incredible way.

"Whoa, what happened to my bad boy?" I say with a laugh.

"Don't worry, doll. He's still very much here." And to prove his point, he walks to me, runs his hands up my thighs and lifts me onto the kitchen counter.

"We don't have time for this, Carter."

"That's a real shame, because you are looking fine right now."

"Let's go and spend a few hours supporting our friends and then when we get back, I'll let you do whatever you want." I lift my legs around his waist and dig my heels into his arse, successfully pressing him harder against me.

"Anything?"

Biting down on my bottom lip, I nod at him in a way that I hope is sexy. It must hit the mark, because he growls and dives for my lips.

"Nope, I've just done my lipstick."

"You're joking?"

"Nope. And hear that horn?" I pause for a moment so he can. "That's my brother getting impatient. So if you want to get out of here without getting another fist in your face, then I suggest we get moving."

"Fuck's sake. I never cockblocked him with Biff. I think me and him need to have words."

"Good luck with that," I say over my shoulder as I rearrange my dress and head for the front door.

Biff smiles and waves when we eventually emerge, but

Zach's face is set hard. He glances at me before looking over my shoulder and directly to his best friend.

"What took so long?" he barks.

"Sorry. I was screwing your sister in her kitchen," Carter says flippantly.

Biff barks out a laugh while Zach turns tomato red.

"For your sake, I fucking hope you're joking."

"For me to know, man." Carter winks at Zach and pulls the back door open for me.

"He's kidding," I whisper to my brother as I pass. "Cool your jets, asswipe."

"Thank you so much for doing this with us," Biff says once we're both settled and Zach's pulled away.

"I wouldn't miss it for the world."

"You think they'll allow us to stay?" she asks. She says it light-heartedly, but I can see the concern in her eyes when she glances back at me.

She tries so hard to let go of what her parents think about her life, but it's so deeply ingrained that sometimes she struggles to do so.

"Only time will tell. If they boot us out, then we'll go and have our own fun."

Silence descends on the car. It's a little awkward, what with our impending day out and the fact that none of us have really talked about what happened in Vegas. Thankfully, Carter breaks the tension.

"So what is this thing today?"

"Ugh, it's some kind of charity event. Silent auction, I think. I want to say it's raising money for a library or something, but to be honest, I stopped listening once she told me the date. I'd been waiting for the right time to introduce Zach, so I thought, why not?"

"You think doing this in public is the best way to go?" I ask sceptically.

"We both know that no matter how this happens, it'll be a disaster. At least this way we'll get some amusement out of it."

"I really hope so."

"Jesus, please don't tell me this is your parents' place," Carter says as Zach turns the car into a massive driveway that leads towards a giant house on a hill.

"No, don't be silly. My parents live in a town house in Chelsea. Whoever is organising this thing probably hired it. Holding a charity event is like the ultimate opportunity to show off. Each one gets more glamourous and expensive than the last. It's exhausting."

"Riiight," he agrees.

Whenever I've attended something like this with Biff, or even met her parents, it only makes me more grateful for my own. Yes, they are part of the same group, I guess, but their close group of friends are much more down to earth. They've never dragged us to anything like this. I'm pretty sure it's equally their idea of a bad day out.

We park alongside an array of fancy cars before climbing out.

"It'll be fine," Zach whispers to Biff before pulling her into his side. They're both dressed similarly to us. Biff is in a pretty summer dress, although I notice when she turns around that it's almost backless and clearly reveals her ink, and Zach has his sleeves rolled up to ensure his is on display too.

"Let's do this shit," Carter announces, although I suspect he has no idea what he's about to walk into.

As we follow the handmade signs that lead us around to the garden, the scent of the rose garden surrounds us.

"I feel like I should be going to a wedding, not an auction," Carter mutters beside me.

It would be a beautiful place for a wedding. I keep my thoughts to myself, not wanting to worry about my own issues when we're about to walk headfirst into Biff's.

The garden emerges, and, much like I imagined for a wedding, tables litter the grass area. There are marquees with lights strung up and a band over in the corner.

"Christ, I think I may have underestimated this," Carter whispers, but none of us get to respond because there's a high-pitched squeal.

"Tabitha, darling. It's so good to see you." Her mum walks towards us with her arms held wide open, her eyes firmly fixed on her daughter. Her hands land on Biff's upper arms before she leans in for a double air kiss.

The three of us watch as she totally ignores that Biff has company and her mother begins roasting her for not being in touch.

At one point, her mother glances up at us all, but her lip curls as she looks to each of us before turning and lacing her arm through Biff's and attempting to lead her off into the mass of people loitering on the grass, waiting for whatever's going to happen next.

"Wait, Mum. Is Dad about? I need to introduce you both to someone." The quiver in her voice is clear.

"Um... okay." She once again glances back at us nervously. If she has any recollection of who I am then she doesn't show it.

She turns and calls to her husband, who was busy talking to a group of men in suits, no doubt trying to drum up some business associates.

"Honey, Tabitha would like to introduce us to someone."

"Hello, sweetheart. So nice to see you at last." Anger seeps into my veins as they stare at their daughter, getting impatient already that she needs their attention, despite the fact they're moaning that they've not seen her for a while.

"Yeah, um... This is..."

"Hi, I'm Zach. Tabitha's husband," Zach says, stepping forward and helping Biff out.

The looks on Biff's parents' faces makes whatever is going to happen next totally worth it. I just really hope that Biff got to see the shock before both they turn red with anger.

"Haha," her mum laughs, but it's anything but amused. "Nice try. But I think the house party you're looking for might be in a different part of town." She barely gives Zach the time of day before looking back to her daughter. "Tabitha, who are these people?"

"Mother, do you ever listen?" Pride swells within me as I watch her stand up for herself, probably for the first time. "This is Zach, he's my husband. And you know Danni, she's attended events with me before, and this is... Carter, Zach's friend and Danni's..."

"Husband," I answer for her, and I'm so glad I do when Carter's hand squeezes mine tightly. It's the first time I've really acknowledged what we really are, and it feels good.

Biff's father stands there with his lips pressed into a thin line while her mother's mouth hangs open.

"I think it might be better if we discuss this in private, don't you?"

"There's nothing to discuss. We got married last week. He's my husband. You either accept that, or we'll leave."

"Inside the house. Now, Tabitha."

Her parents storm off, leaving us all a little shell-shocked.

"Well... that went well," Carter muses.

"Did you see their faces?" Biff asks, spinning to look at us. The smile on her face is wide and triumphant.

"If I didn't know better, I'd think you only married me to piss off your parents," Zach jokes.

"Just an added bonus," Biff quips.

"So what now?" I ask.

"We go inside, tell them how it is, and leave if they want us to," Zach announces before Biff gets a chance to make a decision.

"Are you sure?"

"Of course."

"Okay." Biff shakes her arms at her sides, steeling herself for what's to come before they walk off in the same direction her parents had, hand in hand.

"Is it just me, or are you kind of gutted they've taken the show inside?"

"It's not just you. Shall we see if we can find alcohol?"

"Yes. There's no way I can put up with these snooty fuckers without it."

We make our way through the people towards what looks like an outside bar. When we get there, we find they're only serving one drink. I guess it should have been obvious.

"Pimm's, darling?" Carter sings at me.

"Oh my god," I mutter. "Was this a huge mistake, bringing you here?"

"Probably."

We've both got a glass each and we're hovering on the sidelines of this event when an unfamiliar, deep and slurred voice hits my ears.

"Well, well, well, who have we here?"

"Oh fuck," Carter mutters, turning to look at the man who the voice belongs to. I follow his lead as my eyes fall on the approaching figure. My breath catches.

"Holy shit." Carter's hand slips into mine and squeezes. I return the gesture, assuming that he needs the support right now.

"Well, I can honestly say this a surprise. Who the hell invited you to an event like this?"

My chin drops, I can't help but think I must look just like Biff's mum not so long ago.

"That's enough," Carter barks, not even bothering to answer the question.

"It's so funny, you know this is a silent auction, right? That means you need to read what each lot consists of. Who the fuck thought it was a great joke to bring you? Not only can you not afford to support the cause, but you have no fucking clue what each lot its. And the final joke is that we're raising money to refurbish a library. You ever even stepped foot inside one, brother?"

"Enough," Carter barks, taking a step closer to his twin. The similarities between them are unnerving now they're side by side. Logan looks exactly like the profile picture I spent so many hours looking at. Freshly shaven, styled hair, suit. But under all that, it's seems he's a massive arsehole.

"Do our parents know you're here? They're going to have a fucking field day when they find out."

"Jesus, Logan," I say stepping in front of Carter. His eyes widen in shock. "I'm Danniella, your sister-in-law. I would say it's nice to meet you, but it seems to be turning out to be very much the opposite."

His eyes flick between me and his brother, disbelief

written all over his face. He lifts his glass of scotch to his lips and drains it. Fuck knows where he managed to get that from. Christ knows how many of those he's had, but the way he's running his mouth I'd like to hope a lot.

"Sister-in-law. Fuck off. No one's stupid enough to marry that." His eyes flick over my shoulder, and I lose my shit.

"What the hell is your problem?" I shout, my palms lifting ready to slam down on his chest. I might not have met this dickhead before, but the fact that he's Carter's brother is all the connection I need to give him a piece of my mind.

"Whoa, Danni." Carter's strong arm wraps around my waist, and I'm pulled back into his chest. "Don't cause a scene," he whispers in my ear. I nod, but I don't relax. My fists curl with my need to hurt that arsehole.

"What happened, bro? You never used to need a girl to fight your battles for you."

"I don't. I could have your drunk arse on the floor in the blink of an eye. But I refuse to give these bunch of pricks the satisfaction of you making me lose my shit. It's what they expect of me, and I won't give it to them."

"Well they sure as shit don't expect you to go and read out the auction lots, that's for sure." Carter tenses, the tightness of his arm around my waist almost painful.

"Enough," he grates out.

The two stare at each other as things start falling into place in my mind. Catching Carter talking into his phone, although he wasn't on a call. Getting me to read his messages when most guys would refuse point black. Even his sketched cooking instructions.

Fuck.

"Logan, what are you... oh. Carter," another male voice

says from around a tree that Carter had managed to hide us behind. When he emerges, I find I'm staring at an older version of my husband. "I wasn't expecting to see you here."

"Me either," he grunts.

"Didn't think this was your kind of scene." Logan scoffs but their father ignores him. "You need to get out of here before Logan makes even more of a spectacle of himself."

"Me?" Carter asks in disbelief. "Shouldn't he be the one leaving? He's drunk off his arse and running his mouth."

"He needs to be here. You don't."

Carter tenses, and I expect an argument to fall from his lips, but instead, it's like all his fight leaves him.

He releases me and takes a step back.

"Fine. I hope you fucking enjoy yourselves. Look after my wife." And with that, he storms away.

"Carter, wait," I cry, racing after him, but I'm stopped when a warm hand wraps around my wrist.

"Let him go. He'll need to cool off."

"How the fuck do you know what he needs? You don't even know him," I shout at his dad. I might not know the whole truth, but things are seriously starting to fall into place. The issues with education, him never feeling like he's not good enough. All of that is the fault of the two arseholes standing in front of me. Carter might let them get away with it but I sure as fuck won't.

"I think I know him better than anyone. I spent years and tens of thousands of pounds trying to make something of him."

"He doesn't need your pity money," I snap. "So what he didn't go to uni and get a fucking degree. It doesn't make him any less of a person. He's incredible, not that you've ever given him the chance to show you."

"Dan, what's going on?" Zach's voice booms from behind me. I don't turn to look at him. Instead I keep my eyes trained on Carter's dad.

I sense the moment both Zach and Biff come to stand either side of me.

"Either of you to ever met Carter's brother or father?"

"No."

"Well, you're in for a real fucking treat."

"Where's Titch?" Carter's dad rolls his eyes at the nickname.

"Gone. These two wankers ran him out of the party."

"What?" Zach roars.

"Let's go," Biff says softly, taking my hand and pulling me away from the car crash I was in the middle of.

We're back at the car in no time. Zach floors the accelerator and we race from the car park in search of Carter, assuming he'll be walking along the road somewhere.

"I didn't know Titch had a twin," Biff muses as we look out the window for signs of him, reminding me that we've still not talked properly.

"I think he wishes he didn't."

"He was a dick. Nothing like Carter."

"Was he drunk?"

"Off his face. It's barely four PM in the afternoon at a charity event. Who does that?"

"Logan, apparently."

We don't find him, so without knowing where else to go, we head back to my flat.

"What if he's not here?" I ask as we walk towards the front door.

"Then we'll try other places. He can't have gone very far. He keeps his circle small."

We race inside, hoping to find him relaxing on the sofa, but there's no sign of him.

"Motherfucker. Where are you?" Zach barks.

"So?" I ask, already losing patience with this. I need to know he's okay. I need to tell him that I don't care about anything his brother said. I need to prove once and for all that he is enough.

"The studio. Spike's..."

"The boxing gym."

Zach narrows his eyes at me, but I don't have the time or energy to ask why he looks at me that way.

"Come on then," Biff says, walking from the flat, as impatient as I am.

Zach steps to follow her. "Zach, wait." He turns back to look at me. "Logan said..." I hesitate, questioning my need to ask because deep down I already know the truth. "Logan said that Carter can't read. Is that true?"

"Not really. He can read, he just finds it really hard. He's quite badly dyslexic. His family thinks that makes him an idiot, and it was drummed into him so much as a kid that he still believes it despite knowing it's not really true."

"That's fucked-up."

"Family," Zach says with a shrug as we both head for the door.

The studio is empty—well, that's not true. Spike and D are both busy with clients on their chairs along with ones waiting in reception. But neither of them have seen Carter and both look equally concerned.

"Do you think he'd..." Spike trails off while we all stand in his doorway.

"I don't know, man. He hasn't for months." My stomach drops, because I have a very good idea of what he's talking about.

"He has," falls from my lips without instruction from my brain.

They both turn to me in shock. "L-last weekend. Haven't you seen his bruises this week?"

"Yeah but he said... fuck," Spike barks. "If he ends up in the fucking hospital because of that cunt, I'll fucking kill him."

The woman on his chair with half a tattoo blanches but doesn't say anything as Spike begins to pace.

"Where does he go to fight?" I ask, assuming they don't all just rock up to the gym for it. With the whispered conversations I witnessed, I've got a suspicion that these fights aren't all above board.

"He used to get a text with the address and just disappear."

"Great, well that's fucking helpful."

"Let's go to the gym, see if anyone there knows anything."

"Go to our place first. We might be wrong. He could be hiding there and be perfectly fine." Spike tries to sound hopeful, but I'm not sure any of us really feel it.

In only a few minutes we're back in Zach's car.

"Tell me about these fights," I demand. "I know he's done cage fighting. I saw him fight last weekend. I—"

"He made you watch? Jesus," Zach interrupts.

"No, it wasn't like that. He didn't take me there for that, just to work out. One thing led to another... not the point. This fighting circuit is underground, right?"

"Yes."

"How didn't I know about this?" Biff sulks.

"It's not exactly something he advertises. Plus, he's not been involved for ages. He got a concussion on his last fight and was advised he should stop."

"What?" I ask, blanching. "So this is even more dangerous than I thought. Fucking hell."

"This is Spike's place?"

I look up and down the street. I'm not sure I could imagine a more suitable location for two bachelors to live. "They live next to Pulse?"

No one answers—they don't need to. The sign is right there in front of us.

"Fucking hell, you'd never guess that Titch had moved out. Look at the state of this place," Zach mutters as we walk inside and find the mess.

"Is that a pair of..." I don't finish my thought, because the small bit of red lace hanging from the lamp in the corner could only be a pair of women's knickers.

"Spike's a dog. I think most of the strippers from Pulse have given private shows up here."

"You think?" Biff asks, her hand on her hip.

"Uh huh," is all he gives her before disappearing down the hall.

We stand in the middle of the chaos, not knowing where to look.

"He's been here. Look." When Zach emerges, he's holding Carter's phone.

"Please tell me there's an address on that thing."

He shrugs. "It's locked."

"Give it." I tap in his passcode and open his messages.

"Clapham. Let's go."

"I should drop you two back off. You don't need to do this," Zach says before moving the car.

"No fucking way. Drive there now or I'll call an Uber and get myself there."

"I'm with her," Biff says. "Now go. We need to get him."

Zach's wheels screech as he takes off towards the address Biff put into his GPS.

27

Carter

If I had any suspicion *they'd* be there, then I never would have agreed to the fucking charity event. I knew my parents got involved with that kind of stuff, but what were the chances of them being at the exact same event? High, apparently.

The second his slurred voice hit my ears, I knew everything was about to go to shit. My brother is an over-privileged prick at the best of times, but give him some alcohol and he's just a straight-up cunt. As proved by what immediately fell from his lips.

I wasn't keeping my issues from Danni per se, I just didn't really want to talk about them. I spent all of my childhood having to fucking talk about it with everyone my parents paid to try to 'fix' me.

I'm dyslexic. Not fucking diseased.

But that wasn't good enough for them. They wanted the perfect, intelligent boys who always made them proud. Well... they got that with one of us. Logan was the golden boy. Gifted at school, excelled at all kinds of sports. He got the grades, went to university, and ended up working as a banker, all the while I flunked the lot and vented my issues via my fists. Something that my parents hated, just like the rest of my life. Drawing on people's skin for a living wasn't the 'real' job or career they wanted me to have, and their idea of sport was golf or fucking cricket, not cage fighting. But ever the disappointment, that was who I was.

My first instinct the second I saw him was to fight. What I'd really love to do is slam my fist into his smug fucking face for all the years of hell he's put me through. It wasn't his fault that he was the apple of our parents' eyes. However, it was his choice to play to it. To use every opportunity, every one of my fuck-ups to make himself look that little bit better. And today was no exception. He couldn't cope with the fact that I might have been invited to the same stuck-up party he was, so he had to belittle me. Drag up my weaknesses to make it seem like I didn't belong there. He really didn't need to. I felt like an outcast from before we'd even arrived.

My intention was to walk off the frustration and go home, but I was barely off the grounds of the massive house when my phone chimed in my pocket.

Pulling it out, I found a name staring back at me that I hadn't seen in a long time.

Mickey: Tonight. You in?

My hand trembled as I stared down at it, but this time,

the words were loud and clear, and they were exactly what I needed. I hit the speech to text button and replied with one simple word.

Titch: Yes

The address of tonight's fight was immediately sent to me. It's still early, but knowing I can't sit at Danni's and wait, I call a car and head for the old flat I shared with Spike. Most of my clothes are still there. I'll grab a clean pair of shorts and head to the warehouse early. Mickey will be there, and, if I'm lucky there will also be a bottle or two of alcohol.

The house is a dump. I always used to joke that Spike would be happy living in a pig sty, and it seems I was right. There are clothes, bottles, and empty take-out cartons everywhere.

Ignoring it all, I go straight to my room and pull open my drawers to grab what I need.

Finding there's a hell of a wait for a car, I decide against it and set off running. The warm-up will do me good.

By the time I jog through the closed industrial estate to locate the building where this fight is taking place, my lungs are burning, but it's a fuck load better than feeling the lingering anger from my brother's arsehole words.

My fists clench.

Fighting has been the only way I've been able to rid myself of the feelings of uselessness they all fill me with. They make me feel like nothing, pointless, and fighting proved to me that I am worth something. I am capable of something even if, like everything else, they don't approve.

To my surprise, the place is almost packed when I

push through the doors. I guess we're starting early tonight.

"Titch! My main man," Mickey calls when he spots me. "I gotta be honest, I wasn't expecting you to agree."

"If you'd have asked me six hours ago then I probably wouldn't have."

"You got shit going on?"

"Yeah, enough to get me pumped for this."

"Come on then, let's get you ready. I've got a few guys lined up before you. Get the crowd in the mood and then the floor is all yours. They're gonna fucking love having you back, man."

"I'm not sure—"

"It's going to be epic," he continues, ignoring that I even said anything.

The roar of the crowd makes me wince as a couple of naïve looking kids step into the centre.

"Fucking hell, where you finding them these days, primary school?"

"Don't let their looks deceive you. They've got potential."

"Potential to be flattened," I mutter.

Mickey leads me out the back and away from the action so I can get ready.

"Who am I fighting?"

"Ace."

"Ace? You're fucking joking." Ace is massive. I might have been out of the game for a while, but I can't imagine he's got any smaller, or slower in that time. I, on the other hand, am very out of practice.

"Nah, man. You can take him."

I picture my brother and father and the way they

looked at me earlier, and it stirs within me exactly what I need. Hate.

"You got any fucking whiskey?"

"Just one," Mickey states.

"Whatever." He disappears for a few minutes before bringing me a bottle.

I neck a few shots before it's swiped from my hand.

"Being half cut won't help."

It feels like one second that whiskey is burning down my throat and then the next I'm approaching the ring with a cheering crowd in every direction.

The MC announces my name and they fucking erupt. I didn't really expect anyone to miss me when I stopped fighting, but it seems I might have been wrong.

I push everything from my head and focus on that feeling that constantly sits heavy inside me. The need to prove myself. The need to show I'm worthy. Everything else vanishes, and when I look at Ace, who's smirking at me like he's already fucking won, all I see is my brother's face.

The second the horn sounds signalling the start of the fight, I fly at him.

I don't think of the consequences, of the reason I gave this up, and I sure as fuck don't think of her.

My fists fly, making contact with my target, but I'm not the only one.

I grunt as his knuckles connect with my ribs. My chest burns as I fight to drag in the air I need.

"Motherfucker."

The sound of the crowd is silenced as I focus on my task.

Taking this arsehole to the ground.

Proving myself.
Being worthy.

28

Danni

"What the fuck is going on?" I bark at seeing yet another road closure.

"Essential road works," Zach mutters—not that it's necessary, anyone with eyes could see all the warning signs.

"This is bullshit. It would have been quicker to run."

"You want to?" he asks, sounding a little more serious than he should.

"Run? I was joking."

"Yeah, well. We're not fucking getting anywhere, and he might..." Zach trails off, and the ball of dread already sitting in my stomach only grows.

"Just turn around and try another route. If that fails then we'll run," Biff says, sounding a little more rational than the two of us. "Danni, have you messaged Spike?"

"Y-yes. He said he was finishing his client and then coming to meet us."

"Okay, good." The fact that Zach thinks we're going to need Spike makes my stomach turn.

"What about D?" Biff asks.

"No, don't tell him. Not until we know what's actually happening. He'll lose his shit if Titch is fighting again."

Silence fills the car as Zach turns around and tries another way.

Thankfully, other than a few temporary sets of lights to keep the traffic moving, we manage to make some progress, albeit slow.

The sun is starting to set by the time we get to the other side of the city. Zach reassures me that the fights usually start late, so there might still be a chance of catching Carter before he does something stupid.

"Well, this looks ominous," Biff says as we drive over the giant potholes of the industrial estate the GPS directed us to.

She's not wrong. With the sun now very low in the sky it casts a daunting orange glow over the seemingly deserted place.

"Which one is it?" Zach asks, prompting me to look at Carter's phone once more.

"Keep driving." He follows the track around a little until a couple of dim lights catch my eye. "There."

It's so weird to know that there are probably a ton of people inside, yet there are no cars or signs of life.

Zach pulls the car to a stop and the three of us jump out.

"Maybe you two should wait here."

"And maybe you should shut the fuck up, asswipe."

I storm past my brother towards a set of double doors that are slightly ajar.

Pulling them open, I find a single flickering bulb hanging from the ceiling. The stench of sweaty bodies and blood hits me along with a cheering crowd somewhere in the distance, and I know I'm in the right place.

I take off into the building, not knowing if Zach and Biff are behind me but equally not caring. I need to get to him. I need to stop him doing something he might regret.

I need to tell him how I feel.

My steps falter, the magnitude of those feelings slamming into me. I reach out to the wall to stop me from losing my footing.

I'd fallen for him when he was just a face online. But with one look at that real face today, I realised he was right. That photograph was the only trick; the person I was speaking to was purely Carter. It was his words, his dreams, his ideas that I fell for. Not the appearance. And although there are similarities between them, mostly their eyes, there are so many differences, and not just in appearance. Carter is kind, thoughtful and compassionate, whereas Logan today was just cruel. I could never be attracted to anyone who speaks to someone they're meant to love like that.

The realisation of what I should be doing right now has me pushing from the wall. At the same time, Zach comes up behind me and takes my upper arms in his hands.

"Wait outside, I'll sort this."

"No. No, I need to do it."

I struggle out of his hold and race forward, ignoring whatever it is he mutters at me.

As I move down the empty space, the crowd gets

louder, but it does little to cover the loud thunder of my heart at not knowing what I'm about to walk into.

"I'm sorry, miss. You can't just walk in there," a guy I didn't even notice hovering at the door announces. He's huge, his wide shoulders almost filling the entire doorway.

"Uh... m-my husband. I-I t think he's fighting."

"Even more reason for you not to go in."

"No, I think you'll find that's every reason why I should be inside." I step up to him, wanting to prove that I'm not intimidated by his sheer size.

"I'm sorry, sweetheart, only approved members are allowed in."

"This is bullshit. Get Mickey."

"What the fuck is going on?" Zach asks.

"He won't let us in."

"Zach, man. How's it going?" I look to the Hulk's arms. Full of ink.

"Not great, we really need to get in there. Do us a favour, would ya? I'll do your next tat on the house?"

A conflicted look passes over his face before he glances behind him and into the chaos.

"Fine. But if I get caught, you'll be doing more than one!"

"Thank you," I cry, squeezing through the small gap he leaves and entering the giant space beyond.

The noise of the crowd is almost unbearable. I walk around the outskirts and I lift up onto my tiptoes in an attempt to see what's going on in the centre, but there are too many bodies.

It's not until I get around to the other side that there's a gap in the sea of people and I get the briefest of glimpses of what's going on in the centre.

"Noooo," I scream, although I doubt anyone hears me.

I blink and he's gone, swallowed by the crowd cheering him on.

The image of his bloody face fills my mind and tears sting my eyes. If I thought last weekend was scary, then it's nothing compared to right now.

My legs move without me realising until I can see him once again.

I climb onto a box, a box I probably shouldn't be on, but I don't give a shit. I'll do anything it takes to get him out of the ring.

My eyes find him immediately as he lays into his opponent. It's immediately obvious how tame the fight last weekend was. This is vicious.

Both of them are covered in blood and darkening bruises as the crowd screams for more.

"Carter," I cry, feeling totally helpless.

There's no way he can hear me, yet not two seconds later when his opponent stumbles away, he looks up and our eyes connect. They hold for the briefest of moments, but it's enough to see his confusion and shock before his momentary lapse of focus means he's at a disadvantage.

His opponent crashes into him and they stumble away. Carter takes too many punches to count before he somehow manages to get control of the situation.

He moves with such intensity, such passion and determination. Even more so I'm sure since he's seen me, and he doesn't stop until the other guy is rolling around on the floor.

A guy steps into the ring with them and lifts Carter's hand, announcing him as the winner. A weird sense of pride washes through me that's he's won, but it only lasts for the briefest of moments because Carter drops to the floor.

"Noooo," I scream, jumping from whatever it is I'm standing on and fighting my way through the crowd.

It's takes forever to force my way through. Everyone is too intent on watching the fallout from the fight to pay any attention to me.

When I finally get to the front after a lot of elbowing people in the ribs and standing on their toes with my heel, I run to Carter's lifeless body.

The other guy is nowhere to be seen. It's just the MC guy and Mickey who are standing over him, looking concerned.

I drop down on my knees, my fear ensuring I don't notice the pain as I connect with the concrete floor.

"Carter, come on, baby. I'm here. Wake up." I gently touch his face, taking in all his injuries before looking down to his chest and stomach. The bruising and swelling is already showing itself, but it's the amount of blood that worries me more.

I take his wrapped, bloody hand in mine and squeeze gently as my first tears fall.

"Don't do this, Carter. I need you. I fucking need you."

When his voice breaks through my panic, it's rough and barely a whisper. To start with, I think I'm imagining it.

"I'm okay."

"Carter, I—" My sob cuts off whatever words might have been about to fall from my lips.

Mickey says something above me about the next fight, and red hot anger fills my veins.

"You," I say jabbing him in the chest. "What the fuck were you thinking, allowing him to do this?" I screech.

"You knew he wasn't ready for this. This is your fucking fault. If anything happens to h-him—"

"He'll be fine."

The flippant way he says it while Carter is flat out on the cold floor astonishes me. I guess in order to run this kind of thing, you need to be a cold-hearted bastard.

"Do you even care about any of these guys? Is this just all about money for you?"

"Dan, that's enough," Zach booms from behind me. "Titch needs your energy right now."

I blow out a long breath. He's right. Mickey doesn't matter.

Turning my back on him, I look down at Carter, who's staring back at me with total disbelief in his eyes.

"What the hell were you thinking?" I bark at him. My words might be harsh, but when I reach for him, my touch is anything but. "Fucking hell. I thought you... I thought you were fucking dead, Carter."

"I'm okay," he repeats, but the weakness of his voice doesn't support the words in any way.

"We need to get you out of here, man," says another voice, and when I look up, I find Spike standing behind Zach. His muscles are pulled tight, and there's fury burning in his eyes. "Are you okay if we lift you?"

"Yeah, I'm good."

It's a barefaced lie, we all know that, but it doesn't stop Carter from attempting to get himself to a sitting position and for both Zach and Spike to reach down for him. The three of them are like a well-oiled machine, and it makes me wonder how many times this has happened before.

I stand back and allow them to get him to his feet.

"He'll be okay," Biff says. I'd forgotten that she was here, but the sound of her voice is exactly what I need.

As I turn to her, she opens her arms and I sob on her shoulder.

"You've fallen for him, haven't you?"

"I... I..."

"It's okay." Her hand rubs up and down my back in support. "Come on, lets help them out."

Biff and I hold the doors open, and finally we leave the crowd behind. Zach and Spike are carrying all of Titch's weight by the time we're out in the car park, and his head is hanging on his shoulders. I've no idea if he's passed out or what, and it makes me panic.

"Be careful, you don't want to hurt him more," I snap.

"I'm okay, doll." His voice is barely above a whisper, but I hear it loud and clear in the silence of the car park. The hustle and bustle of London might only be a few minutes away, but none of that can be heard right now. It's eerie, and it only makes this situation seem worse.

I snort, because Carter quite clearly is anything but fine.

"Get him in the car," Spike demands, and Biff runs around them to open the door.

I climb into the other side and gently place his head into my lap once they've managed to manoeuvre him inside.

My fingertip trails down his cheek. His eyes flicker open as much as the swelling will allow, and my breath catches when we connect.

"You came," he whispers.

My heart slams against my chest as realisation of what he means floods me.

"Oh, Carter." I run my fingers lightly over his sweat-damp hair. "You've no idea, do you?" I hesitate, trying to put into words just how I feel about him, but when I look to find his eyes again, they're shut. "Carter?" Nothing. I panic, I've no idea if I should be allowing him to sleep right now or not, but I'm distracted when both the front doors are pulled open and Biff and Zach climb in.

"How is he?" Zach asks.

"He's fallen asleep. Should I wake him? He probably has a concussion."

"Leave him until we get back. Just keep an eye on him." I nod, a huge lump forming in my throat.

Zach starts up the car at the same time the loud roar of an engine comes from beside me. When I glance out the window, I find Spike pulling on a motorcycle helmet and gunning his engine.

Zach sets off behind him and we head back into the city.

"Where are we going?" I ask when the turning to the nearest hospital comes and goes.

"Your place."

"Zach, he needs to go to a hospital. Look at him."

"Dan, it's okay. We'll get him looked at. I won't let anything happen to him. You've gotta trust me."

"Trust you? He's passed out on my lap and covering my legs in blood." I can only assume the last part, but there's something suspiciously damp down there and I know it's not from me.

"I know, I know. This freaks me out as much as it does you, I assure you. But we know what we're doing."

"How many times have you done this before?" I'm not sure I want the answer, but the question falls from my lips anyway.

"Too many."

"Fucking hell," I sigh, my head falling back for a few

moments before I remember that I should be making sure Carter is still with us.

I dig around in my small clutch to find a packet of tissues so that I can attempt to stop him bleeding quite so much. I press one to his lip and the other to his eyebrow that's once again split open, but there's not much else I can do, and I feel totally useless.

Running my eyes down his body, I take in the emerging bruises that seem to cover his entire torso. There's blood there too, but I'm sure it's just sprayed from his face and probably from the other guy's fists.

My stomach turns over at the thought of another man slamming his curled fists into what's mine.

Mine.

I find his face once more, and for the first time since I met the real Carter, I allow everything I feel for him out. A sob bubbles up my throat, and I fight to keep the words in that I want to tell him.

"Is he okay?" Zach asks in a rush from the front.

"Y-yeah. Nothing's changed."

"Why the sudden tears?"

"It's... nothing. I'm just a bit emotional."

I notice Biff's hand come out to rest on Zach's thigh, and I'm grateful that she's stopping him from asking any more questions. I might have admitted to Biff how I'm feeling, but the first person I need to tell is Carter, not my brother.

Silence descends on the car. It's heavy and oppressive, but at least it means I can hear Carter's low breathing loud and clear.

I keep my hands on him, hoping that he can feel my presence. Feel my support. My love.

Before too long, we're pulling up in front of my flat.

Thankfully, there's a space right out the front and Zach parks quickly before killing the engine.

There are lights on in Harrison's house above, and dread sits heavy in my stomach. I hope to God that they don't look out of their window in the next ten minutes. That is not the way I need them to be reintroduced to Carter.

I breath out a sigh as the rumble of Spike's bike comes to a stop behind us somewhere and Zach and Biff step out.

Their muffled voices filter into me for a few seconds before the doors open and we somehow manage to get Carter from the car.

With Carter's body hanging limply between Zach and Spike, we slowly make our way down to my flat. Thankfully, no one comes rushing from upstairs, and I breathe a sigh of relief. The last thing we need right now is our older brother getting involved.

"Danni," Spike barks halfway to my bedroom. "Open Titch's phone. Find Doc and call him. Tell him what's happened and give him your address."

"Uh... okay." I pull his phone from my bag and do as I'm told. It's not until the call connects that I question who the hell I might be about to talk to.

"Yes," a deep male voice says down the line.

"Um, hi. I've got C-Carter... um... Titch Wright. He's been in a fight and—"

"Motherfucker. Where are you?"

I rattle off my address. "I'll be there in twenty." The line goes dead before I get to say any more.

"Who was that?" Biff asks.

"I've no idea, but we're going to meet him in twenty minutes."

"Right."

Putting his phone down, I rush through to the bedroom. The guys have Carter laid out in the centre of my bed. They've removed his shoes but are otherwise just standing and staring at him in total disbelief.

"What happened, man?" Spike asks softly, in the hope that Carter will wake up and explain, but sadly nothing happens. His chest is still rising and falling evenly, so I guess there is that.

"I'll get my first-aid kit then. Start cleaning him up."

Zach nods as he takes the chair in my room. Spike falls on to the edge of the bed and drops his head into his hands. I might not know all that much about Carter's previous roommate, but it's becoming more than clear how much Spike cares for him.

I retrieve the box that until Carter moved in was mostly untouched and fill a bowl with warm water. When I re-join them in the bedroom, the scent of coffee floats through the air and I glance into the kitchen as I pass the door to find Biff busy getting mugs down from the cupboard.

Crawling onto the bed, I place everything on the bedside table and come to a stop beside him. I dip a cotton ball into the warm water and begin gently wiping his face. In only seconds, the bowl of water is pink with his blood, but at least he's starting to look a little better.

None of us say anything—we're too lost in our own heads—but that doesn't mean I don't feel the weight of their burning stares as I clean their friend up.

When Spike's voice breaks the silence, it's so loud it makes me startle.

"You're really good for him," he muses.

"I'm not so sure that's true. Look at him."

"That wasn't because of you."

"Wasn't it?" I can't help wondering if it was the fear, the shame from his brother's words that led him to this more than it was the words themselves. He's clearly been hiding that part of his life, his struggles, from me. He didn't want me to know, and the second I found out, he ran and did this.

"No. This is about him and his own demons. Demons you help push away."

I sob. "I- I didn't even know. He didn't tell—"

"He would have. He just didn't want to ruin what you thought of him."

"Why would that ruin anything? I don't care about any of that. It's what's inside that matters, what I've fallen—" Thankfully, the doorbell rings, cutting off my admission.

Spike jumps up and goes running.

"I never would have put you two together in a million years," my brother muses, "but I've got to be honest. I think you're kind of perfect together."

"Yeah?" I ask, a smile pulling at my lips.

"Yeah. You're kind of the yin to his yang."

"Aw, Zach. Biff making you all romantic?"

"Something like that," he mutters, standing as we're re-joined by Spike and whoever Doc is.

29

Carter

Voices I recognise but can't place fill my ears. Light that feels as bright as the sun burns at my eyes despite the fact that they're closed. Everything hurts. Every-fucking-thing.

What hap—fuck.

Memories hit me almost as hard as he did. Logan drunk and spewing my fucking secrets to Danni. The text. The fight. My muscles tense as I remember being in that ring. I've never been worried about fighting, about whether or not I'd get to walk away after, but last night was the closet I've come to it. I was out of practice and slower than I'd like. But Ace? He was anything but slow.

His first punch to my ribs ripped the air from my lungs, and I knew it was going to be one hell of a fight from the off.

Most of my memory of it is a blur. I don't even remember who won. From the pain radiating through my body, I'm guessing it wasn't me.

"Get him to take two of these when he wakes. He can have two more every four hours. If they don't help, call me. If he gets worse, call me."

That voice. I know that voice.

"Are you sure we shouldn't be taking him to hospital right now?" I know that voice, too. It's soft, caring, and sexy as hell. My aches and pains are forgotten for the briefest moment as I focus on it and the sensation it sparks up in my body.

Danni. She's here. Wherever the fuck here is.

"No. Other than the broken ribs, it's nothing more than cuts and bruises. He'll be just fine with a little TLC."

TLC, now that sounds like a fucking good idea. I open my mouth to agree, but nothing comes out. Well, only a moan.

"Carter?" In a heartbeat, she's at my side. The warmth of her hand burns into mine as her other gently lands on my cheek. "Are you awake?"

"Y—" I fight to swallow, my throat feeling like a fucking desert.

"Wait." The sound of her moving fills my ears before a straw is pressed against my lips. "Drink," she demands, and I can't help but smile at her tone.

I do as I'm told, and thankfully it makes me feel a little more human.

"Can you open your eyes?"

I pause. I want to, I really fucking want to see her. To see the look in her eyes. My need to know if she's here because she feels like she should be after what she's discovered, or if it's because she wants to be. I'm terrified it's the former, but what if she does care? What if I'm not good enough for her either?

I suck in a breath and crack my eyes open. I thought it was painful just being awake, but as the electric light from above pours in, I can't help but groan.

"Turn the light out," Danni says to someone before the softer glow from the beside lamp illuminates the room.

The first person I see is Spike. And he looks fucking furious.

Jesus.

Turning my head slightly, I find her.

The second our eyes connect, I know I had no reason to be scared. The concern, the fear, the anger within them tells me everything I need to know. She didn't come to me tonight out of pity. It was because she wanted to. Needed to.

"Dan," I whisper, the lump in my throat getting the better of me and cutting off any other words. Since the first time I looked at her, she's had walls up. They were so bloody obvious, and I thought higher than I'd be able to scale. But suddenly they're gone. There's nothing clouding her eyes as she stares at me.

"Fucking hell, Carter. I thought you were dead." She takes both of my hands and squeezes gently. I can only imagine the state of my knuckles right now, despite them being wrapped. Her eyes fill with tears, although none fall. "I thought I'd lost you."

"I'm right here, doll. I'm okay."

A scoff comes from the other side of the room, but I don't look to him. I already know I'm in for a Spike ear-bashing. He's warned me enough about fighting again, and I promised him I wouldn't. But look at me now. One word from fucking Logan and I walked straight into that fucking ring without a second thought.

"I'm not going to ask you why, because I think I get it. But I need you to promise me something." I nod—it's all I'm capable of right now. "Next time you need to blow off steam, use me," Danni begs.

"Fucking hell." Spike walks from the room, pulling the door to behind him, but he doesn't leave the flat.

I ignore her previous comment, knowing that if I think about that offer too much then I'll want something I'm not capable of right now.

"He's mad."

"We all are, Carter. Do you have any idea how it felt running into that warehouse, not knowing what we were going to find?"

My lips part, but no words come out, because as much as I can imagine, I've no clue.

"Think about the person you care most about in the world. Now, imagine they're in danger and there's nothing you can do to help." I nod, squeezing her hand, hoping she knows it's my way of telling her that she's the one I care about most without actually saying the words. "A-and now times that by about a million." Her voice cracks, and it physically hurts, knowing that I caused her pain. Made her feel as useless as I do on a daily basis.

"I'm sorry. How did you find me?"

"You left your phone at Spike's. We found the message with the address."

I nod, absorbing her words. I was so desperate to escape reality that I didn't even notice I'd left it. "About what Logan said. I—" Her warm fingers press against my lips, cutting off my words.

"Not now, Carter. You need to rest. We've got plenty of time to talk about that."

"But—"

"But nothing. I don't care about what he said. None of that matters. That isn't what makes you. What's in here is what makes you." She presses her hand gently to my chest, right above my heart. "And I think that's pretty incredible, so…" She trails off, slowly leaning forward. "As long as you promise to never run off like that again, then I think you might be stuck with me." Her lips brush against mine as she says the words, and my heart swells.

"For real?"

"Yes." She kisses me gently, but when I try to deepen it to make it what I really need, she pulls back. I groan, and she laughs. "Doc said you had to rest, not get ideas."

"Doll, you're in bed with me. I'll always have ideas."

"I'm not *in* bed with you, Carter. I'm sitting on the edge. Now, you're going to take these painkillers and then you're going back to sleep."

"Am I?"

"Yes."

I nod as she pops two pills from the pack beside her and helps me to sit a little to take them. My ribs scream at my movement, but it's not something I've not dealt with before. A broken rib or two kinda comes with the territory of cage fighting.

Once I'm settled, she stands from the bed, but not before I catch her fingers in mine.

"Don't leave."

"I'll just be out there, speaking to the others. Call if you need me."

"I always need you." Conflict flitters through her eyes.

"I'll be right outside the door." She drops a kiss to my forehead and pulls her hand from mine. It doesn't take all that much effort, because I'm weak as fuck.

I shut my eyes the second she pulls the door closed behind her, and, after listening to their hushed voices for a few seconds, I drift back off to sleep.

The next time I come to, the room is in darkness and the pain in my body is a little bit less than before, but it's not the most notable thing. That's the small body curled up beside me.

Lifting my hand, I gently brush a lock of hair from her cheek and push it behind her ear. She's so fucking beautiful, and with her eyes closed, I no longer see the fear I put there tonight. I fucking hate myself for it. I should have been stronger than to go running back to my old ways the second Logan opened his fucking mouth. I should have trusted her to stand by me, to fight for me, even if she had no clue what she was fighting for. I've asked her to trust me time and again, yet I didn't give her the same courtesy.

"Fuck," I bark, irritated with my actions.

Her eyes fly open and connect with mine.

"Shit, I'm sorry. I didn't mean to wake you."

"Are you okay?" She pulls herself up so she's looming over me, her eyes flitting around my face, looking for more injuries.

"I'm fine. Lie back down."

"Do you need more painkillers? A drink? Something to eat?"

"Do you know what I really need?"

"If you even think about saying sex, Carter, then I'm gonna—"

"Lie with me. Just lie with me." I hold my arm out for her and gesture for her to settle against my side.

"I don't want to hurt you." She hesitates.

"It's the other side that's broken. Please, doll. I need you."

"Fucking hell, Carter. The second it gets too much, tell me and I'll move."

"Of course," I lie. I don't give a shit how much it hurts, as long as she's in my arms.

She rests her head on my chest and I fight not to react when my entire upper body burns with pain. It's worth it. *She's* worth it.

I drop my nose into her hair and breathe her in. "I'm so sorry. It was—"

"Just rest."

"No, I need to get this out. I need to explain."

"You don't—"

"Do as you're told, doll," I say with a laugh.

She nods against me, making my breath catch, but she says no more.

"I was wrong to do that yesterday. Running and blanking everything out with someone else's fists is just how I've always dealt with it." I blow out a breath as I replay what Logan said in my head. "Everything he said was true. Well, no, that's a lie. He over-exaggerated. I can read. I can write. It's just... it's just really fucking hard. It's why I draw. It's so much easier to get across what I'm trying to say with images than it is with words." She traces over the ink on my chest as I speak. She trails the mountain tops that I've spent my life trying to climb and continues onto the broken and battered heart.

"I get it," she whispers, but I don't let her words stop me explaining more.

"My parents have high expectations. They wanted us both to be the most intellectual kids ever born. Logan fell into that role easily. Even in the early days he was a level above his reading age. He could write his own name, hell he could write mine better than I could.

"I was always looked at as the slow one. The stupid one. It didn't matter that I was better than Logan at other stuff, because none of that mattered. I wasn't what my parents classed as intelligent, and that was that. I endured years of extra classes, special tuition, everything they found that might help me. 'Cure' me. They refused to accept that there was an actual reason why I couldn't do these things. They spared no expense, as they liked to remind me often, yet I was still too stupid to understand.

"It was exhausting. I constantly felt like a failure while I got to watch Logan do everything I couldn't and lap up all the love and acceptance from our parents.

"When everyone left me alone, I discovered that I did have a use for the pen and paper they were always shoving under my nose. I started drawing when I was about six, I think. I found it was the perfect way to get my feelings out without having to actually write, or even think about, the words.

"I drew all sorts. Whatever popped into my head. But I kept everything hidden under my bed in a box. I was a constant disappointment, so I had no reason not to believe they'd be disappointed in them too."

"Carter," she breathes. She tilts her head as if she

wants to look up at me, but I can't deal with looking into her eyes right now.

"Don't," I demand as softly as possible.

If she looks at me, then she'll see the tears that are threatening to escape, and the last thing I need right now is her pity. Or worse, for her to think I'm weak.

She stops moving the second she hears my voice and thankfully does as I ask. Her fingers continue following the lines of my ink, most of which has been put on my body by her brother.

"I was lucky, I found a job not long after I finished school and was able to rent this really shitty room in a house share and live my own life. But my parents' judgement was never far away, and Logan's bragging at what he was achieving wasn't that far behind either. He sailed through his A-levels and was accepted into Oxford. Fucking Oxford," I repeat with a laugh. "Our parents had never been prouder as they watched their boy go to one of the finest universities this country has to offer. And when people asked about me, do you know what they said?" I don't allow her time to answer, because of course she has no idea. "They told them that I've gone travelling to 'find myself'. They were too ashamed to admit I'd moved out and got a job." I sigh, thinking back to how much that all hurt. "I'm pretty sure that had I not been given a chance at the studio, then I wouldn't be here now. The only other thing I had in my life was anger and fighting. I've no doubt that would have killed me by now."

The silence that follows those words is heavy, but I won't take them back. It's true.

"Well, I'm grateful for whoever it was that gave you that chance."

"You know him," I whisper, suddenly feeling tired again after such an emotional rehash of my past.

"Oh?"

"D. He's got a thing for broken teenagers." I laugh. "He helped create Titch. I was a scrawny teenager on the brink of destruction. He's the father I never really had." I don't register her response, because I fall back to sleep.

30

Danni

I lie there for the longest time, thinking over what Carter just told me. My heart breaks for the boy who was rejected over and over again by his family. No child deserves that.

One thing I do know: his parents made a massive mistake, because he's no failure. He's incredible. So what, he didn't follow his brother to Oxford. He's made a very good career out of a talent that most people could only wish for.

I'm once again reminded of how incredible my own family is. Guilt cripples me that I've not admitted to them what happened in Vegas. I've not even introduced them to Carter as my boyfriend, let alone anything else. How must that make him feel?

Fuck. I never want to do anything to make him think for even a moment that I might be ashamed of him.

Vowing to take him to meet my parents properly as soon as possible, I watch as the sun begins to rise. I've only got a small window in here, but it's enough to watch the light change to a warm orange as the spring day starts.

With Carter snoring lightly beside me, I slip from the bed and make use of the bathroom before finding one of his hoodies and pulling it over my head. Spike is sleeping out on the sofa, so I can't walk around in my barely-there satin pyjamas like I usually would when it's just me, or just the two of us now.

Once they were happy that Carter was okay, Biff and Zach headed back to his flat, but Spike point-blank refused to leave. That was fine by me, as long as he was happy to crash on the sofa. I could see the concern filling his eyes, and I knew that he needed to be here to see Carter first thing this morning, just to settle his own mind.

I'm not expecting him to be awake, so I slip into the living room as quietly as I can, hoping that I can grab a coffee and go and sit outside in my morning sun trap to allow them some peace. But when I look to where he should be sleeping, I find a set of eyes looking back at me.

"Shit," I gasp. "I wasn't expecting you to be awake yet."

"Sorry, I didn't mean to scare you. I couldn't sleep."

"Sorry, the sofa isn't very comfortable."

"It's fine. That wasn't the issue." The same shadows from last night fill his eyes.

"He's okay. He was awake a couple of hours ago, talking to me."

"He really doesn't get how awful it is for those around him when he does shit like that."

"I know it's no excuse, but I think he's too used to believing no one cares."

"Ain't that the fucking truth," Spike groans, lifting

himself up so he's sitting on the sofa, the blanket I gave him pooling at his waist. I can't help my eyes dropping to his ink. He must notice because he reaches out and grabs his shirt before pulling it over his head.

"Coffee?" I ask, side-stepping the sofa and going for the kitchen.

"Yes. Make it strong."

"You got it."

I make us a mug each before taking it over and curling myself into the other side of the sofa.

Spike takes a sip despite it clearly being too hot.

"How... um... how many times have you had to rescue him from a fight like that?" I ask hesitantly, not knowing if I really want the answer.

"Too many. I thought he was done. I thought he'd taken the concussion warning seriously. He promised me he was done. I guess I should have learned by now that he doesn't fucking listen to me," he mumbles to himself.

"He does. And I'm sure if it weren't for Logan yesterday then he wouldn't have needed to break that promise."

"Logan's a fucking cunt... sorry," he winces, glancing over at me.

"Don't. I fucking agree. It just proved that I met the right twin the day I turned up for a date and Carter was waiting for me."

"I told him not to do that either." Spike rolls his eyes. "I told him it would end in disaster."

"Has it?" I ask, and he looks over with his brows pulled together.

"Has it what?"

"Ended in disaster."

"I guess that all depends on what comes next." He falls

silent, but it's clear it's only because he's trying to find the right words. "Titch is... one of a kind. Any woman would be lucky to have him..."

"But?" I add, encouraging him to say more.

"Yeah, go on. I'm intrigued too," an amused, deep voice comes from the doorway.

"Aw fuck," Spike laughs.

I jump from my seat and run to where he's propping himself up against the doorframe. "Are you okay?" I ask in a rush, looking him over.

"Yeah, doll. I'm good." His voice is deeper than usual, and the pain is clear in his eyes.

"If you needed something, you should have called me."

"I needed a piss."

"Okay, well, you should go back to bed." His hand lifts, his fingers threading into my hair and forcing me to look at him.

"I'm okay. You can stop worrying."

"I'll remember to say the same thing to you after you think you've found me dead on the floor, shall I?"

His eyes narrow. "Not funny."

"I'm well aware."

"I think I'll come and join you for a bit. Your conversation seemed stimulating."

Spike chuckles. "What? I wouldn't be your friend if I didn't warn her what you're really like."

"A man needs to have some secrets," he complains.

"Don't worry, I won't tell her how you had an obsession with the Spice Girls. Oh... whoops. Sorry!"

Carter launches a cushion at his friend while we all laugh. Carter winces in pain as he moves, and I hate that I can't do anything about it right now.

"Do you need any more painkillers?"

"Nah, I've taken the ones you left beside the bed."

"Okay, good. Coffee?"

"I thought you'd never ask."

The guys chat away while I make us all a fresh drink. "You hungry?"

"You plan on cooking, doll?"

"I can try. Or I'm much more skilled with ordering something? What do you fancy?"

"McDonalds," they say in unison.

"What's that, some kind of tradition? Carter gets the shit kicked out of him and you both enjoy a McMuffin after?"

"Yeah, something like that," Spike mutters, suddenly sounding less excited about the food.

"Hey, I didn't get the shit kicked out of me," Carter complains, pulling me into his side once I've placed the mugs on the coffee table.

"Really?" Spike asks, his eyebrows almost hitting his hairline. "Do you even remember if you won or lost?"

"No," Carter mutters sadly.

Reaching up, I press my lips to the rough underside of his jaw. "You won," I whisper, not wanting him worried that he can't remember.

I can't see his lips but I feel his smile. "Fuck yeah, I did."

"I didn't tell you to stroke your ego." He shrugs, because it seems that's all I did.

"Don't look so fucking pleased. It shouldn't have happened," Spike barks, pushing himself to the edge of the sofa.

"I know, I—"

"No, Titch. I don't think you do." The two of them stare at each other, tension crackling.

"I'm... uh... just going to use the bathroom, leave you two to..." I trail off, feeling like I'm imposing on a conversation they need to have alone.

Carter squeezes my hand as I move, as if he doesn't want me to leave, but I'm not sticking around while they hash this out. It's between them.

I close the bedroom door behind me as their silence continues. Blowing out a long breath, I gather some fresh clothes and take them through to the bathroom.

The deep rumbles of their voices start to fill the flat, but I turn the shower on and leave them to it. If Spike needs to rip Carter a new one for his behaviour last night, then he is more than welcome.

By the time I wrap a towel around my body, I feel like I was able to wash a little of last night's anxiety down the drain, and now knowing that Carter is going to be okay, I breathe a little easier. That is, until a raised voice from the living room fills the now quiet space around me.

I can't make out what Spike is saying, but it's obvious that he's angry. Furious, actually.

I rush to drag on my clothes before pulling the door open and stepping into the bedroom. His voice is clearer, but it's not until I get to the door that I can decipher the words.

"I don't know how you've done it, but you've got a fucking good woman in there, and for some reason she's fighting for you right now. Trust me when I tell you that there aren't many of those in this world.

"This is what you've spent so long looking for, so why the fuck are you pulling this shit now? You'll fucking lose her, and you'll end up back where you started with meaningless hook-ups with women who aren't worth fuck all. She won't stick around and watch you self-destruct like I have for past fuck knows how long.

"Do you have any idea what it's like for us to watch you do that to yourself? Fuck, man. Just because your family are a bunch of cunts, it doesn't mean that we all are. We fucking care about you. We want you fucking safe."

When Spike's voice gets even louder, angrier, I pull the door open and step into the room. The last thing we all need is these two fighting. Thankfully, when I look around, I find Carter sitting where I left him, looking a little sheepish, but the man who really captures my attention is pacing back and forth in front of my kitchen with his fists clenching and the muscles in his neck pulled tight.

I glance between the two of them before walking towards him.

"Spike," I say softly, coming to stop in front of him and placing my hand on his forearm. He stops, but he doesn't look at me. Instead, he just blows out a long breath.

"I'm... I'm sorry." When he risks a glance up at me, all I see is the concern for his friend.

"It's okay. I get it."

"You can stop whispering about me now."

A chuckle falls from Spike's lips at Carter's words. "I think I need to go and get some fresh air. Maybe you could get him in the shower or something, he fucking stinks."

"Fuck you, man."

Spike shakes his head, finds his shoes, and disappears from the flat.

"Well that was heavy," I mutter, thinking back to Spike's little rant.

"It's nothing less than I deserve. I promised him I wouldn't do it again, and look." He pushes from the sofa, albeit slowly, and holds his arms out at his sides. "He's a good guy, and I betrayed him. He has every right to be hurt."

I nod, totally agreeing. "Things aren't always that black and white," I mutter as he stalks towards me. It doesn't matter that he's covered in yellow and purple bruises; my core still clenches with desire as he approaches.

"Nope. Never," I whisper.

He doesn't stop until there's only an inch between us. The heat of his body seeps into mine, making me wish I was in his arms once again. But as much as I might want to wrap my own around his waist, I know I can't. It'll hurt him too much.

He lifts his hand and wraps it around the back of my neck as he stares into my eyes. His swelling has reduced a little now, so he's able to open his almost properly.

"Thank you," he whispers. It's so sincere that it has a ball of emotion clogging my throat and tears burning the backs of my eyes.

"W-what for? I've not done anything."

"That's what you might think. But to me, you've done everything. You found me, you came for me, you... accepted me."

A sob rumbles up my throat at the crack in his voice.

"Carter," I sigh, wrapping my hand around his forearm, hoping it's a safe place to touch because I need this connection with him right now. "You're incredible. Accepting you was never an issue. It was accepting how you made me feel that was the problem."

His eyes search mine, begging for me to say more, but

I don't get the chance. The buzzer rings out loud through the flat, putting an end to the words I've been building up to say to him.

"Fucking hell," he spits. "If that's Spike, tell him to take another trip around the block."

Carter steps back and allows me to go to answer the door. I don't know why, but something tells me it's not Spike. He needed more breathing time than that.

Dread sits heaving in my stomach as I lift my hand to the door. I tell myself that it's because it's probably my parents making an impromptu visit and I'm going to have to explain the battered and bruised man in my house. As much as I might be dreading that conversation, I won't shy away from it. He's my husband, and, planned or not, I won't allow him to doubt this, us, any longer.

Pulling the door open, every muscle in my body pulls tight at the person I find staring back at me.

"What are you doing here?"

"Is he here?"

"None of your business. How did you find me?"

"It wasn't hard once I discovered your name, sweetheart. So I'll take your avoidance of the question as confirmation. I need to see him."

"No."

His eyebrows almost hit his hairline. "I'm sorry?"

I guess no one says no to him very often.

"I said no. You're not welcome here. Not now, and not ever."

"Fucking hell. Fair play." He lifts his hand and runs it through his dishevelled hair. He turns as if he's going to leave before spinning back to me. "Look, I just wanted to apologise. Yesterday got out of hand."

"You think?"

"Just let me see him. Let me say my piece and I'll be out of your hair."

"You don't deserve to see him."

Logan's chin drops, but only a second later Carter's voice calls from inside the flat.

"Just let him in, doll. Let's see what he's got to say for himself."

"But..."

"It'll be fine. *I'll* be fine."

I blow out a breath. It hasn't even been twenty-four hours yet since these two were face to face, and that nearly got Carter killed. This isn't going to end well.

I stand aside and allow him to walk in. My heart thunders in my chest as I imagine the worst outcomes from this. I tap my back pocket, ensuing my phone is in there in case I need to call for someone.

Spike will be back soon, it'll be fine.

I don't need to give Logan directions, seeing as once you're past the entrance my flat is open plan.

I know the moment his eyes land on Carter, because he sucks in a deep breath.

"Fucking hell, what happened?"

"You did," I seethe from behind him.

"What? I didn't do this."

"No, but you caused it."

"Enough, Dan," Carter says softly, although his hard, angry eyes never leave his brother. "Let's hear what he's got to say, then hopefully he'll fuck off as fast as he came." He tilts his head to the side and waits.

"I'm... I'm sorry, okay?"

I scoff, not accepting his words. I might have only met him once, but it's going to take a hell of a lot more than one pathetic apology to make up for what happened yesterday. "I'd had too much to drink, and I let my mouth run away with me."

Carter is silent as they stare at each other, their identical green eyes locked onto one another. I've no idea if they have any kind of twin connection, but, as silent words pass between them, I assume there must be something there.

"I was harsh, I know. But you've no idea what it's like."

"Being the perfect one who always makes our parents proud. Yeah, it must be really fucking hard for you." Carter rolls his eyes.

"It's not like you imagine. They're over the top, overbearing. Constantly wanting more from me. Nothing is ever good enough. The pressure, it's... unbearable."

"So you drink?" I add, assuming where this is going.

He hangs his head, an uncomfortable silence settling around us.

"If you want my sympathy, it's going to take a little more than this sob story to get it."

"I don't. I just... fuck. I don't know. I'm lonely. Miserable. And..."

"You thought I might want to be your friend after all these years?" Carter pushes from the sofa, pain etched into his features. His shoulders are set as if he wants to fight, and I panic. I step forward and between the two of them, hoping like hell that my presence will be enough to stop him.

"No, I just..."

"Wanted to apologise," Carter says, sarcasm oozing from him as he takes a step closer.

"Carter," I warn quietly.

"I won't," he mouths silently.

"I'm checking myself into rehab on Monday, I just

thought you should know. I won't be contactable should you..." he trails off. I can't imagine these two talk regularly, so it's not really an issue. "I was hoping that once I've sorted myself out, maybe we could... start again."

"We'll see." There's no emotion in Carter's tone, and it scares me. "You can see yourself out."

"Oh...okay. Yeah. I... uh... hope that heals soon."

"Do you?" Logan goes to reply, but the front door opens and heavy footsteps head our way. "Oh fuck." The edge to Carter's voice only increases the dread already filling my body.

It takes only a second for me to turn from Carter to see what's about to happen, but even that is long enough for Spike to have Logan pressed up against my living room wall with his hand around his throat.

"You're not fucking welcome here," he spits in Logan's face. Spike's voice is low and menacing. It shows a whole other side to him that I wasn't expecting.

"I... I... was just..."

"I don't give a fuck. You. Are. Not. Welcome."

Spike pulls his arm back. Carter and I both call for him to stop, but it seems nothing will get through his red haze as he slams his fist into Logan's face.

"Fucking hell, Spike," Carter calls, his body vibrating with his own anger and his need to do something.

"Don't," I warn, holding my hand up to him. He does not need to get in the middle of this right now.

"Spike," I cry, turning to him and tugging on the arms he's holding Logan up with as hard as I can. "Enough, Spike. Enough."

He throws another punch, Logan's nose spraying blood everywhere before he seems to come back to himself.

He looks from Logan to me and his eyes widen in shock.

"Get the fuck out of here," I bark at Logan. "And if Carter wants anything to do with you, then he'll find you. Not the other way around. You got that?"

With one last look at his brother, Logan turns with his shoulders lowered and leaves the flat.

Once I know he's left and shut the door behind him, I turn to the two still standing in my living room. Both of their eyes are dark with fury and their fists are curled.

"What was that motherfucker even doing here? Why the fuck did you let him in?" he snaps at me.

I open my mouth to respond, but I don't get a chance.

"Out, Spike," Carter roars, his voice like I've never heard before.

"But—" He turns to his friend, but the second they lock on each other, a little of Spike's fight leaves him.

He nods before turning, muttering an apology to me and leaving the flat.

"Carter, what's—"

"Do you stand by what you said last night? What you made me promise?"

"Uh..." I try casting my mind back, but I feel like I've just got whiplash.

His hand lands on my waist and slides up, his thumb grazing my nipple, making it pucker under his touch. It continues higher until his fingers are around the back of my neck and his thumb caresses my cheek. His body presses against mine, his hard cock against the softness of my stomach.

"Carter," I half moan, half chastise. He shouldn't be doing this, he's in too much pain.

He leans forward, his lips brushing the shell of my ear

and making me shudder. "You made me promise to take it out on you. That if I needed to fight, I had to use you."

I swallow, and I swear it's the loudest fucking swallow of my life.

"I need you, Danni." The hand that's still on my hip clenches almost painfully.

"Yes. Yes, whatever you need. Take it." I gasp when his tongue runs up my neck. "Take. It."

Everything falls from my head. My concern for him. My anger at his brother. My shock at Spike's reaction. Everything but him and what happens when we connect.

He drops his hands to my arse and lifts me. A grunt of pain falls from his lips, but when I glance at him to tell him not to, the look of determination and need that's written all over his face stops me. Instead I hold on to his shoulders in the hope of taking some of my weight and follow his lead.

By his own admission, this isn't the first time he's been in this state. I need to trust that he knows what he's doing and when to stop.

My arse connects with the granite countertop and he releases his hold on me in favour of pulling my oversized jumper over my head.

"Naked. I need you fucking naked." His eyes are wild as they flit over my body. My muscles clench as I wonder what he's got in store for me.

Reaching behind my back, I undo my bra and pull it from my body as Carter drops his joggers and kicks them off.

His length is hard and desperate. I want to reach out for him, but he stops me by dropping his lips to my exposed nipple and sucking hard.

"Fuck," I cry as he bites down.

"Need you," he mutters, kissing across to the other side. "Need you so fucking bad." My chest swells for this incredible but broken man before me. He's so much more than I ever could have imagined that night I walked into the restaurant, expecting someone who looked totally different. But as it turns out, he's exactly what I needed.

I let go of all my preconceived thoughts about the man I thought I wanted and jump in with both feet.

My fingers thread into his hair as he sucks and nips at me.

"Carter," I moan, encouraging him and fully giving myself over to him.

He begins kissing down my stomach, but he gasps in pain as he tries to bend.

"Stop," I say, tugging lightly at his hair.

"Dan, no. I need—" I place my fingers against his lips, halting his argument.

"Shush, I know." I hop down from the counter and take his hands in mine. "I was just going to suggest we do this elsewhere."

The smile that curls at his lips is wicked, and it hits me exactly where I think he intends.

"Oh, well, in that case."

He allows me to pull him towards the bedroom.

"Now lie down."

"But—"

"No buts. You're not in charge right now. I am." I wink at him and spin on my tiptoes. Pulling my phone from my pocket, I pull up my music and scroll until I find something suitable. I stop on Usher's name, because I'm sure whatever comes on first will have the exact beat I'm after.

I hit play and wait.

The music fills the space around us that was previously only filled with our heavy breathing.

"Doll?" Carter asks, his voice the encouragement I need.

"You need a distraction? I'll give you a distraction."

Channelling my inner stripper, I spin back to him and wiggle my hips in time with the music. This would probably be better if I weren't already half naked, but it's not like I'm going to re-dress now.

Tucking my thumbs into the waistband of my leggings, I make a show of pushing them down my hips. I turn my back on him and bend, giving him full view of my thong-clad arse as I push my leggings down.

He groans. "Are you trying to fucking kill me?"

I chuckle to myself, but when I turn and get a look at his tense, bruised face, I take pity on him.

Pushing my last remaining item of clothing down my legs, I step towards the bed and press one knee into the mattress.

"You're so fucking beautiful." His eyes drop from mine in favour of my body, and I still to allow him the time he needs.

"Get up here." He juts his chin out, showing me exactly where he wants me.

"I don't want to hurt you."

"My need to taste you is more insistent than my pain."

"But—" He lifts a brow, and it cuts off any more argument I might have had.

Crawling towards him, I place my knees either side of his head as his hands wrap around my thighs.

"Make sure I hear you scream even with your thighs pinning my ears." I flush with heat, knowing what's about to come.

His fingers tighten, and I've no choice but to drop down and allow him the access he needs.

I cry out as his tongue presses against me for the first time. My thighs tremble and my toes curl as he circles my most sensitive part like a pro.

"Carter," I cry out as he sucks on me.

His tongue slips lower, spearing me, making me clench around him, needing more.

"Shit, fuck. Shit."

His hands lift, his fingers tickling up my stomach until he takes the weight of my breasts in his palms.

"Oh god," I moan as he pinches my nipples at the same time as biting down on my clit.

He continues, driving me crazy until I'm so close to losing control that I can see stars. It's at exactly that point that he stops and pushes me away from him.

"Fuck me. Now."

I eagerly crawl down his body, being as careful as I can not to hurt him more than I probably already am.

The second I'm over his waist, I wrap my fingers around his hard length and immediately move over him. My eyelids flutter closed as I sink down. My muscles tighten, sucking him in deeper and reawakening my previously lost release.

"Fuck, doll. So fucking good," he groans, his eyes closing and the muscles in his neck straining.

His fingers grip onto my hips, and he helps me to move while his own hips thrust upwards.

"Look at me," I demand, needing the connection between us. Needing to show him that I can do this for him. That I can be exactly what he needs.

His breath catches when our stares lock, telling me he's seeing it all. All the truths I've been covering up, how

I really feel. I've known it since we started messaging all those weeks ago, but I convinced myself after finding out who he really was that it was all make believe, a fantasy. No one can start falling for someone when they've never met. It just proved my point that you don't really know someone until you meet them in person. But then, it seems, he's so much more than I thought back then. Yeah, he's different. He's not what I was expecting. But fuck, he's like no one I've ever met before. It might have only been a short time, but I know, and I fully accept, that this man is it for me. The bruised, the broken, all the slightly bent pieces of him.

I sit down on him harder, taking him deeper, and he grunts as I take him by surprise.

Resting my palms on his bent knees behind me, I use them as leverage to lift almost all the way off him before dropping back down.

"Yes, doll. Yes."

"Carter," I cry, as the sensation begins to get too much, the orgasm he brought me to the brink of earlier racing back. I lose control of my actions as I chase the release. "Carter, Carter, Carter," I chant, our eyes locked on each other's. He tilts his hips just so, and I fall. I fall into mind-numbing bliss.

My body twitches above him, and I'm forced to close my eyes as I ride it out.

I'm just coming down when his fingers dig into my hips and his cock swells inside me. He stills for a beat before roaring out his release as he fills me.

I stay frozen on top of him as I watch the pleasure and release wash through him. My heart races and my pussy clenches once again at the sight, little aftershocks rocking my body.

Gently, I climb off and lie down beside him. His eyes stay closed for a beat, but, when they open, they're full of emotion.

Reaching out, I place my hand on his rough cheek.

"Carter," I breathe, not knowing what to say or where to start.

"Thank you," he whispers after a beat. I nod but don't say anything, sensing that he has more. "Thank you for fighting for me. For giving me this."

"Anything. I'm yours." He sucks in a breath as those two words hit him.

"Yeah?" The beginning of a smile twitches at his lips, but it doesn't break free quite yet.

"Yeah."

His fingers brush over mine. It's the first time he notices that I'm wearing my wedding ring. His eyes widen as he stares down at it.

"Could you get something for me?"

"Of course."

"In the zip pocket of my bag, there's a little box. Could you bring it over?"

"O-okay."

I've no idea what's going on, but what I'm not expecting to find is a velvet covered little black jewellery box.

He holds his hand out for it and I pass it over.

"Carter...what—"

"One day, I'll do this properly, I'll get on one knee without my body reminding me of the massive fucking mistake I made last night, but I can't wait any longer." I bite down on my bottom lip as my eyes fill with tears.

He flips the top open, exposing the most stunning princess cut, platinum engagement ring.

"Carter..." I breathe, not knowing whether to look at him or the shining diamond.

"Danniella Abbot, will you be my wife?"

"Yes," I cry, crawling onto the bed and gently wrapping my arms around his shoulders.

A sob rumbles up his throat, and it makes my own tears fall.

I pull back so he knows just how much this means to me.

His eyes search mine, and I hate that it feels like he's questioning me, making sure I just gave the right answer because how could I possibly want him? But I do. Every last piece of him.

Reaching out, I take his face in my hands. "I love you, Carter. I love what's on the outside, but more importantly, I love the man in here." I drop my hand to his heart. It thunders under my touch, and I smile. "You are enough, Carter. You're everything. You're my everything."

"Fuck," he barks, attempting to swallow down his emotions, but I see them. I see it all. He leans forward, crashing our lips together and utterly consuming me.

When he pulls back, we're both fighting to breathe.

"Here," he says softly. "We should see if it fits."

Lifting my hand, he pulls the ring from its cushion and slides it up my finger.

"It's perfect. Thank you so much."

He stares down at it for a beat, almost in disbelief. "You have nothing to thank me for, doll. I'm the one who should be saying those words."

"Enough," I soothe. "This is it for us now. I want this. I want us. The good, the bad, and the ugly."

"Me too," he murmurs. "I love you."

He kisses me once again. It's full of passion and desire,

but it's softer than before. As he sweeps his tongue into my mouth, I feel everything he's feeling, and hope pours into me. This is a new start for both of us. Yes, it's early, and most will think we're crazy, but hey, we're already married so why not jump in with both feet?

My stomach grumbles, making him laugh and reminding me that I never got to order that McDonalds earlier.

When I pull back and look at him, it's obvious that he's struggling. His eyes are heavy with his exhaustion.

"Why don't you lie down for a bit? I'll go and order us some food and I'll wake you when it's here."

I can tell he wants to say no, but it's pointless. He knows as well as I do that he needs to rest.

"Okay."

He lies down and pulls me with him. I stay beside him for a few minutes, but he almost instantly falls asleep. I watch him before my stomach rumbles again, reminding me of what I should be doing.

As I sit up, my ring catches my eye and I smile.

31

Carter

I wake with a wide smile on my face as I remember what happened only moments before I fell asleep. I gave her the ring I've been carrying around with me since we got back.

I felt ridiculous, walking inside the jewellery shop that I had to pass on my way to work that first afternoon, but I couldn't help myself. As far as I was concerned, Danni was it for me. She already had my wedding ring. Granted it was around her neck, but I was hopeful, or just downright stupid, because I wanted to see it on her finger once again, along with an engagement ring that I'd chosen for her.

I only spent a few minutes in that shop. The second I saw it I knew it was the one and I bought it there and then. I had no idea when I would get to give it to her. I had to hope the perfect time would present itself. I was happy to wait as long as it took for me to show her that we were meant to be. So what, we had an unconventional start? It's us. Our story. For me, the crazier the better. It'll only be more entertaining for our grandkids.

The scent of food filters into the room, and I'm reminded of what woke me in the first place. The front door. For a second, I fear he's come back. I roll my eyes. Logan has had a drinking problem for years. Our parents could be part of the issue, but I think that might just be the surface of it. I do hope he finds what he's looking for, but I sure as fuck won't be helping him. I've got my own life now with someone who's worthy of my time, and I intend on making the most of that every day.

The door pushes open, and the woman herself steps into the room. She's wearing one of my t-shirts. It's massive on her, but fuck if it doesn't look a million times better than it does on me. But as incredible as she looks, it's what's in her hand that really makes my mouth water.

"My breakfast."

"Well, we were too late, so actually it's lunch, but..." she shrugs.

"It's good. That's all that matters right now."

I sit up and make a right song and dance of trying to prop the pillows up behind me, so much so that Danni abandons our lunch on the bed to help me. I fucking hate having to rely on someone for shit like this. Although, I must admit that she's a much more attractive nurse than Spike ever was.

Guilt hits me as I think of him.

"What? What's wrong?"

"I need to call Spike."

"He's okay. I spoke to him while you were sleeping. He's gone home to shower and change. He'll be back later."

"I can't believe he hit Logan."

"Nor can I. I thought he was the nice one."

I can't help but chuckle. "Oh, doll. It's probably time you learned that none of us are nice."

"Oh, I don't know. There's a sweet guy in there somewhere," she says as she sits back from getting me comfortable. "I've got the ring to prove it."

"Meh, maybe I have my moments. Now get that fucking shirt off. I'm not eating this while you're dressed."

Her eyebrows almost hit her hairline. "Oh?"

"It'll help with the pain."

"Oh, so you're going to blackmail me into getting naked."

"I was going for the sympathy vote, but I can resort to blackmail if that's what it takes."

"Lucky for you, I'm easier than that." I watch as she lifts up on her knees and curls her fingers around the hem of my shirt. Slowly, fucking painfully slowly, she peels it up her body. My eyes lock on her full tits before the fabric releases her hair and a mass of curls falls down around them.

I find her eyes. They're soft and so full of love. She didn't need to say the words earlier. From the moment I looked up at her when I was on the floor of that fucking warehouse, I knew. She wouldn't have been there, wouldn't have fought her way to me, if she didn't.

"What?" she asks when my attention doesn't leave her.

"I really fucking love you."

Her wide smile steals my breath. If I didn't already know that I'd do anything for this woman, then I would have just realised.

"I really fucking love you too. Now eat. Then you need more pain meds, and then…"

"Then?" I taunt, wondering what the hell she wants me to do today when I can hardly move.

"Yes, then you're having a bath."

"With bubbles?" I ask, unwrapping my burger and taking a huge bite.

"Of course."

"What about you?"

"What about me?"

"I want bubbles and you."

"You're meant to be relaxing."

"I will while my hands trail around your wet and bubbly body." Her nipples pebble at my words and she squirms slightly. It's all I need to know that she's fully on board with my plan.

"Fine, but no sex. You need to heal."

"We'll see."

"You're right. We will."

"I feel like you're setting a challenge here. You are aware that you stand no chance, right? Once I turn on the charm, you'll be like putty in my hands." She laughs, and the last remaining weight from last night and Logan's morning visit lifts.

"Oh really?"

"You can't resist me, and you know it."

She shrugs, and I know that I've already won.

"I can't remember the last time I had a bath," I admit as I sink down into the bubbles. "Why is there grit in it?"

"It's the salts. They'll dissolve."

"Or go up my arse."

She rolls her eyes and shakes her head. "They'll help relax you."

"Really?" I ask sceptically. "I'm pretty sure you can do a better job." I lift my hips, my already hard cock protruding above the bubbles.

"Are you ever not ready to go?" She places her hand on her waist and juts her hip out. The move does not help my situation at all.

"With you naked? Never. Now, are you going to join me?"

"Carter, I—"

"Just get in," I demand, cutting her off. "I want you in my arms."

She hesitates for a few seconds before stepping in between my legs.

"Good job it's a big tub, huh?"

"You trying to say I'm fat, doll?"

"Oh yeah," she says, running a fingertip down my abs. "Massive."

I capture her wrist before she gets any lower. "Go further and I won't be held responsible for my actions."

She stops, but I know given half a chance she'd continue, despite her warnings about me relaxing.

We get ourselves comfortable with her lying back against my chest. It hurts like fuck, but I'm not about to tell her that. I wrap my arms around her waist and try to keep my breathing steady and even.

"This is nice," she murmurs.

"And I feel less like a pussy in a bubble bath while I've got you naked in my arms."

She laughs. "You're an idiot," she jokes for a second before stiffening in my arms. "Shit... I didn't mean—"

"Danni, don't. Don't censor yourself because you're worried that you'll offend me. You won't."

"Okay," she whispers. "I'd just hate for you to think—"

"I won't ever compare your words to theirs, if that's what you're going to say. If I even for a second thought you had the same opinions, then I never would have married you."

"Were you sober enough to have a say?"

"Of course. One of us had to be the sensible one."

"Sensible? Right. So, about our wedding," she muses, tilting her head up to look at me. "Please, will you tell me how it happened?"

I consider her question for a few seconds just to make her stew. She asked a couple of times when we were in Vegas as she freaked out about not being able to remember, and I refused. Mainly because when I told her what I did remember, I wanted it to be because she wanted to remember the moment, not because she wanted to remember a mistake.

"We carried on dancing after Zach and Biff left. We had a few more shots, we laughed, joked. Everything was just so... easy. It was like I was out with my best friend, only she was a chick and one I really wanted to fuck again." She chuckles, but I don't allow her to say anything.

"You suggested we move on, that you wanted to experience Las Vegas by night. We bar-hopped down the strip, getting a shot in each and moving on. We were fucking steaming. It was probably one of the best nights of my life, because whenever I looked at you, my world seemed the right way up for once. You didn't care about anything other than having a good time. It felt incredible."

"So how did we go from bar-hopping to a chapel?"

"You asked me if there was anything I wanted to do

while we were in Vegas. I told you that I planned to go to Rebel and get some new ink. You told me that there was no way in Hell anyone was putting a needle anywhere near your skin, but that you wanted something to remember the few days by. At this point we approached a jewellery shop. You stopped and stared in the window. I thought you'd seen something you wanted. Well... I guess you did. I just didn't know you were looking at wedding rings.

"Eventually, you turned to me. A wicked smile curled at your lips and my heart damn near burst at how happy you looked. "Marry me," you blurted out. "Let's get married, and that can be our memento." I thought you'd lost your mind, but you wouldn't give up. You dragged me inside and chose our rings.

"Well, one thing led to another, and not even an hour later we were inside a wedding chapel and all booked in."

"So you weren't lying? I really did ask you?"

"You really did, doll. I thought I'd won the fucking Lottery."

"You didn't think about saying no?"

"Sure, I could have. I could have easily distracted you, no doubt. But I wanted it. I wanted you. I had since the moment I saw you online. Standing beside you in that little jewellers, it was no different. And it still isn't now. I want you, and if you'll have me, I'll keep you forever."

"Wow," she breathes. "I need you to know that I've never been that spontaneous in my entire life. It might have been a one-time thing, if you're expecting something similar regularly."

"I don't know. You've been pretty spontaneous since we met. You let me fuck you on Biff's sofa, despite the fact that she could have walked back through the door at any moment. You agreed to let me live here with you. And, you just said yes to me again."

"Huh. Clearly you bring out the crazy in me."

"I just so happen to like your crazy." Leaning forward, I brush my nose against her ear and delight in the shudder that runs down her body from my touch. "So we got married after a few weeks, how long do we wait for what comes next?"

It was meant to be a joke, but suddenly the idea of her belly swollen with my baby is the only thing I can see. Fucking hell, I think I've lost my mind a little over this woman.

"One thing at a time, Carter. We've not even told my parents yet."

"It'll be fine. They already love me."

EPILOGUE

Danni

Once I made the decision to tell all to my parents, I soon became impatient to rip that plaster off and get it over with, but I knew that turning up with a beaten and bruised Carter and then announcing that he was my husband after our family's third shotgun Vegas wedding probably wasn't going to go over too well.

So in the end, we waited a month. We jokingly decided that if we hadn't killed each other by then, maybe we weren't so crazy after all and this could actually work. As we laughed about it, we both already knew that we were in this for the long run, but having some more time just the two of us so that we could really get to know each other was exactly what we needed.

There was no more hiding how we felt or feeling awkward about not knowing how we tied the knot.

Everything was just... easy. Carter was turning out to be everything I ever wanted.

Once he was strong enough, we drove over to the flat he used to share with Spike and packed up all his stuff. Thankfully there wasn't any bad blood between the two of them after the showdown with Logan. If anything, I think it might have brought them closer, despite the fact that Carter's now officially moved out.

It's been the two of us ever since, living as a real married couple and doing all the domesticated things expected of us. Carter's changed his hours at the studio so that we have some more time together, and I'm still learning the art of delegation so that I can spend a few less hours in the office being a control freak. It's not easy, but coming home and walking into Carter's arms makes it totally worth it.

My family knows about us. It wasn't exactly an easy secret to keep, seeing as I live beneath my older brother and his family, but thankfully they've all respected our wishes to be just ourselves for a few weeks while we find our feet. Mum rings or texts daily asking if she can meet him again, but I've put her off until now. Today is the day, and as I sit at my dressing table attempting to tame my wild curls, my stomach churns over with nerves.

Glancing down at the rings on my finger, I sigh. *It'll be fine*, I tell myself.

I blow out a long breath.

"It'll be fine." His voice startles me, and when I look up to the mirror, I find him leaning against the doorframe, watching me.

"How long have you been there?"

"Long enough to know you're freaking out."

"I just know they're going to be so disappointed."

"We've got a plan, doll. It will be fine."

I nod. I know what he's saying is true. We've spent a lot of time talking about what we do next.

"We'll give them a wedding. Your mum will get to go dress shopping and do all the things she's probably been imagining since she gave birth to you. She won't miss out. Plus, I have a feeling that once we tell them the rest that they'll forget all about missing our wedding."

I blow out a shaky breath as I think about our recent discovery. "I know, but we agreed not to tell them about that yet. I want to make sure everything is okay before we announce it to the world. Plus, I think one life-changing announcement at a time is probably better for Dad's heart."

Carter walks into the room and pulls me into his arms. "Whatever you feel is right. I want you, and this little one," he says, placing his palm to my stomach and making me giddy with excitement, "happy at all times."

"I still don't think it's really settled in."

"Tell me about it."

After Las Vegas, Carter's fight and us trying to find our new normal, I'd totally spaced out on the fact that I was meant to get my period. It wasn't until my box of pills fell from the shelf in the bathroom cabinet one morning that it hit me.

I bought a test on the way to work and did it the second I got into the office. I knew before I even looked at the result what it was going to be.

I remember it as if it were only a few minutes ago. The fear, the excitement, the trepidation about telling Carter.

Much like everything else in our relationship, it wasn't planned. But I figured that everything else has so far worked out okay, so this will too.

"You're growing our baby. I told you that you were spontaneous."

I laugh. "Only with you. Every other aspect of my life has been planned to perfection."

"I'm glad I could throw in a curveball."

"You certainly did that."

"Are you ready? We probably don't want to be late."

"Yeah," I say on a long breath. "Let's do this."

Thankfully, Carter drives to my parents'. My hands are trembling so bad that I think it would have been dangerous if I did.

I fiddle with my rings. "Should I take them off?"

"Do what feels right."

I hesitate with my fingertips on them ready to slide them off, but removing that part of my life, if only for a while, feels wrong.

I need to go in there and rip that plaster right off. If I hide them, it means I won't have to confess right away, and if I don't, there's a chance I'll avoid it all afternoon.

"They're staying. Let's do this."

Carter pulls up outside my parents' house, and my stomach turns over. I've no idea if it's the nerves or the start of my morning sickness, but I'm on the verge of throwing the door open and emptying the contents of my stomach on my parents' driveway nonetheless.

"The longer you sit here putting it off, the worse it'll get," Carter says, jumping from the car and coming around to open my door. He probably thinks he's going to have to drag me from the seat. I hate that my reluctance to face this head-on could make him think it's about him, but it's not, it's far from it. I have zero doubts about him, our relationship, and our future. I just hate disappointing my parents.

"Come on, then. Let's get this over with and see if we're still welcome for lunch."

"They won't kick us out. They're good people."

"I know."

"Here they are at last. We were starting to think that all this time alone was a way of avoiding us for some reason," Mum says as we join both her and Dad in the kitchen. They both give me a hug and greet Carter as if they've met him more than once before in their lives.

"Not at all," Carter says while I panic. "We just needed to adjust. Everything happened so fast."

"You don't say. One minute you're Zach's best friend, and the next you're our baby's boyfriend."

"About that," I say, the blood draining from my face.

Mum turns her narrowed eyes on me. "Oh, for the love of god, please do not tell me that—"

"I knew it!" Dad announces happily, turning to Mum. "Cough up, baby. I won."

"What?" I screech, looking between the two of them. Mum looks like she's about to burst into tears whereas Dad has a shit-eating grin on his face.

"We had a bet. You turn up and announce that you're our third child to get married in Vegas and I get to go on a two-week golf holiday. You didn't, and I have to endure a two-week sun and beach holiday somewhere exotic with this one," he says, pointing at my mother.

"You had a bet on us?" I ask, utter disbelief lacing my voice.

"We did."

"I can't believe this."

"Why? We bet on you lot all the time." My eyes widen in shock. "Got to say though, neither of us were risky enough on betting on Zach getting married any time soon."

"Jesus, I can't believe I'm hearing this."

"So, come on. Tell me the good news so I can go and call the boys."

"You don't even know what they've got to say, I wouldn't be so smug yet," Mum sasses at Dad, but it's pointless. I think we all know which way this conversation is about to go.

"Fine. We got married in Vegas."

"Yes," Dad calls, punching the air in celebration. All the while, Mum cries in disbelief.

"I can't believe you lot," she mutters, giving Dad a hard stare and stepping towards me. "Congratulations." The sadness in her voice as she says it guts me.

"We're going to have a wedding, Mum. We're going to do it properly. I want to do it all properly."

"Really?"

"Yes, really. I want us to go dress shopping and cake tasting. It's not going to be a big event, but it will be a wedding that you can help me plan from beginning to end."

"Thank you," she sobs, pulling me into a tight hug.

"I'm so sorry. It wasn't exactly planned."

"Please tell me you remember it," she begs when she pulls back. She just groans when I shrug. "Well, at least tell me he got you a good ring." She reaches for my hand and looks at my finger. "Oh, boy did good."

She releases me and turns to Carter. "Welcome to the family," she says before pulling him in for a hug while Dad gathers me up in his arms.

We spend the afternoon giving them some brief details of our drunken wedding, but we focus on the wedding we're going to have here to celebrate. I don't want anything as big as Summer and Harrison recently had, just a small affair with our nearest and dearest. Carter is still in two minds as to what to do about his family. I've told him I'll support him no matter what he decides, but as of yet, we've not had any contact with any of them. I'd like to think the prospect of a grandchild might make them reconsider their actions, but then again, do leopards ever really change their spots? I'm not sure I want those kinds of people around my child. They did enough damage to their own, I don't want them and their opinions to taint anyone else I love.

By the time we say our goodbyes later that evening, Mum looks a little less sad about the whole thing. I now just need to hope I can keep her reined in to stop her going overboard with the plans.

"Thank you so much for lunch," Carter says, as Mum pulls him in for another hug.

"No, no. Thank you for securing where I'll be holidaying this year."

"Hmmm... yeah. Thanks for that."

"Well, if you will bet on our lives, at some point you're probably going to lose."

"Okay, double or nothing that they're pregnant by the end of the year." Mum groans and swats Dad's shoulder. Thankfully, she doesn't look straight at me, because I'm sure my face would have given me away.

We say our goodbyes and climb into the car.

"See. That wasn't so bad."

"True. I can't believe they bet on it though."

"I think it's hilarious. I want to still have fun like that after that many years of marriage." Carter laces his fingers with mine as he drives us back into the city.

"Yeah, now you put it that way, I'm happy to torment our kids for our own amusement."

"Kids? You planning on more than one?"

"I think we've already determined that planning doesn't work for us. Let's just go with the flow and see if I screw up my pill again or not."

Carter laughs, the sound making my chest swell. "Sounds good, doll."

Carter

"Are you sure you're going to be okay?" I ask Danni, who's sitting on the sofa with a glass of water.

"Yes, I'm fine. Lauren will be here in a few minutes. You're more than welcome to stick around and enjoy some girl talk if you don't want to leave me."

The thought fills me with dread, but I'd do it for her. I'd do pretty much anything for her.

"Get out of here, Spike is waiting for you."

"Fine. I'm going." I'd rearranged all my clients for today so we could see Danni's parents, then Spike announced that he was finishing early and taking me out for a drink to get over what my day might have held. I'd originally told him no, but the second I explained the plan to Danni she got straight on the phone to Spike and told him that I'd love to go out with him. He was delighted, seeing as he keeps sulking about missing out on not one but two stag dos with both Zach and me getting married in Vegas without him. He's not told me what he's planned for tonight, but it doesn't take a genius to work it out.

Danni's phone pings on the coffee table. She leans forward to look as I shove my feet into my shoes.

"Your Uber's outside."

I swipe my wallet and phone from the counter before dropping to my knees in front of her.

Reaching out, I wrap my hand around the back of her neck and pull her forward to kiss me. "I'll miss you," I mumble against her lips.

"With all the strippers dancing around, I doubt it."

"I'd have you over every single one of them any day of the week."

"Good to know. If you're a good boy, then maybe I'll be your personal stripper when you get home."

My cock swells at the thought. "I'll hold you to that." Her eyes darken as she stares at me, and I regret ever agreeing to this when I could spend the evening in bed with my girl.

"Stop getting ideas. Lauren doesn't need to walk in on any of that happening." As if she'd timed it, the buzzer rings, putting an end to my torture.

I give her one more quick kiss before telling her to stay put and that I'll let Lauren in on my way out.

"Be good," Danni calls after me.

"Good? When aren't I good?" Her laugh rumbles down to me. "I love you, doll."

"I love you too. I'll be here waiting."

Thoughts of how I might find her when I get back fill my mind, but I soon push them aside as I'm forced to greet her friend.

We met the night of Zach's birthday all those weeks ago, but we've all been out for drinks since then. After saying a quick hello and goodbye, I climb into the awaiting car and head for my old flat.

"Jesus, what happened in here?" I ask, looking around at the mostly tidy living room.

"Been trying to get my act together. No woman wants to come back to a shithole."

"Ah, now it all makes sense. The smell was stopping you getting laid."

"What? No. Nothing ever stops me getting laid. I was just feeling sorry for Ann having to clean up after me. I'm sure she's already on the verge of asking for a pay rise."

I shake my head at him as he throws me a beer and I fall down onto the sofa. "So what's the plan?"

"I'm gonna hit the shower, get my junk smelling fresh, and then we're hitting Pulse."

"You're so predictable, man."

He shrugs. "There could be worse things."

"Less of a pain in my arse would be a good start." He flips me the bird as he leaves the room.

I look around the place. I lived here for years before I forced Danni to make me her new roommate, but even though it's only been like, five weeks, it feels like a lifetime ago that I called this place home.

"Ready?" Spike asks as I drain the last of my drink.

"Yep, let's do this shit," I say, crushing the can and standing to leave.

"She looks good on you, man. I don't think I've ever seen you smile this fucking much."

"You trying to tell me that I was a miserable fucker before her?"

"You had your moments."

"Jesus. Let's go before you start getting deeper into feelings and shit. I've got a girl for that now."

"Don't I fucking know it. This place is seriously fucking quiet these days."

"What, even with all the pussy you get? Ow," I complain when he slugs me in the shoulder.

"I need a fucking roommate."

"No, you need a live-in cleaner."

"Do you want to end the night without another black eye?"

"Do your worst, just know that my girl will be after you if I come home with any kind of mark on me tonight."

He shudders in mock fear, but I know the threat hits home. I see the way he looks at Danni, like she's a creature from another planet. He has no idea what to do with a woman I trust wholeheartedly. He's believed for years that not a single one of them can be trusted beyond owning a nice warm and wet pussy to slide into, so we're a weird concept for him to get his head around.

In only minutes, we're greeting tonight's doorman and making our way inside. Seeing as Spike is a regular, he nods at one of the waitresses, holds two fingers up, and heads to his usual table.

Our arses have barely hit the seat when she appears with a tray in her hand, a whiskey, and three shots of something neon for both of us.

"Cheers, Krissy," Spike says with a wink before downing two of the shots. "To the stag we never got to have," he says, lifting the third towards me and drinking that one as well.

"We are having a wedding. There will be a hen and stag do then, you know."

"Yeah, but it's ages away. I wanted to celebrate now."

"By celebrate, you mean get drunk and fuck a stripper?"

"Uh, I'm pretty sure that's the same thing, right?"

Laughing at him, I take my first shot. It's fucking awful and burns all the way down.

"Good, right?" he asks, watching as I splutter.

"No, it's really fucking not. So, where's Zach tonight then?" I ask once I can feel my tongue again.

"Pussy whipped by Biff," Spike mutters into his whiskey.

"He's still at the studio, isn't he?"

"Yeah."

His attention leaves me when a spotlight illuminates the stage and a couple of girls walk out. He slouches down in his chair a little to enjoy the show.

"Now this is what I'm talking about. A night with my boy and some hot as fuck pussy."

"You really need a girl of your own." I intend for it to be so quiet that he doesn't hear, but apparently he's got sonic hearing tonight, because his glass pauses halfway to his lips and he turns to look at me.

"No. No I fucking don't. I don't do relationships, as you full well know. I'll leave you to enjoy your one pussy for the rest of your life. I like to be a little more... experimental."

"Don't I know it," I mutter, thinking of all the things I've walked in on over the years.

The waitress he first waved at continues to refill our drinks as the night goes on. It's not long before I've got a nice buzz going, although it's still not enough not to be pining for my girl at home and ignoring the tits that are on display all around me. Most are too fake for my liking, anyway.

Spike excused himself to do fuck knows what with fuck knows who about fifteen minutes ago, leaving me to bat away the offers of a lap dance from the girls prowling around.

"Thank fuck for that," I say when he re-joins me. I don't miss the slight smile playing on his lips, so I can only assume he got some action in one of the backrooms. Fucking dog. "I was one proposition away from going the fuck home."

"She's turned you into a right pussy, you know that?" The slur in his voice points to the fact that he's already had one too many of those disgusting shots, but I can't help feeling for him. I don't think he'd ever admit it, but he's lonely now I've left. This night out is him trying to make us 'normal' again, to be like we were. But sadly, for us, everything's changed. I just wish he had someone he was able to move on with as well.

"Do you know what? I don't even care," I admit with a sappy look on my face.

"Ugh, it's sickening. First Zach, now you. If D finds himself a girl in the next few weeks, I might just end it all and put myself out of my misery."

"Dramatic much?" I mutter.

"Nah, I'll save that for you lot with the girls. They're the ones who bring the drama. I can't believe you've both fallen for their charms."

"You've no idea what it's like, man. When you find that one, she buries herself so deep under your fucking skin that there's no way of getting rid of her." A look passes across his face. It's one I've seen before, but I've never discovered what puts it there. He shoots me down every time. "And don't forget, you were the one who pushed this. You were the one who told me to move in with her, to prove that she's mine."

"Yeah, well, aren't you glad you listened to some of my advice, even if you ignore most of it?"

"Got me here in the first place, man." I wave my wedding ring at him and smile.

"Whatever. I need another drink." He sits back in his chair after waving to the waitress, and his eyes scan the room. "It's not going to be the same without you."

"I'm sure you'll find something to distract you."

The waitress lowers our fresh drinks to the table and quickly disappears with our empties.

"Have you put an ad out for a new roommate yet?"

"Nah, thought I'd better get the place sorted first."

"Good plan."

We fall silent as the lights on the stage before us change once again. Everything goes dark for a few moments before they illuminate one woman dressed in a tiny school uniform.

I run my eyes up her but stop when I get to her face. My eyes widen and my chin drops. I must be wrong. It can't be.

"S-Spike," I say, nudging him in the shoulder to get his attention.

"What?" he barks, lowering his drink.

"Is that... Is that Kas?"

He looks towards the stage, his body still for a beat before the glass that was in his hand falls to the floor. It smashes around our feet, but that doesn't stop him.

"Motherfucker," he grunts before he stands with such force it knocks the table over. Everything goes crashing to the floor, successfully causing enough noise to alert everyone and have all eyes turning on us, including Kas'.

She doesn't register us to start with. She probably can't see much with the blinding spotlights on her, but the second Spike pulls himself up on the stage, all the colour drains from her face and she starts backing away.

It looks like Spike might have found his distraction project for a while.

Shaking my head at his over-the-top protectiveness of our little family, I lift my whiskey to my lips and take a sip as he marches her from the room, much to her irritation. The little pocket rocket looks about ready to kill.

> Are you ready for Kas and Spike's story?
> Defy You is OUT NOW!

ACKNOWLEDGMENTS

Aww, I'm so sad to be at the end of Danni and Titch's journey. I loved their story with this epic banter and Titch's attentiveness and belief in his feelings for his girl.

These Rebel Ink boys have utterly stolen my heart, and I can't wait to dive into what's still to come.

As always I need to say a huge thank you to Michelle for alpha reading Trick You as I wrote it and putting up with all my typos.

Once again my betas, Darlene, Deanna, Keeana, Lindsay, Nicole, Susanne, Tracy. Thank you so much for dropping everything to dive into Danni and Titch's story, and as ever for giving me your honest thoughts.

Evelyn, as always, thank you so much for polishing everything up and fixing my repeated errors. Gem, for proofreading and making Titch as pretty as possible.

A huge thank you to Samantha, I literally couldn't do any of this without you. Thank you so much for everything you do.

And I need to say a huge thank you to you, for supporting me, reading, reviewing and helping to share my words. I wouldn't be doing this now without all my readers. THANK YOU!

Spike and Kas are coming your way later this year. I have a feeling it's going to be a wild ride!

Until next time,

Tracy xo

ABOUT THE AUTHOR

Tracy Lorraine is a *USA Today* and *Wall Street Journal* bestselling new adult and contemporary romance author. Tracy has recently turned thirty and lives in a cute Cotswold village in England with her husband, baby girl and lovable but slightly crazy dog. Having always been a bookaholic with her head stuck in her Kindle, Tracy decided to try her hand at a story idea she dreamt up and hasn't looked back since.

Be the first to find out about new releases and offers. Sign up to my newsletter here.

If you want to know what I'm up to and see teasers and snippets of what I'm working on, then you need to be in my Facebook group. Join Tracy's Angels here.

Keep up to date with Tracy's books at
www.tracylorraine.com

ALSO BY TRACY LORRAINE

Falling Series

Falling for Ryan: Part One #1

Falling for Ryan: Part Two #2

Falling for Jax #3

Falling for Daniel (A Falling Series Novella)

Falling for Ruben #4

Falling for Fin #5

Falling for Lucas #6

Falling for Caleb #7

Falling for Declan #8

Falling For Liam #9

Forbidden Series

Falling for the Forbidden #1

Losing the Forbidden #2

Fighting for the Forbidden #3

Craving Redemption #4

Demanding Redemption #5

Avoiding Temptation #6

Chasing Temptation #7

Rebel Ink Series

Hate You #1

Trick You #2

Defy You #3

Play You #4

Inked (A Rebel Ink/Driven Crossover)

Rosewood High Series

Thorn #1

Paine #2

Savage #3

Fierce #4

Hunter #5

Faze (#6 Prequel)

Fury #6

Legend #7

Maddison Kings University Series

TMYM: Prequel

TRYS #1

TDYW #2

TBYS #3

TVYC #4

TDYD #5

TDYR #6

TRYD #7

Knight's Ridge Empire Series

Wicked Summer Knight: Prequel (Stella & Seb)

Wicked Knight #1 (Stella & Seb)

Wicked Princess #2 (Stella & Seb)

Wicked Empire #3 (Stella & Seb)

Deviant Knight #4 (Emmie & Theo)
Deviant Princess #5 (Emmie & Theo
Deviant Reign #6 (Emmie & Theo)

One Reckless Knight (Jodie & Toby)
Reckless Knight #7 (Jodie & Toby)
Reckless Princess #8 (Jodie & Toby)
Reckless Dynasty #9 (Jodie & Toby)

Dark Halloween Knight (Calli & Batman)
Dark Knight #10 (Calli & Batman)
Dark Princess #11 (Calli & Batman)
Dark Legacy #12 (Calli & Batman)

Corrupt Valentine Knight (Nico & Siren)

Ruined Series

Ruined Plans #1

Ruined by Lies #2

Ruined Promises #3

Never Forget Series

Never Forget Him #1

Never Forget Us #2

Everywhere & Nowhere #3

Chasing Series

Chasing Logan

The Cocktail Girls

His Manhattan

Her Kensington

FALLING FOR THE FORBIDDEN SNEAK PEEK
CHAPTER ONE

Falling down on my bed, I blow out a long breath and tell myself that everything will be okay.

I had plans for this summer—a few weeks of fun before uni starts. The girls and I had been looking at last-minute holiday deals, and we had tickets for a music festival...but then my dad swooped in, in that way that he does, and ruined everything.

I knew it was coming.

I just wasn't expecting it quite yet.

I'd hoped agreeing to study what he wanted me to and working for him was enough—apparently not.

I decided a few years ago that I wasn't going to move away to study. I mostly love my life in London, and I loved living with Mum. I'm not ashamed to admit that she's one of my best friends. It was only as I started looking at universities that my dad piped up and told me that I would be studying accountancy and finance at The London School of Economics. He'd done his research and decided it was the best place for me to learn my trade so I could enter the family business.

I just about managed to contain my laughter when he emphasised the word *family*.

I've no idea how long I lie on my bed trying to convince myself that moving into his house with his new wife and her son isn't the worst thing to ever happen to me, but eventually my stomach rumbling has me moving. I sit on the edge of the bed and take in all my half-unpacked boxes. A large sigh falls from my lips. If I don't find everything a home, maybe I won't have to stay. I know it's wishful thinking. This is it for me now.

Disappointment floods me as I make my way through the silent house. It's not that I was expecting a welcome party or anything, but someone being here would have been nice. Someone to help me carry everything up to my room would have been even nicer. Since Dad moved in with Jenny a few years ago, I've been told to treat this place like my home.

It will never be.

It's just a house, a show home, a shell in which I'm scared to touch anything for fear of making a mess. Home is a place with character, with mess from day-to-day living, with people who love and care for you.

My dad isn't a bad man, per se, but he's not exactly what you'd describe as a doting father. Everything he does is for his own gain—if it happens to help others in the process, that's just a bonus.

My step mum, Jenny, is lovely. She really is, but I can't help feeling like she's just a little bit...broken. She makes all the right comments and does all the right things. She's a great mum. But there's such sadness in her eyes.

The fridge is full, as usual. It's strange, because I've never witnessed anyone eating more than a slice of toast or an apple in this kitchen.

I fix myself a salad with the unopened packets of fruit and vegetables, but it doesn't really have the effect I needed it to have. Being here makes me feel kind of empty, and no amount of lettuce leaves is going to fill the void after moving out of the flat Mum and I shared for the past few years.

Rummaging through the cupboards, I can't help smiling when I find a stash of naughty stuff hiding at the back.

Pulling my hair back into a messy bun, I put my thoughts to the side and set about making something that will make me feel just a little bit better.

The sun's just about to set, casting an orange glow throughout the kitchen. It almost makes it feel warm and inviting—almost. My mouth waters as I pour melted chocolate over the crushed biscuits and marshmallows I've managed not to eat already. Standing in only a vest and a small pair of hot pants, I decide to make myself a hot chocolate, grab a blanket, and enjoy my bowl of goodness out on the deck with a magazine. Chocolate makes everything that little bit better. If I eat enough, it might make me forget what this summer's actually going to be like for me.

I'm just waiting for the kettle to boil when a shiver runs down my spine. I'm sure it's just the size of the house that freaks me out. I've seen enough horror films to know there are plenty of hiding places in a place this big.

I'm still for a second, but when I don't hear anything, I continue with what I was doing. That is, until a deep rumbling voice has every nerve in my body on alert.

"Wow, step daddy sure is attracting the young ones these days." His voice is slurred, his anger palpable. It makes goosebumps prick my skin and a giant lump form in my throat. "You look too pure. Too innocent to be with that prick," he spits.

There's no love lost between my dad and my stepbrother, that's not news to me, but the viciousness of his voice right now makes me wonder what their relationship is really like. My dad might be many things, but he wouldn't cheat on Jenny—he loves her too much.

I can't remember the last time I saw him, but there's no way he can't know it's me. Who the hell else would be cooking in his kitchen? Deciding he's just trying to rile me up, I go to collect my stuff and get out of his way. Unfortunately, he seems to have other ideas.

His breath tickles up my neck moments before the heat of his body warms my back.

"You came here for the wrong man. I can put that right, though." The alcohol on his breath surrounds me. It's a reminder that there's a good chance he has no idea what he's doing right now.

The softness of his nose running up the length of my neck has tingles racing through my traitorous body. I don't realise he's smelling me until he blows out a long breath and the scent of alcohol hits me once again. I turn to leave, but his hands slam on the counter behind me and cage me in.

"Look at me," he demands.

"Let me go, Ben."

If he's surprised to discover it's me, he doesn't show it. If anything, his eyes shine with delight as he takes in every inch of my face before focusing on my lips. My stomach flips, knowing where his thoughts are.

Something passes over his face but it's gone too quickly to be able to identify. He pushes himself from the counter and away from me. No more words are said, but when he gets to the door, he looks back over his shoulder and runs his eyes over my body. They hold a warning I don't really understand.

Once he's disappeared from sight, I sag back against the counter. What the hell was that?

After putting half of the rocky road on a tray in the fridge, I forgo sitting outside and instead take my spoils to my room to hide. There's stuff everywhere in my room and, unlike the rest of this house, it makes me feel a little more relaxed.

Since the day Ben and I were introduced by our parents, we've not really had any kind of relationship. He's pretty much stayed out of my way and, in turn, I've done the same. It's not all that much of a task. When I'm here, he spends almost every minute somewhere else. When he's home, he's moody, arrogant, and generally a prick, so I'm more than happy to stay out of his way.

It's just a shame he's so damn pretty to look at. As the years have passed, he's only become more attractive, too. I've no idea if it's just his job or if he works out as well because every inch of him seems to be toned to perfection.

Jenny spends most of her time apologising for his attitude and trying to explain that he's got a lot going on. I'm yet to discover what that is. As far as I can tell, he seems to be your average twenty-year-old guy who'd rather be off his arse drunk or with a woman than spending time at home with his parents.

By the time I've dug my way to the bottom of the bowl, I feel pretty sick. There's still no sign of my dad or Jenny, but the music pounding from Ben's room across the hallway leaves no doubt as to what kind of mood he's in.

DOWNLOAD NOW to continue Lauren and Ben's story.

Printed in Great Britain
by Amazon